The Tomboy & The Captain

by USA TODAY bestselling author

GINGER SCOTT

For Brenda and Tammy.

laney price

I'M NOT sure if it's the room I smell or me. It's probably a combination of both, though I fear I may be causing the brunt of it. Patient zero. My armpits, back, and nether regions are soaked in sweat after more than twenty trips from my old third-floor apartment to my best friend Ivy's pickup truck on the street.

"I know it's August, but seriously . . . ninety-one? I hate Iowa sometimes." Ivy kicks the front door open wide as she shuffles through with the last box.

"You say that in the winter, too, you know. I think you just have something against Iowa." My arms are held down by the disheveled pile of clothes I scooped up from the floor of my old bedroom. Right where my ex left them. When he moved out a week ago. Correction, when he had *people* move him and most of our things out.

"Not true. I love Iowa. In April. And a sliver of October."

I snort out a laugh at her assessment. Ivy's from Illinois, so Iowa—not that different.

"College students should be given at least three full credit hours for constantly moving. Bonus points for humidity." I blow up at the hairs stuck to my forehead. They literally go nowhere.

Stretching my pinky finger out from my grip, I manage to hook the door handle and tug the door closed behind me. How I haven't tumbled down the concrete stairs during one of these trips to Ivy's pickup, I have no idea. I can't see my feet which, being five-eleven, is rare for me. I can *always* see my feet. I can see freaking everything.

"Remind me again, why did Cam decide to break the lease early and not just let you stay through the fall?"

Ivy knows why. She just wants me to bash on Cam some more because this move has been miserable. And she never liked him. Turns out, neither did I. Cam is what's called a micromanager, and he wants a woman who likes to be managed. I could not be further from that type, if that even is a type.

"Because I said no to his grandmother's ring," I grunt out as I lean into the guardrail for a short break after the first flight of stairs. I adjust my hold on my clothing. Things are starting to slip, and the last thing I want to do in this hot afternoon sun is scatter garments on the pavement thirty feet below.

"That's right. I forgot," she says in a flat tone.

"I'm sure you did," I punch out through a laugh, rolling my eyes as I pivot to take the next set of stairs.

Ivy warned me the proposal was coming, and thank God she did. She spotted the ring when she was snooping through Cam's desk drawer one day while waiting for me to get dressed for our girls' night out. The fact that I was working through the best way to end my relationship while Cam was plotting our future is proof of how far apart we were as a couple. Seems my failing to reciprocate those three little words never registered to him as a red flag.

Truth is, I shouldn't be half of a couple with anyone. Not believing in love is sort of a dagger to the heart of a successful relationship. I certainly have no delusions about real fairytales. I was always upfront with Cam. I *liked* him, well enough. At least, I liked the roommate arrangement we had going. But I would never be the perfect wife. He considered my volleyball playing a hobby. I consider it a career. I wasn't going to follow him to Chicago for law school and give up my last year of sports eligibility.

I suppose we made sense on a certain level. Pre-law students in mostly the same classes. Only children from divorced parents. Of course, his parents were amicable, basically friends. My father hasn't shown his face since my thirteenth birthday, but that doesn't stop my mom from threatening to bash it in with a meat tenderizer anytime his name comes up. And it comes up more often than it should thanks to his empty promises via phone calls and letters.

I'll pick you up for a birthday dinner.

I'll see you on Christmas this year.

I'll be at your big game. Save me a seat!

I don't save seats anymore. And I don't answer his phone calls. I read his letters, texts, and emails because I can't stand the way the words taunt me when they go unread. I'm never surprised, though. I'm also no longer let down.

I guess I should be grateful that I fell in love with volleyball before my dad had a chance to ruin it too. Bobby Price walked away from his family in Pittsburgh to live the beach life and make the pro tour out in California before his knees got too old. He's got his own brand of sunblock now, and those checks paid for a lot of travel team play for me.

Funding my passion was the least he could do since he couldn't be bothered to show up or volunteer to coach like so many of the other volleyball-playing parents on my teams.

When I went down with a shoulder injury last season, a small part of me expected him to finally step up, or at least swoop in with some motivational speech or advice. A shoulder injury is what took him out of the game in college. He got his second chance thanks to the beach tour, so I suppose his comeback dulled his ability to feel empathy. Clearly, being of his own flesh and blood doesn't matter.

I give the garments weighing down my arms one final heave into the back of Ivy's truck as she slides the last box into place and flips up the tailgate.

"I can't believe we have to do this all again, only in reverse." She chuckles while heading to the driver's side.

"At least it's the first floor at your place. I mean, unless you want to give me your master suite." I shoot my friend a grin as I climb in the passenger side.

"You'll prefer the first floor. Right by the laundry. Better water pressure."

I stare at her profile while she starts the engine and eventually she meets my gaze.

"You made that last part up," I challenge.

"Yeah. There's no way I'm giving up that bedroom. Even for you." She reaches over and pats my thigh, then shifts into drive to take me and my life's belongings to my new address, right across from the laundry room.

Unloading is a lot easier than packing, and in less than an hour, Ivy and I have every box stacked at the foot of the bed and most of my clothes hung in the small walk-in closet. Her old roommate left behind a queen bed and one dresser along with some pretty wild pink curtains and a lot of hot-pink

LED lights. As long as I have the basics, though, I've got all I need until graduation. Hopefully, by then I'll be planning my next move to one of the start-up markets for the new pro volleyball league.

"You're sure Matt is going to be cool with me taking the room?" Ivy shares this place with her brother. They've been trying to find someone to fill the empty room—and take on a third of the bills—for a few weeks. He's been out of town for the last week, living his best summer with one last hurrah out in California. He got invited to some influencer camp for "wannabe frat boys," as Ivy says. Her brother is actually pretty decent at the social media marketing thing, though. He went viral with a few posts on our college hockey team last year. I'd love for him to work something up for me this season and maybe up my profile before the pro draft.

"Oh, I told him. Not that he reads his damn messages. I swear if it's not a hashtag or mention on some social account, he doesn't consume it." She rolls her eyes. "Seriously though, he is going to be so relieved. He literally has interviews lined up to find a new roommate this week. He was starting to freak out with rent coming due. Speaking of . . . rent's due Tuesday." She puckers her lips and holds out an open palm. I let her linger for a few seconds, but before she makes the actual grabby motion, I give in.

"All right, hang on. I have cash like you said." I snag my wallet from the bare mattress in my new room and pull out the four hundred bucks I took out this morning. It's a steal compared to what I was paying with Cam.

Ivy leaves me to unpack on my own, and after about two hours, I have most of the basics in place—workout things folded in the drawers, toiletries organized along with makeup. I bought a new comforter and pillow set, so the bed actually looks inviting, and I'm about to throw in the towel for the evening and collapse face first into it when Ivy raps on my door and pushes it open wide.

"Don't you dare think you're getting out of drinks at Patty's." She bends down and picks up the sneakers I just took off and set by the door, then tosses them on the bed.

"Aw, Ives, I'm beat! Raincheck?" I flop down on my ass to untie one of the shoes, knowing my friend isn't really big on no for an answer, especially when it comes to free drinks. I promised her I'd pick up the tab if she helped with the heavy lifting today. My shoulder is pretty much healed, but the last thing I want to do is set myself back by overdoing it with a few moving boxes.

"And throw a new shirt on while you're at it. Maybe swap out that bra too. You look . . ." She swirls her finger in front of her as if trying to conjure the right word.

"Like I've spent the day moving my shit from one place to another?" I respond, slipping my foot into my shoe and lacing it.

"Yeah, like you moved here from an alley. Like that." She snaps and leaves my room.

"That's not exactly what I said," I holler after her. Her snicker echoes down the hallway and back at me. I scowl but also sniff the sleeve of my shirt.

I take her advice and toss on my favorite cotton bralette and my Team USA crop shirt. I twist my hair up into a messy bun and splash a little water on my face both to wake up and to bring a little color back to my cheeks.

Patty's is two blocks from the house we're renting, which makes getting home after a few drinks a lot easier. And now that I'm sliding onto one of the stools and feeling the cold curve of the mug in my hand, I'm a lot less irritated at my friend for dragging me out tonight.

The Bears preseason game is on every TV in this joint but one—the tiny set boxed in between the mixed drink bottles behind the bar. While Ivy hits the restroom, I manage to convince the bartender to tune it into the volleyball World's match going on right now, and I'm finally beginning to relax. I blow on one of the tater tots from the basket I ordered and test it with the tip of my tongue.

"Practicing for me later tonight?"

I drop the crispy snack from my fingers and cringe at the sound of my mortal enemy's voice. Cutter McCreary has been a pain in my ass since our freshman year at Tiff University, when he led the charge for his precious hockey team to take over our locker room. I swear he did it because I refused to give him my number the night before at a party, where he acted like an entitled frat boy simply looking to hook up. He swears the locker room was in the works all along.

Thing is, I know guys like Cutter. They aren't used to rejection. And when they get it, they act out. And our coach was promised our locker room was safe from budget cuts days before it was ripped away from us. Cutter's response to that? He said the locker room wasn't cut. It simply changed ownership.

Asshole.

"Shouldn't you be figure skating or some shit?" I give him side eyes. His chest puffs up with a silent laugh.

"Cute, Laney. But nah, we just won our scrimmage against Northeastern. I guess you couldn't get a seat for tonight's game. Tiff hockey sells out and all. We don't have all those open seats like you guys do."

I meet his glare and tighten my lips to keep my words inside. *Do not engage, Laney. That's what he wants.*

Cutter's been the captain of the hockey team since his sophomore year after his older twin brothers were drafted. He's obnoxiously confident, drowning in dimples, and literally the face of Tiff U. It helps that this town is hockey-crazed, and the team—*and fine, Cutter*—are good. Three-time conference champs. But so are we. And unlike the hockey team, Tiff women's volleyball has been to nationals. We're expected to go again this year, my year. Nobody talks about that, though.

"You know, Cutter . . . I bet it keeps you awake at night wondering what your so-called fans would think if you couldn't skate and swing a stick at the same time." I twist in my seat and cover my chest with folded arms just as Ivy walks up behind him.

"Oh, great. I leave you alone for thirty seconds and you're already picking a bar fight," she says, slipping into the space between Cutter and me to grab her beer. She gives me a stern look as she backs away, which irks me because why would any so-called bar fight be my fault and not his?

"What?" I huff.

She purses her lips before bringing her mug to her mouth and taking a slow sip. Cutter chuckles and raises a hand to get the bartender's attention. "Pitcher for the back. Make it two."

Half a dozen of his teammates stream in and head toward the back tables, and the clack of pool balls being racked breaks through the pulse throbbing with heat in my ears. I blink a few times and will my attention away from my nemesis for a beat, but then his pitchers are delivered, giving him an excuse to slide from his stool and brush against my thigh with his bulky and admittedly hard body.

With one palm flat on the bar top, he bends down and leans into me, his breath warm at my ear. I shift my gaze to take in the sharp line of his jaw but keep my head still. My molars gnash together and I fantasize about turning with a hefty right hook so I can punch him in the dick.

"You know I am up all night, Laney. But it ain't because I'm thinking." The soft chuckle that slips from his lips and blows against my ear sends shivers down the left side of my neck. My shoulder scrunches up out of rote reflex, and I hate that he sees it. I wait until I hear his teammates cheer at what I assume is his presentation of two pitchers of beer before I shift in my seat and glance over my shoulder. The pub is filled with adoring fans, most of them women. And they're all clamoring for Cutter's attention. It's nauseating.

Ivy bumps her elbow into mine to draw my attention from the back of the room.

"You know he fucks with you like that because he's attracted to you, right?" She smirks through a sip of her beer and twists her finger in one of the blonde ringlets that frame her face.

"Yeah, I know. Boys pulling pigtails and all that. It's all so basic. And I hate how much attention and funding and resources and—"

"Yeah, yeah. It's a man's world and female athletes work just as hard, blah, blah," Ivy cuts in.

I frown at her and she sighs.

"Sorry. It's not that I don't agree with your position. It's just that I've heard it so many times, and I lifted a lot of heavy shit today so I was hoping to maybe enjoy some drinks without a lesson on the patriarchy. If that's all right."

She shrugs and holds her mug toward me. I stare at it for a few seconds then lift mine and clank it against hers.

"Deal. Just promise me one thing." I lift a brow.

"What's that?"

"You won't start dating a hockey player while I'm living with you." I give her a hard stare because Ivy is as much a playboy as Cutter.

She snorts out a laugh after a few seconds and answers, "That's a deal."

We both drain our mugs and slam them down on the bar, and I wave down the bartender for another round. He swaps our glasses out and Ivy starts to laugh.

"What's funny?" She's not drunk yet, so something must genuinely be tickling her.

"Nothing, it's just that . . . I've already hooked up with most of the team anyhow. And I don't like seconds."

I shake my head and muse over her proud sexuality. Cutter McCreary might not be the biggest player at Tiff after all.

"Baseball players are hotter," I add.

We toast to that, and don't mention the men's hockey team for the rest of the night. I just keep looking at them—at *him*, really. And his stupid hot face and even hotter body. That's the beer talking, though.

cutter mccreary

THE FRESHMEN DON'T GET it yet. You can't celebrate a scrimmage win like it was a championship. You have a beer or two, then you go home and get your ass ready to fix whatever things Coach didn't like during practice the next morning. I watched some of those young dudes down those beers they begged us upper classmen for like they were water. I'll give them this, at least they showed up for skating this morning. Granted, they've collectively filled the trash bin Coach put out at center ice with vomit.

Coach blows the whistle a little longer to signal *stop* and a few of the freshmen collapse on the ice, pressing their bright red cheeks against the cold.

"That's only going to get them more lines," I mutter under my breath. Chuck, our goalie, coughs out a laugh and leans into me.

"As long as they don't piss him off enough to earn all of us more lines."

My mouth drops at his warning. I took it easy last night, but not *that* easy. I stuck around Patty's until Laney and her friend took off for the night. Not because I'm into her, but because that girl pisses me off. She blames me for her team losing their locker room three flipping years ago, and she won't let it go. I was as surprised by the news as anyone when one morning the athletic director slapped the hockey logo on the door.

It doesn't matter how many times I explain that to her, though. She needs to have an enemy and I'm that guy for her. So fine, whatever. I'll be her enemy. She's still the hottest girl on campus—maybe in Iowa. All legs, long brown hair, dark eyes, and a sexy, raspy laugh I only get to hear when it's at my expense. Being her enemy is kind of fun, especially when her cheeks heat to a candy red because of something I said.

But does she have to make those little digs anytime the press interviews her about Tiff U athletics? I swear, Laney Price brings up my name more than anyone when it comes to pressers. If they win a championship this season, I won't be shocked if her speech goes something like, "And no thanks to that loser Cutter McCreary for this trophy." Even last night I thought about buying her and her friend a round as a gesture of goodwill, but I stopped short because I immediately imagined her pouring the drink over my head.

"Stoddard and Droshky, you're on clean-up duty!" Coach shouts, and I breathe a sigh in relief. The two freshmen who fell to the ice first scramble to their knees, then skates, and make their way to the disgusting bin on the ice. They both wrap their faces behind their elbows and forearms as they drag it to the maintenance area to wash it out.

"Suckers," Chuck says over his shoulder.

I snort out a laugh and drag my tired ass behind him into the infamous locker room. I stop in front of my locker and slip out of my practice jersey and pads. I'm not in game shape yet and I felt it today. Thankfully, Coach was too preoccupied with the rookies and didn't fixate on how slow I was. I'm going to have to put in some extra time to get my legs and lungs in shape for this season.

I've put skating last the past month, taking care of things for my mom after her breast cancer diagnosis, even though she insisted I worry about my life. That's how she is, though —the woman is going through chemo on her own and is so damn afraid of being a bother. My oldest brothers can't help much from Colorado, and they have families of their own. The twins are in Bakersfield for their first AHL season so it's not like they can put things on hold and come home to southern Iowa to take care of Ma for a few months. Since our dad passed last year, that leaves me. And I don't mind. I'm just going to have to dig deep and put in some extra time to get back into form.

Chuck and I slam our doors in unison and head to the showers. It's been a while since I really took note of this place, but so many things in here are still incredibly female-centric. Stalls instead of urinals. Oh, and a tampon machine that I'm pretty sure is still full. This wasn't just for volleyball —women's basketball shared this space too, along with field hockey. They all got moved to the new facility, but I guess volleyball got left behind. I don't know the inner politics of college athletics. I do know that they pay my tuition if I keep slapping pucks in the net.

"Hey, you ever get shit from the women's teams for us having this space?" I ask Chuck, hanging my towel on one of the metal hooks before drowning my head and shoulders under steaming hot water.

"Nah. I don't think they really care anymore."

"Huh." I chew at my lower lip and nod. "Maybe not the team, but Laney Price still sure fucking cares." That look on her face last night flashes through my mind—the way her lips scrunch up with disgust when she talks to me. The little roll of her eyes.

"Dude, Laney Price hates you. That's all," Chuck laughs out.

"She doesn't hate me," I protest. Even I know that's a bullshit statement.

"Yeah, okay. You hold on to that fantasy if it makes you happy," he teases.

I breathe out a heavy sigh and turn to let the water pound against my face.

"Laney's opinion is the least of my problems. I still need to find a place to live."

I've been in the condo my parents bought as an investment for three years. Since Flynn and Todd took off, it's been just me. After our dad passed, things have gotten tight financially. Selling the condo makes sense to help with Mom's bills.

"Dude, still no leads? That sucks, man." If he could, Chuck would take me in. But he's already sharing a room with one of the guys, sleeping on an air mattress and living out of his suitcase. Half of our team is in the dorms, but I couldn't go back into campus living even if I wanted to. The dorms are full this year thanks to record enrollment. The irony is it's the success and popularity of our hockey team that's led to the attendance surge. *Doesn't seem to earn any of us more housing funds, though.*

I finish showering and get dressed at my locker. I still have a few days before I need to be out of the condo completely, but classes start Monday. This is the last weekend I'm going to have before regular season games start.

My gear tucked in my bag, I zip it up and drop it at my feet, then grab my phone and wallet from my locker. I slide open my messages and scroll back to the one that Matt dude who runs our social media sent me last week when I put out a plea for anyone seeking a roommate. He seems cool enough, I guess, and he did say he had a room. I was hoping to find someone I knew better, but I'm not in a position to be picky. I press CALL and sling my bag over my shoulder as it starts to ring.

"This is Matt. What up?"

I cringe at his greeting and contemplate ending the call right now. I could just live in my Jeep.

"Hello?"

Ugh.

"Yeah, sorry. Hi . . . this is Cutter. You responded to my message in the group chat? About needing a place to stay?" I close one eye and hold my breath, not sure whether I want him to tell me the room is mine or it's taken.

"Cutter! Yeah, man. Of course! Sorry, I've been in Hollywood for this influencer gig. Lots of rooftop bars and celebrities and all that shiz, ya know?" He sounds like my brothers after they've mainlined Redbulls. He's a bit intense, but I'm homeless so what the hell.

"Yeah, cool. That all sounds . . . cool. Anyhow, about the room?"

I toss my bag in the back of the Jeep then slide into the driver's seat and sync my phone to my speaker.

"It's yours, Cut. All yours. This is great!" My speaker only makes Matt louder. Also, I'm not a fan of being called Cut. But we'll get to all that, I'm sure. Or maybe I won't see him much. Or maybe I'll become a reality show on his social feed. Shit, this is a bad idea.

"Utilities included, or rather, kindly picked up by my parents every month," he tosses in before I nearly back out.

I'm not going to find a deal better than this.

Fuck it.

"Okay. Should we set up a time to meet? I hate to sound desperate but . . .I'm kind of desperate. I really need to get out of my place asap. When can I move in?"

"Sure, Cut. I get it."

"I don't really go by Cu—"

"If you've got time, you can move in today. So, listen, bud . . ."

Bud?

I pinch the bridge of my nose and fend off regret. I hate being called *Bud* more than *Cut*.

"I just got back in town and haven't been home yet, but there's a spare buried under the red-hatted gnome in the flower bed. Trust me, you'll see it. I'll text you the address so you can let yourself in to check it out. It's five hundred a month and rent's due, so if you can, leave cash on the counter. I'll let my sister know."

"Sister?" I arch a brow, a little intrigued. Of course, if she's anything like her brother, I'm going to need to invest in locks and earplugs.

"Yeah, it's me and her upstairs. You'll be in the downstairs room. Sorry about the décor in there. Our last roommate was really into pink and she left some shit behind."

"I can deal with pink." My phone buzzes in the center console so I glance at the screen to see the address Matt texted.

"Cool, bro. Well, I sent the digits. I'll see you later tonight. We can hang." He ends the call before I can respond, not that I know how to. I guess I can live with *bro* if that one sticks, especially for five hundred a month.

I press for directions to the address Matt sent and head south to Center Street. I pull along the curb in front of a gray and white brick townhome with a flagstone walkway leading up to the door. The house is maybe five minutes from campus, which is nice, and from the looks of the cars all parked along the street, I'd say most of us are students renting.

I leave my Jeep and head up the walkway, stopping at the small flowerbed at the end of the concrete porch. A six-inch gnome with a red hat and holding up two middle fingers greets me and I chuckle.

"Yeah, it's easy to notice all right," I muse.

I bend down and lift the small statue, then dig into the soft dirt with my index finger. I feel the sharp edge of a key about an inch in the ground and work it out. Not the safest setup. *Note to self—lock bedroom door.*

I open the front door and pop my head inside to look around.

"Hello?" My voice echoes back at me thanks to the slick tile floor and massive entryway ceiling.

It's a nice place, and you can tell a chick lives here. There aren't piles of socks and random shoes around the front door like there always are at my place. I'd like to say I've been neater since my brothers moved out, but that would be a lie. If anything, my slob-like tendencies have increased without the competitive desire to be the best brother. At least the *cleanest* brother.

I step fully into the house and close the door behind me. Holding my breath, I listen for any signal that someone's home. It's eerily quiet. There's an open living room straight ahead with a large sliding glass door that leads out to a patio and what looks like some forest preserve beyond that. I slide open one of the hall closet doors to my right and eye the decent space leftover in there. Might be nice to store my gear in here rather than in my bedroom for once.

Shoving my hands into my jean pockets, I step further into the space and glance at the simple kitchen to the left. It's a nice space with a big island and stools. I could maybe have some of the guys over, which I'm sure Matt would love. I'm not stupid—I know part of the perk of me living with him is he now has access. The guy's good at the social media stuff, though, so what's the harm? *I might regret that thought.*

I pass the stairs and walk through the living room to the hallway that abuts the garage. To one side is the laundry room and a decent-sized bathroom, to the other a dark bedroom still very much filled with someone's crap. I flip the light switch on the wall and step into the center of the room, stretching my arms up and dusting my fingertips against the ceiling before spinning in a slow circle to survey the stack of boxes by the foot of the bed.

"She left some things behind . . . *my ass.*" I unfurl one of the box's flaps and find it filled with sweatshirts and jeans. I pick up the Tiff U gray hoodie on top and poke around the box a little, maybe a small part of me hoping to find lingerie underneath. It's just more sweatshirts, though. From the looks of things in this room, it seems their old roommate is still packing.

"Welp, I guess I can do her that favor," I mutter, cracking open the closet door to find dress clothes still hung up. There's an empty box by the door, so I drag it over and grab a handful of hangers and do my best to fold the clothes into the box in a way that will make them easy to pull back out and hang. It takes me maybe ten minutes to get the closet completely cleared, and maybe a few more to empty the two drawers that were still full of things. Within an hour, I've got the room mostly cleared out and have this girl's boxes stacked neatly in the foyer, ready to go. It will take me the rest of the afternoon to gather up my clothes, along with the house crap like dishes and appliances that I don't want to put into storage.

I pat my pocket to feel for the key and glance around the bedroom one last time before I head out. I would never have paid attention to the Tiff jacket hanging on the back of the bedroom door if it weren't for the name on the back. In bright gold stitched satin letters, it reads PRICE. And the giant volleyball logo under the name sure shrinks the odds that this is a coincidence.

I'm moving into Laney fucking Price's old room.

That's some ironic shit right there.

3 /
laney

I'M NOT sure why I bothered to call my mother. She doesn't get angry about the same things I do, which only makes me more frustrated by the end of our call.

I've been cleared to practice by my medical team. I feel zero pain. I'm strong, and in the unsanctioned practices I've had without coaches present, I'm hitting the ball hard. Maybe even harder than before. But because some person in an office at the NCAA hasn't checked a box or submitted an email or something that says I've been approved to play, I had to spend the entire day today on the phone making pointless pleas with our athletic director and the various people who apparently aren't qualified to clear me officially. And I had to do it all with my backup taking swings and earning a lot of praise a dozen or so feet away from me.

Mom's takeaway from my thirty-minute rant as I walked home in the dark to my new residence?

"Maybe you can still get into the Chicago law program this semester. It would have been nice for them to let you know that you wouldn't be allowed to play volleyball so you could have made an informed decision."

I did make an informed decision. I decided that I have no desire to be a lawyer. Or to be married. My mom doesn't even believe in marriage, but for some reason she made an exception for Cam. Because he comes from money. And he doesn't have starry-eyed pro-sports dreams like the loser who walked out on us. Just because I love this game doesn't mean I'm anything like my father, though. I love this game despite him. I'm good . . . despite him.

I swing my bag around to the front of my body to feel around for the key just as my phone buzzes in my palm with a text. It's from my mom. And it's a link to the late enrollment dates for Chicago.

"Gah!" I growl before dropping my phone into the zipper pocket of my bag as I fish out the door key.

I open the door, prepared for the empty house. Ivy told me she would be working late rounds tonight. She's a nursing student and she's at the bottom of the food chain. I slept like a brick last night after the bar, but I'm still exhausted tonight, so finishing unpacking is going to have to wait.

Bumping the door shut with my hip, I twist the lock and step into the entry, making it maybe three feet before running into a tower of boxes.

"What the—"

I pat the side of the box and wait for my eyes to adjust to the dark house. Within a few seconds, I'm able to see my own handwriting on the cardboard. My stomach drops, and irrational thoughts fly around my head as I drop my bag and feel around the wall for the light switch.

Is Ivy kicking me out? Maybe my room flooded. Shit! Did my room flood?

I flip open one of the box tops and see my clothes—

garments I spent the afternoon hanging thirty hours ago—folded in half and still clinging to their hangers. This is a bad sign. Everything I spent the day moving in is pushed against the wall, and my jacket is slung over the back of the couch. I run my hand over the stitching around the letters of my name as I walk past it and round the corner to head to my room. There's a soft glow of light spilling onto the hallway floor through the cracked-open door. My heart pounds in my chest, then instantly stops when a figure passes across the light.

"Ivy? Matt?" I freeze and contemplate running to the kitchen to grab a knife.

"Hello?" The voice responding from behind the door sounds familiar but I can't place it. It gives me a dose of comfort, though, that whoever is here isn't a total stranger. Or my brain is tricking me into a trap and I'm about to be murdered. I ball my hands into fists and hold them at chest level, ready to swing and run. I'm about to pop the door open with a swift kick when the intruder opens it for me and we come face to *goddamn-you've-got-to-be-kidding-me* face.

"Get out of my fucking room!" My fists turn into hard, flat palms that I shove into Cutter's bare pecs with enough force that they make a smacking sound and leave red imprints behind. My booming pulse pushes against my eardrums as I step into my room and scan for clues. The bed is covered in some heavy black comforter. The dresser is covered in a pile of men's workout clothes while the top drawer is filled with what looks like boxers and mismatched socks just tossed in and not paired.

"You moved out!" Cutter shouts with this annoying sense of authority that sends me down a momentary rabbit hole of what-the-fuckness.

"I moved *in!*" I correct him, my palms pressed against the sides of my head, thumbs rubbing pointless circles into my temples.

"No, that's not what happened. I moved in. And you moved out. Matt said this place was—"

"I don't care what Matt said. Ivy and I moved my shit in yesterday! How are you even here? What the hell is happening?" I'm spinning in a slow circle, trying to decide what action to take first. Cutter starts pacing, and the woody scent of whatever body wash he used makes me nauseous.

"Oh, my God! Did you use *my* shower?" I point out the door to the bathroom across the hall. My eyes scan along the floor to Cutters feet, which are bare. There's a damp towel on the floor—the carpeted floor—so I lunge at it and snatch it in my hand.

"And you're leaving wet towels on the floor? What is happening?" I march the wet towel across the hall and toss it in the sink. My eyes widen at the razor, shaving cream and aftershave all sitting where my brush and body spray were when I left this morning. My white towels are gone, too. Instead, these gross navy blue ones are basically shoved onto the rack.

"No. Just . . . . no." I fly back into the room and immediately begin to roll up the blanket on the bed. Cutter grabs it before I can hurl it into the hallway, and our eyes meet mid tug-of-war. He's holding his phone against his ear.

"Yeah, you need to get here now. There's an issue with your former roommate." His eyes sear into me as he listens to what I'm guessing is Matt on the other end of the line. I jerk the blanket, hoping to catch him off-guard, but he's too quick, pulling back almost immediately and drawing my body into his.

"Ugh!" I shove the blanket into his body and push away from him. His eyes dim and he smirks. Asshole.

"See you in a minute. Thanks." He tosses his phone onto the bed, along with the balled-up blanket.

"Matt will be here in a minute. He's parking out front." He crosses his arms over his smug self and I cough out a laugh.

"You think Matt is going to somehow make you right? Matt's an idiot. Screw this. I'm calling Ivy." I march out to the main room, snag my bag, and take out my phone. I put it on speaker as it rings and walk back into the bedroom where Cutter is annoyingly tucking his clothes into dresser drawers.

"What's up? I'm here until two. You all right?" Ivy's wired on coffee, which makes her loud. Good, because I need my loud, aggressive friend right now.

"We have a problem, Ives. Seems your brother moved in a Neanderthal." I scowl at Cutter, then grab the pair of sweatpants he just put in the drawer and toss them to the floor.

"What? Hold on. Let me step into the break room." Ivy's voice muffles as she moves. I grab another pair of pants from the drawer and toss them on top of the last pair.

"Okay, now, what is happening?" Ivy asks.

"I'm standing in my room . . . along with Cutter McCreary. And my things are all in boxes by the front door. And Cutter's things are all in my room. Hence, the problem." I think I summed that up nicely.

Matt jets into the room with a bag of fast food in one hand and a pair of sunglasses in the other. It's night. No need for shades.

"Hey, man, what's . . . oh, hey, Laney!" Matt says as he catches a glimpse of me in his periphery. He slings one arm around me and drags me into him for a hug that I do not reciprocate.

"Matt, what the fuck did you do!" his sister screams through the phone I'm still holding in my palm.

"Ivy?" He squints and reads her name as I hold up my screen.

"Yeah, Matt. What the fuck did you do?" I pile on.

His eyes flit to mine and a wave of confusion passes behind his pupils, practically drowning him.

"I went to LA. And now I'm back. I stopped for Chicken and Go on my way home. Was I supposed to pick up food for you, Ivy?"

I would yell at him on his sister's behalf except I can tell by his expression that he's dead serious. He has no idea that there seems to be two of us here for the one room.

"Matthew Chester Grossman. Do you ever listen to your voicemail like an adult? Have you read any of my text messages?" Matt sets his food down and pulls his phone from his back pocket, likely to do what his sister just questioned him about doing in the first place. It takes about five seconds for reality to hit him.

"Oh . . . yeah. Shit." He hooks his sunglasses into the neckline of his black T-shirt, then runs his fingers through his messy hair.

"Ivy, I didn't know. My bad, Laney." He gives me a sheepish grin, and because he's Matt and has always been, well, like this, I soften a little. Not completely, because I still have the issue of my belongings sitting in boxes once again and the man I hate most taking up my space.

"Dude, bro." Matt spins slowly to meet Cutter's waiting hard stare. He holds his hands out to either side and shakes his head yet doesn't utter another word.

"You told me this room was mine, man. Class starts tomorrow. I have a game soon. *Dude, bro?* That's your solution?" Cutter's jaw flexes and I swear he's going to crack a molar.

My phone clutched in one hand, I move toward the dresser and scoop up a stack of Cutter's sweatpants and carry them out the door.

"That really sucks, Cutter. I'll help you box your clothes back up." I'm a step away from the door when Cutter swoops in front of me and clutches his pants in both hands, jerking them back from me.

"Oh ho ho, hell no! We had a deal. I brought your cash. I am not moving my shit back out of this room." He plants his stack of sweats back where I snatched them from, then folds his arms across his chest. Which is still bare. It's annoyingly distracting.

"Well, I'm not going anywhere, and I was here first," I declare, setting my phone on the dresser so I can hold my fists on my hips.

Cutter snickers, then pinches the bridge of his nose.

"I've already moved your shit out," he argues, and my eyes narrow on his stupid smug face.

My lips pucker as I struggle not to blurt out the dozens of names I want to call him.

"Cutter, you're going to have to move in with Matt and share a room," Ivy suggests. I snap and smile at her brilliant solution and Matt shrugs. He seems fine with it.

"Works for me," I say, reaching for the stack of sweatpants again a second before Cutter's heavy palm lands on top.

"Hell no! No offense, Matt, but rooming with you . . . I'd

kill you. You know it," Cutter says, shaking his head. Matt's face scrunches, a little hurt.

"Well, that's a risk you're going to have to—"

"You move in with Ivy!" Cutter blurts out. His lip quirks up on one side, proud of his solution.

"No offense, Cutter, but I pay the most rent and I work crazy shifts at a hospital," Ivy says, beeping from the emergency room doors blaring in the background. "I'm not getting bunk beds, and my best friend was given the room first. If you want, you can stay on our couch until you find another place."

I shift my gaze from my phone screen back to Cutter. His mouth is a hard line as he stares down at the floor, but I have a feeling he's about to give in. His cheek dents as he chews at the inside and his gaze darts to mine.

"We'll share," he says, shifting his weight, a daring smirk threatening to form a dimple on one side of his face.

I try to read him, tell if he's kidding, but he doesn't crack. I spit out a sharp laugh.

"That's ridiculous!" It's also my biggest nightmare.

"Why? You afraid you'll fall in love with me and then this whole act you have going about hating my guts will be nothing but a lie?" He lifts a brow as I cock my head to the side a tick.

"That's stupid." I huff out another stunted and frustrated laugh before crossing my arms over my chest and tucking my hands deep into my pits. I'm not okay with the direction this is going. But I'm also not letting Cutter McCreary steal another thing away from me.

"If it's stupid then it shouldn't be a big deal. I mean, how often are we going to be here at the same time?" He shrugs as if that's the only thing to sort out with his absurd plan.

"Uh, we'll both be *sleeping* here. That's the big deal."

"I can handle sleeping next to you. At least for a semester." He seems so sure, but I know better. Cutter would be hitting on me nonstop, probably even in his sleep.

"You wouldn't keep your hands to yourself. And I can't sleep with one eye open every night. This season is too important for that." I shake my head vehemently, as if somehow my action will shake the idea out of Cutter's head too.

"Wanna bet?" He purses his lips, a cocky smile faintly curving the edges of his mouth as he holds out a palm. I glance down at his hand and laugh it off. He nudges his palm a little closer. "I'm serious. We'll make it a bet. We'll share the room and whoever catches feelings first has to leave."

His challenge piques my curiosity, along with my competitive side.

"When you put it like that, it sounds like a sucker's bet," I say, unfurling my arms from around my body and holding my palm up yet still not out to shake his.

"Then what do you have to lose?" His mouth twists into this arrogant pucker.

"You won't make it a week," I laugh out, giving in and shaking his hand. His fingers wrap around my palm and he gives me a slight squeeze. There's a roughness to his skin.

"Ha, okay. You think you're that irresistible, huh?" He breaks our hold first, and I take that as my first tiny win.

"No, I just think you're that weak." I snatch up my phone and take my friend off speaker. I hold my phone up to my ear. "You hear all that?" I ask her.

"Yeah, and I think it sounds like a really bad idea." Ivy sighs into the phone, and I pass by Matt, who is still standing in the center of the room wearing a dumbstruck expression.

"I can handle anything Cutter McCreary can throw at me," I profess, and I make sure I say it loud enough that Cutter hears as I leave the room and march into the living room to grab the first batch of my many boxes.

"Yeah, maybe. Just remember what you're supposed to be focusing on this year. Beating Cutter isn't going to make or break your future," Ivy says. I pause at the first stack of boxes and push my tongue into my cheek as I nod.

"Fair point. I promise to hardly notice he's here until he's gone."

"It's a good plan. Look, I've gotta get back. We'll catch up more tomorrow when I'm off." We both say our goodbyes and I tuck my phone into my sports bra to free up both hands so I can carry my moving boxes into my room for the second time.

Matt is streaming video on his phone as I walk in, putting his own spin on things and likely turning this into a public spectacle. "Team hockey versus team volleyball is happening under my roof, y'all. Your boy Cutter is facing off against Laney Price for the last room near campus. And the tension in this place is unreal!" I roll my eyes, then drop my boxes on the floor before smacking Matt's phone out of his hand and sending it tumbling into the hallway.

I shoot Cutter a challenging glare.

"Dude, Laney. Come on," Matt whines as he makes his way out of the room, leaving Cutter and me on our own to sort out the details of this arrangement.

"Well, are you going to just stand there or are you going to help me move back in?" I tug the closet door open and push the hung dress shirts, jackets, and hoodies to one side, then snap my gaze back to him. " I hope you don't think you get the closet to yourself."

"Of course I'll help. I'm nothing but a gentleman." Cutter snags a white T-shirt from one of the drawers and slips it over his head. I subconsciously study his forearms and then his abs as he works the shirt down his body, halting my ogling when I realize I've been caught.

"You prefer I keep this off?" he teases, tugging at the hem of the shirt and stepping into the doorway. I let my eyes roam down the center of his chest again then back up to his eyes before I shrug.

"I prefer you don't exist," I say before slipping by him and willing myself not to commit his freakishly perfect abs to memory. I add some extra sway to my hips while I'm at it since he's now walking behind me. If I want Cutter out of here in a week, I'm going to need to turn up the heat a little.

"Afraid you're stuck with me, Laney. All. Night. Long," he says, drawling the words out in a way that seeps into my stomach and warms my insides.

Shit.

"I'm sure I'll barely notice," I toss over my shoulder before training my focus on the next stack of moving boxes. I bend down and hoist them into my arms, but as I turn, Cutter is waiting with a grin and open palms to take the load from me. I let him, but then quickly realize as he walks away that now I'm the one left watching his ass and broad shoulders and stupid wavy hair that tickles the back of his neck.

Nope. Nothing to see here at all.

cutter

I TOOK the high road last night and slept on the couch. Which is too small for my body. And left me with a massive crick in my neck this morning. Nothing like waking up to skate at the crack of dawn when your body is literally clicking like a LEGO man's. I could tell everything was going to be a battle, though. And the more Laney thinks of me as a nice guy, the easier it will be to win her over in other ways. Since she pretty much hates me now, I've got a steep climb.

"Dude, no offense but you look like shit today," Chuck says as he shoots the pucks back to me. He wanted to get some extra defensive work in this morning, and I needed to hit shit hard, so it works out for both of us.

"What looks shittier? My shot or my face?" He better say my face. I haven't shaved in three days, and my beard grows fast—and kind of wild.

"Hard to say," he coughs out. I rear back and slap the puck at his chest. He snags it with his glove, then laughs.

"Fine, just your face. How's the roommate situation going?" Thanks to Matt's popular social stream, the entire team knows I'm living with Laney Price. Word even got to

Coach, who made a point of sternly warning me not to stir up World War III.

"Well, last night I slept on the smallest couch ever invented, so . . . not great, man. Not great." I nod to him and he readies himself in the goal. I take a few shots and slip one by him, which pisses him off. Good. He called my shots shit, and I don't think he was sincere when he took that back.

"You just going to let her have the room, then?"

I grimace at him because while that would definitely be the less stressful route to take, I'd still be left with nowhere to stay. The couch is not a permanent solution, and I doubt anyone wants to see me transforming the living room into air mattress central. The two-plus hours to drive from my mom's house down south to campus isn't an option either, so, no . . . I'm in this to win it.

"I was being a gentleman. Tonight, it's her turn." I tap the ice and line up another puck. Chuck sinks into position, and I send the puck to the back of the net through the slight space he left under his five hole.

"Damn it!" He tosses his glove on the ice and tips his mask up. "I'm done for the day. I'm frustrated."

Too bad. I'm frustrated too, and this was helping.

Chuck and I skate in and hit the showers. I leave him to grumble on his own since I have my first photography class in twenty minutes. Apparently, every Tiff student has to complete two art credits, something I seem to have put off finishing the second part of until my senior year. It feels inconsequential in terms of a business degree, but since I would like the diploma in case I'm not as fortunate as my brothers in terms of going pro, I opted for photography. I've always had a good eye for composition, and my dad had a lot of camera gear. I breezed through the intro class last year, and the advanced classes are mostly project-based, so I should be able to knock out my assignments around my game schedule.

I make it to class with about two minutes to spare, and since I'm the last to arrive and barely fit into the desk-chair setups this school insists on using, I gain everyone's full attention as I fumble my way into my seat. I blow up at the hair dangling over my brow and lift a hand from the desktop when my gaze meets the pair of wide eyes on the girl sitting across from me.

"How ya doin'?"

She flashes me a quick smile, then immediately ducks her head and stares at her phone in her lap, long blonde hair swooping around her face like curtains closing.

Okay, then.

Our instructor pulls the door closed as she enters the room and she immediately starts handing out papers. "Welcome to Advanced Portrait Photography. I'm Nadia Kaufman, and I will be your assignment editor for the semester."

I scratch at my head as I peruse the checklist she just handed me. It's a list of events on campus as well as names of people, and a few stand out to me—Max Syme, our best defender on the hockey team, and Laney Price.

"Everyone will need to complete portrait sessions with two different people on this list. We're doing the administration a favor this semester. All of your work in this class will be used for the various athletic department promo pieces as well as the media guide. What you come up with and create with your subjects is not only a reflection on your ability and your grade, but it is a reflection on Tiff University as well. So . . . no pressure, folks. You have the month to complete this first assignment, and of course use of the tech room and any gear you may need to check out. "

A tall, slender woman in a pair of black overalls that make her somehow look both artsy and like a model at the same time, our teacher stops her pacing at the front of the class and crosses her ankles as she leans into the podium.

"Any questions?" She arches a brow.

I glance around the room, not wanting to be the first person to speak. It becomes clear pretty quickly, though, that I'm the only extravert in this room.

"Can we pick from the list now?" I finally utter.

"First come, first served," she says.

I nod and glance back down at the paper to give myself one more gut check before verbally committing. It seems too good of an opportunity to pass up. Forced time together with Laney, her image in my hands. She's going to have to trust me to some degree.

"I'll take Laney Price and Max Syme."

"They're yours," she says, swiping a pen across her copy of the list.

Laney is mine.

An evil laugh echoes around the inside of my head at the thought.

The rest of the class divvies up the remaining names before we spend the rest of the hour on lighting review and looking at portrait samples.

I go right from class to practice, and Coach runs us long since we have a big match-up coming this weekend. By the time I make it to my Jeep, I've got three missed phone calls from my mom. Missing one of her calls always slams my chest with instant panic and guilt. I call her back as soon as I pull out of the lot.

"Oh, hell. I'm sure I worried you, Cutter. I'm fine. I was trying to remember how to log in to the damn streaming service you set up on the TV," my mom says, rather than just answering with, "Hello."

"It's fine. Yeah, I worried, but I'm glad you're okay. Do you still need help getting logged in?" My mom is not very tech-savvy. She's spent her life working as a craft instructor at the local art shop. She can spin her own yarn, but she can't make a Facebook account to save her life.

"Maybe tomorrow. I gave up, and I might have broken the remote."

I chuckle, imagining her tossing it at the wall in frustration. My dad was always the calm one in the house. The McCreary marriage flips every hockey-family stereotype on its head. Mom? She has always been the hard-ass. She's the Irish temper, and definitely the enforcer. Dad, he was a softy. He let us get away with *everything*.

"You remember when you caught Dad smoking out in the shed?" My lips pucker into a grin at the memory.

"Oh, good God, yes. That man! He stunk like cigars, but in he came trying to tell me someone in the neighborhood must be smoking meat or something. Took me all of a minute to find his stash!" She laughs at the memory, and it makes my smile grow. I love these small talks with her. I know my brothers think I do it to show off being her favorite, but honestly? I think I get more out of it than she does.

"Hey, I'm out of the condo, by the way. I set up some movers to take the rest of the stuff and put it into storage. I'll worry about that over the winter break. Maybe we can sell the things none of us wants." I mentally make a list of everything in that place still—years of accumulated junk. The important stuff is still at my mom's house, but I'm sure there are a few things she'll want to save.

I pull into the driveway but stop short when I realize I'm not sure who's parked in the garage. I back out and instead park at the curb while my mom continues to go through the list of things in the old house by memory. I don't want to tell her the stuff I've already donated or thrown away, so when she tells me just to keep it, I say thanks and move on.

She must be feeling good today. It's refreshing since the last few times she's gone through treatments she's been pretty flat in the days afterward. Apparently, she felt good enough today to drive herself to the grocery store. Of course, I hate that I wasn't there to help with that, but she seems proud of being able to pick out her own produce rather than ordering online and waiting for someone to dump it in her trunk.

I tuck the phone between my shoulder and chin so I can sling my gear bag over my shoulder and make my way inside. My legs are toast and I'm desperate for the shower. I hope I won't have to fight Laney for it.

"I know it's bad timing with the house, but I'll make it up to you with a home-cooked meal. I'm making the stuffed peppers you like. So you'll be here, right?" My mom thinks she has to bribe me over to the house with her cooking. I'd come regardless, but I'm not about to turn down stuffed peppers.

"You keep talking to me like that and I'm coming over right now," I say as I step into the bedroom and come face to face with Laney. She's holding a fat roll of blue painter's tape, and as my eyes scan the room, I realize she's literally marked the space in half.

"Well, you could fix the remote then if you do," she says.

"Yeah, see you Sunday," I confirm with my mom before ending our call and tossing my phone on the bed. I drop my bag to the floor and slowly spin to take it all in—the dresser taped down the center, all the way to the small drawer in the middle. The closet shelves are marked in half, along with the bar and the set of hooks I will never use. The bed frame is rationed into halves with blue tape, and my curiosity can't handle not flipping the covers off the mattress to see what her solution was there. A thick, black elastic band stretches the length of the mattress. I lift it with my fingers and let it snap back before huffing out a single laugh and meeting Laney's gaze.

"Holy crap! You're nuts!"

She grimaces and proceeds to kneel and press a long strip of tape on the carpet from the foot of the bed to the edge of the dresser.

"Was that one of your adoring fans talking dirty to you?" she grumbles as she tears the tape off and presses the end into the carpet fibers with her thumb.

"Uh, no. And more importantly, you do realize we can't cut the door in half, right? One of us has to get in to get over to this side." I hop over her line, assuming she's pushing me to the far side.

She stands and blows up at some loose hairs tickling her forehead and face as she considers my critique. Her eyes flit to me a second before she nudges a sweatshirt I left on the floor to the other side of the tape.

"Guess you'll have to jump. Might make it hard for you to leap out the door to get to whoever is talking to you like that, though, and making you want to rush over right now." She rolls her eyes and turns her back to me before putting the roll of tape into the drawer of one of the night stands. I smirk, amused that she insists I was having a flirt fest with some girl on the phone.

"Right, well. I'll be sure to let my *mom* know that the reason I'm late for dinner Sunday is because my crazy-ass roommate insists I complete an obstacle course every time I want to leave the house."

Laney glances at me sideways. Her red cheeks make me pretty certain she's a tad embarrassed by her assumption.

"I suggest you practice it then, so you're never late," she says, turning her attention back to her own side of the room. "For your mom or any other . . . whatever."

She waves a nonchalant hand over her shoulder, and I cough out a laugh as I wait for her to engage more. She doesn't. Instead, she snags her laptop from her backpack and hops up on the bed with her blanket, stretching out her long legs and covering up with the bright floral quilt before resting her laptop on her thighs and flipping it open to begin typing.

"Practice." I nod and hold my mouth in a tight-lipped smile. "All right then. Practice it is."

I pique her interest enough to glance at me briefly over the top of her screen as I tiptoe to the edge of her tape line.

"This is my half, then? This . . . right here?" I point down at the tape and she shuts her laptop and sits up as if she actually has to check it.

"I mean, I didn't measure, so you may have an extra inch or so that you don't deserve." Her lips form this annoying, arrogant straight line and her head tilts slightly to one side.

"Believe me, Laney. I have plenty of extra inches."

Her gaze darts up as she breathes out an annoyed sigh. I take that opportunity to leap from my side of the tape to the open doorway. Because of the angle, I have to grab the door jamb to maintain my balance. A quick glance back at my enemy lets me know she's still watching, so the balancing act is worth it.

I pull up the bottom of my gray practice shirt, bunching it in a fist at the center of my chest so I can flex my abs with every ounce of energy left after skating for four hours. Her eyes dart lower and I smirk, pulling my shirt up over my head then tossing it into the room—on my side of the floor. I run my hands through my sweat-dampened hair and hold my elbows out so I can flex my biceps and forearms. Yeah, I feel like an asshole with the whole Magic Mike routine, but Laney isn't laughing so I know on some level, it's working on her.

I reach up and grab the top of the door jamb and lean my head to one side, pushing my tongue in my cheek before stretching my mouth into a faint smile.

"Should I keep going?" I quirk a brow.

She shakes her head and shrugs.

"I don't fucking care." Her words don't match the quick dart of her tongue along her lips, though.

"All right, then." I let go of the door trim and hook my thumbs in the waistband of my joggers.

I pause for a second and tick my head a fraction to feel her out. She blinks slowly then reopens her laptop, lifting her knees to prop the screen high enough to block her view. Nothing stopping me now, so I pull my pants off and toss them onto the bed—purposely aiming for the very center.

Laney closes her screen halfway and peers over the edge at my pants, then over to me. Her discipline not to look away from my face is impressive, and probably a good thing because this whole charade has my cock hard. Boxer briefs leave little to the imagination.

She kicks her blanket off one leg then digs her bare foot

under my joggers to give them a swift flick off the mattress and onto the floor. Again, on my side.

"I'm gonna go ahead and shower," I say, an attempt to draw her attention to me one last time. She doesn't look my way again, though, instead opening her screen back up and settling into a pretty swift round of typing.

Huh.

I linger for a few seconds, taking a good look at her toned legs and the white cotton shorts that barely hug her ass. She's wearing an oversized Tiff football sweatshirt, which makes me wonder if she's dating someone on the team. She supposedly moved out from a place she shared with her ex-boyfriend, but that's all I could get out of her last night before she refused to speak anymore and I *kindly* offered to sleep on the couch.

It takes a few minutes for the shower water to heat up, so while I wait I set up the small speaker I keep on the sink, syncing it to my workout playlist. It's mostly rap and a few hard metal songs, which I'm sure Laney hates, so I go ahead and amp the volume up a few extra notches before getting in the shower.

I'm mid-shampoo when I hear the fisted knock on the door.

"Turn that down!" Her voice carries over the sound of the water, but I pretend I can't hear her.

"Sorry, in the shower! What?" I grin as my fingers work the soap into a lather on my scalp.

The bathroom door pops open.

"I'm writing a paper, you asshole." Her voice is crystal clear now.

"Yeah, sorry. I'm showering but I'll take care of it when I'm done. Might have a soak, though."

I chuckle silently to myself. From behind the screen of the shower curtain, I tilt my head back. The water rushes along my forehead and clogs my ears as I rinse away the shampoo. My eyes are closed from the suds, and when I wipe away the remnants with my thumb and index finger to open my eyes again, I find Laney has pulled the curtain open and is staring at my face.

"What the fu—"

She holds my speaker between us and flicks open the back panel with her thumbnail. Tilting the device, she spills two batteries into her palm before pushing the panel back in place and tossing my now useless speaker onto the bathroom counter. She holds the batteries up once her back is to me.

"I'm keeping these." She pulls the door shut behind her with enough force it sends a rush of cold air through the open shower curtain.

Craziest part? I'm still hard as a rock.

**5 /
laney**

KILLING the speaker distraction was easy. Unfortunately, I can't yank the batteries out of Cutter. And now that he's showered—still shirtless and wearing these low-slung gray sweatpants as his massive body takes up the entire half of the bed I allotted him—I'm distracted.

The entire bed wiggles every time he adjusts the crossing of his legs or fidgets with his pillow under his neck, switching hands to rest behind his head while he holds his phone up with the other. I have about five hundred words left in this essay, and in the thirty minutes Cutter's been lying next to me, I've written the same four over and over again.

THIS IS NOT WORKING. THIS IS NOT WORKING. THIS IS NOT WORKING!

He finally flops on his side, propping his head on his elbow. He tugs on my blanket. I jerk it away from him and give him a glare. All that does is make him grin, and shit . . . now he's showing teeth. I bet he had braces. Those teeth are perfect. Bright white. And there's the dimple.

"I'm trying to finish a paper. Can you not act like an annoying little brother *please?*" I shake my head and retrain my focus on my computer screen. It's all pretend, though, since all I'm doing is waiting to see him move in my periphery. How does he smell so good? Seriously, his scent is like a calming spa treatment, or it would be if I could calm my ass down. Instead, I'm stressed to the max about getting this paper done so I can get some sleep.

Shit. How am I going to sleep in here tonight?

"I didn't mean to annoy you like a little brother. I was going to ask to use the edge of your blanket to prop my phone up so I can read."

"You read?" I respond quickly. And wow, that insult did not land with the satisfaction I thought it would. Cutter blinks a few times and rolls to his other side.

"Never mind."

My stomach knots as I stare at his bare back for a few seconds. He takes a heavy breath and holds out an arm, palming his phone. His forearms are somehow more defined than his chest. I squint to read his screen but the words are too small.

"Sorry," I utter, barely audible.

I look back at my computer and delete the last row of THIS IS NOT WORKING. I'm not worried about falling for Cutter, but I'm sure not making it easy for him to fall for me. Not if I keep snapping at him like that. I glance back at him just as he swipes the screen to a new page.

"What are you reading?"

His head shifts and his eyelashes flutter as he stretches to glance from his periphery.

"It's for my marketing class. It's a study on Coke's branding."

Branding, huh?

"Any good takeaways?" I could use some branding of my

own. Maybe I can get something out of these insufferable few days together in this room.

"I'm not sure yet. I mean, Coke is kind of like a brand beast. It's hard to apply what they've done to newer products and ideas because they've been around so long. But the fact you can't help but think of them when you see red and white is pretty impressive." He shifts to sit up, leaning against the wooden headboard as he palms his phone and flips back a few pages.

"Like this part . . . it was pretty cool. And maybe, I could see how this would work for athletes." He hands me his phone and I glance through the section about partnerships. I have made a few deals with Midwestern companies, but nothing major. There was a car dealership that used my likeness last year. I got a free lease for a year out of that deal, but then I got hurt—hence, no renewal and no car this year.

"It's easier for you guys," I say, handing back his phone.

His body shakes with a short laugh.

"How so?"

I give him a sideways look but he's serious.

"Well, for starters, men's sports get way more attention from the media. Your potential for TV deals is bigger regardless of your performance. And that equates to cash in your pocket. Meanwhile, we can go twenty games undefeated and come out of it with BOGO coupons for the burger joint."

Cutter studies my face for a few seconds, and I notice small details around his eyes. His lashes are copper-tinged, and he has faint freckles that fall into the creases when he talks or smiles.

"You know I had nothing to do with the locker room bullshit, right?"

I snap out of my temporary hypnosis and jerk back an

inch or two. I never expected him to bring that topic up with me. My brow draws low and I pull my lips in tight, willing away the tight feeling growing in my gut. I can't tell if he's trying to piss me off by bringing that up or what, but I'm not going to let it fire me up and turn him off even more.

"You personally? Yeah, I know. But *you* as in . . . hockey player, male athlete, campus hot boy? You had more to do with it than you let on." I turn my attention back to my screen, mostly to shut myself up.

"Campus . . . hot boy?"

My eyes flutter closed. My computer screen follows. *Why did I say that?*

"I can see I'm going to have to get up early and finish this paper without you hanging around." I lean to my left and plug my computer in to charge overnight. I'm going to need to get up at 4 a.m. if I want enough time to finish this thing.

"I can be quiet. Sorry. Lips zipped. Promise." He shifts his weight and our arms touch. We both jerk away on contact. Bare skin to bare skin. His body is hot. *Why is his body so hot?* Hot and . . . well, *hot?*

"It's fine. I'll finish it tomorrow. My brain isn't in the right space." I wriggle my feet to pull my socks off as I tug my blanket up my body and sink down into my pillow. I'm not normally a still sleeper. I tend to flop from side to side, stomach to back. Tonight, though, I'm going to do my damnedest to sleep like a corpse.

I bury my head into my pillow enough that the sides form a cradle around my head and close my eyes.

"You know it's only eight-thirty, right?"

My eyes pop open. I shift my gaze to Cutter, who is also in the corpse position but seems way more relaxed. He holds his phone up and shows me the time on it as if I need proof.

"I go to bed early," I lie. I *should* go to bed early, but I'm a horrible insomniac. I usually start the process around nine, and somewhere around one or two I drift off. You'd think with the crazy routine I put my body through, I'd collapse by the end of the day. My mom says it's my busy mind. I'm pretty sure it's the thousands of problems I seem to save for bedtime, when my brain likes to catalogue them.

"Good to know. Well, good night. I'll kill the light. I can read in the dark." Cutter gets up and crosses the room, stopping at the tape mark and leaning over the dresser, every torso muscle showing off. He looks at me over his shoulder, his reach still a foot short of the light switch.

"You can make an exception to turn the light off," I say through a soft laugh.

"Phew, good. Okay. I was starting to worry I would have to really practice that leap from the doorway to my side, practicing all my moves for door shutting and light-switch flipping."

He flicks the light off and returns to his side of the bed. I follow his form, looking at him in my periphery as he sinks down to fully lay next to me. He adjusts his pillow and tucks a hand behind his neck, his elbow dangerously close to my temple. I sigh and roll my head the other way.

"Oh, sorry," he hums, adjusting again, switching arms to give me more space.

"You know, I'd be down with buying twins," I grumble.

"Sure. I mean, if that will help you in terms of . . . well, you know." He ends it there, and several seconds pass while I hold my breath and wait for him to finish that thought. Because *no—I don't know.*

Unable to stand it, I roll to my side and narrow my eyes on him.

"Help me how?"

I'm not surprised to see his lip tick up slightly, but it still pisses me off.

"With the bet. You can't stand being this close to me. It makes you . . . weak." His smirk grows.

"Oh, hell no, buddy! That has nothing to do with it. Your bulky-ass body just takes up too much room." I shove his bicep and he goes nowhere. I don't even think his muscle twitched.

"Well, you're the one who put this line on the bed. I don't care how much room you take up." He lifts the band I put around the mattress and lets it snap.

"Fine, then. Move over," I say, flopping to my other side so my back is to him. I arch my spine and press against his side, urging him to scoot to the edge of his side. He chuckles but moves to give me room.

"You comfortable now? No temptations driving you wild?" His deep laugh fires me up a little more and I shove backward hard, knocking him to the floor.

"Now I'm comfortable." I snuggle into my blanket and pillow and force my eyes shut.

"You're stronger than you look, Price. I'll give you that," he says, still laughing. It pisses me off that I can't seem to piss *him* off. This whole thing is fun for him. It's maddening.

"You have no idea how strong I am," I mutter as I will myself not to react to the feel of his body slipping back into bed. The mattress sinks with his weight and his blanket covers my feet with some extra weight.

No matter how hard I try not to, I keep mentally replaying every word he's said tonight. I imagine having better responses, and I dream of my own bed and a room that he isn't in. But I also refuse to roll over and let him have his way. That's how things are for Cutter. He *always* gets his way. And that's why, no matter how tempting his body heat is at my back, I know I will not suddenly grow feelings for him.

"You're still awake, huh?" he whispers. I'm not sure how long I've been trying to sleep, but I guess it's been close to an hour. The room got darker a minute ago when he put his phone on the charger.

I think about not answering, but he'll just hover over me and test my eyes, so I let out a heavy sigh.

"I don't sleep well sometimes. When I'm stressed, for example."

"Oh, I make you . . . stressed," he teases.

I sigh harder this time.

"Yeah, and not in a good way."

He doesn't have a response to that, and that same guilty twinge that hit my gut the last time I insulted him is back. *Damn you, conscience!*

"I have trouble sleeping too. Sometimes I meditate."

I cough out a short laugh because the visual of him sitting with his eyes closed and his hands on his knees seems ridiculous. He's at least six-four. And he's as bulky as a refrigerator.

"Way to perpetuate the stigma, Price. Classy."

I snap my mouth shut. Even though he was sort of joking with his response, there was sharp truth to it too. It's not fair to assume big guys can't have complex problems. I know better.

"Sorry, again. I'm just grumpy."

"I get it. It's fine." His voice is a little raspy, and I'm not sure whether it's sleep catching up to him or he's trying to whisper. There's something soothing to it.

"What has you stressed? Besides the obvious," he says,

more soft laughter filling our small space. I laugh too, giving in for the night. There's no reason we can't make this easy. Cordial. Maybe even friendly. All on the surface, of course.

"I'm still not officially cleared from injury. I mean, I'm cleared medically, but the powers that be still need someone to sign something or click something or—"

"Right. Put a rubber stamp on a file. I get ya," he breathes out with the kind of sigh that makes me think he's been through something similar.

"Right? So many hoops. You'd think the school was the one injured and not me." I blink my eyes open briefly to disrupt the visual of Chelsea Mickelson playing my position instead of me.

"They might sit me for the first few games." I don't know how I let that confession slip out, but now that my words have hit the air, my chest opens wider and I take a full breath.

"Yeah, but those games don't matter. They won't be conference. And it's just to make sure you come back fully ready. They don't want you getting hurt again." His words echo what my coaches have said. Surely, he gets the truth, though. He knows that's what they have to say. They don't owe me a spot. If someone proves to be better than me, that's the player they're going to get behind.

I shift so I'm on my back again and I roll my head to look him in his waiting eyes. I wonder how long he's been looking at me like this. He's either secretly an incredible actor or he's genuinely interested in what I have to say. His eyes are kind, a slight squint due to the soft smile on his full lips. His hand is propping his head up, his fingers disappearing into the soft waves of brown hair. It's too bad this isn't the version of him I met first—the sober guy with kind eyes. Instead, I got the jackhole at the kegger who was so sure I would sleep with him our freshman year.

"I don't want to think about it. I just need to keep rehabbing and working out as much as I can until I get cleared for the court." My chest squeezes with all the negative thoughts swirling around about my playing time, what that means for my plans, and Chelsea's decent showing at practice.

"I get it. Topic closed. Feel free to open it up anytime you need to, though. I'm a good listener."

My mouth spreads into a fast smile at his response, but before it turns into a laugh I get a good look at the sincerity on his face. He's not being cheesy or fake. So instead, I nod.

"Deal."

I roll back to my other side, maybe running away from the tension I felt just then. Somehow I can tell his eyes are still on me. A part of me likes it. It feels safe in the dark to let him look at me. It makes me want to show off for him, physically. To tempt him, of course. Nothing more than that.

I kick my blanket off and stretch my arm up over my head, knowing it will make my shirt rise up enough to show my midriff and the curve of my hips.

"How old is your little brother?" His question comes out with a tinge of nervous wavering in his voice. He's looking at me for sure.

"I don't have one."

"Oh, I thought . . . when you said I was annoying like a little brother. So. . . any siblings?" His voice is simmering again, soft and deep. I close my eyes and breathe in through my nose.

"Just me and my mom. I mean, I have a dad. Legally. But that's about it." My mind shifts its weight from Chelsea to my father, and that's an easier frustration to deal with. I'm good at that one.

"Oh. I'm sorry, if you even want to hear sorry for that. I get it if you don't."

My thoughts pause and I smile with my eyes closed as I take in his words. Nobody has ever quite reacted that way when I mention having a bad relationship with my father. It's kind of nice to hear sorry. And it's also nice to have the option to reject it.

"Thanks," I say. "How about you? Brothers? Family?"

"Well, you know about my mom already—my hot date for Sunday." He follows up with a soft laugh and I roll my face slightly into my pillow. I'm a little embarrassed about that. I'm sure it came across as jealousy when I thought he was on the phone with some puck bunny.

"My dad passed away last year. He was a great guy, but he lived pretty hard and it basically wore out his parts. Liver, kidneys, among other things."

What he isn't saying is his dad was an alcoholic.

"I'm sorry," I say, biting my bottom lip before adding on, "If you want the sorry. If not, save it for later."

A short breathy laugh leaves him.

"Thanks. And I'll take it. He really was a great guy. He was nothing but kind and warm and generous. None of those stereotypical bad traits that usually go with being the life of the party at the corner bar."

I picture Cutter holding up the pitchers a couple of nights ago and how everyone cheered his name. I wonder if the elder McCreary was adored like that. Maybe that's where his charm comes from.

"And brothers—yeah, I've got those. I'm one of five. Flynn and Todd, you probably know. Then there's Patrick, he's the oldest and has a baby girl. Andrew is next, and he has twin boys. I guess that runs in the family. We all grew up playing hockey in southern Iowa. Our town is called Springs, and it's barely on the map, but . . ."

I'm not sure if it was the timbre of his voice, the way it fell somewhere between late-night radio host and bedtime story narrator, or if it was the blissful tone of his words as he spoke about his family that did it, but something about Cutter McCreary's voice in the dark put me fast asleep.

It's three in the morning and I startle myself awake, a habit I have when I'm in unfamiliar places. This place has yet to feel like home. Cutter's pillow is pulled over his eyes and his arm rests on top to weigh it down. His chest rises slowly, his breath quiet and steady. I spend longer than I should watching him sleep, and when it becomes clear that I'm not going back to dreamland, I slip to the floor and pull my laptop down with me so I can finish my paper in peace and quiet. And without waking Cutter. I refuse to consider why that last part matters.

6 /

cutter

I COULD TELL she fell asleep when I started talking about my twin nephews. I described them in detail, then added made-up traits like tails and horns on their heads just to see if she responded. She didn't, and the way her body remained perfectly still let me know she'd nodded off.

I pulled the cover back over her body. She was showing off for me when she slid it off. I knew what she was doing, and I didn't mind. Laney's sexy as hell when she's not smearing my name out loud or swearing at me. Actually, she's a little sexy then, too.

What's crazy is how fast I fell asleep after her. I usually struggle. I didn't get into it with her last night but that's my biggest worry about sharing this room—and bed—with her for however long it lasts. I'm basically nocturnal. Actually, nocturnal would indicate that I sleep during the day but that doesn't happen either. Maybe a better term for me would be non-turnal.

I'm not even groggy this morning, which is also unusual. I didn't hear Laney leave, but her running shoes are gone, along with her workout bag, so my gut says she went to the gym to prove herself and retake her dominant place on the team. She and I have more in common than she realizes.

Skipping the shower this morning, I pull my hoodie over my jersey and grab a Tiff beanie to pull down over my crazy-ass hair before grabbing my gear bag, keys, wallet, and phone. The living room smells of strong coffee, and I follow the scent into the kitchen where Ivy is pouring half a pot into a tumbler that seems to be holding way too much.

"Aren't you going into the medical field? That feels like a toxic amount you've got going there," I joke as I gesture to what looks to be about forty-four ounces. She shoots me a glare before shoveling a scoop of ice into her container and screwing on the lid, then giving the mixture a good shake.

"Touchy subject. Got it. Do not mention your coffee addiction. Mind if I . . ." I point to the pot that has about a normal cup remaining. Ivy grabs the handle and carries the pot to the sink and starts to pour it out. I drop my gear on the floor and step toward her, tilting my head to the side.

"Come on. You cannot like me all you want, but don't take things out on perfectly good coffee."

She stops pouring and slams the pot down on the counter. I wince.

"Fine. Get your own mug, though. For now, you can use one of Matt's. They're in there," she says, pointing her thumb over her shoulder.

"Thanks," I choke out. Damn, is Ivy intense. I see why she and Laney are friends. I grab a small thermos from the cabinet and fill it with the remnants of coffee.

"And for your information, the medical field basically functions on coffee. This amount?"—she shakes her tumbler —"This is nothing. And I have a test today so there is going to be more when this is gone."

I shoot her a faint grin and for a blip I think she gives me one in return. I maybe imagined it. Regardless, Ivy spoke words to me that were not flanked by swear words and loathing. If I can get Ivy on my side, maybe Laney will soften more too.

"I don't like you, Cutter. And you're going to lose that stupid bet." She points at me as she grabs a backpack practically bursting at the zippers from the stool near the kitchen counter.

"Noted," I say with a wink, putting on a good face. *Yeah, I imagined that grin.*

I snag my gear bag and head out to my Jeep. It takes a crank or two to turn it over, a sign that my battery is on its last leg. I've been putting that off, along with a lot of other small expenses. Money is tight, and I don't like having to ask my mom for spending cash. That's what my summer coaching gig is for. And I'm thankful for those awesome checks that Grandma sends along with her inedible cookies that I will pretend to love until her last breath. More than wanting to defeat Laney, I want to win this housing wager for the cheap rent.

I make a right turn to head toward campus, and spot someone jogging about a block ahead. I'm not one-hundred-percent sure, but I swear that's Laney's backpack bouncing up and down, and there aren't many girls around here who wear their hair in one massive braid that starts at the crown of their head. It becomes clear as I roll up closer that it's her, so I check my rearview mirror to make sure I'm not holding anyone up, then slow to match her pace. I roll down the passenger window.

"It's still dark out. Wanna ride?"

Laney slows to a walk and folds her hands behind her

neck before squinting at me as she pants. The sun is just cresting the horizon behind me, the sliver of light about to blast me through the mirror.

"It's only another mile or so. I'm good." Her cheeks look red, even in the dim light. I'm sure she's in great shape, but this jog is uphill. And if she wants to have legs for jumping when she reaches campus, she should probably take my offer.

"You put in two already. And I will hands-down admit that you are faster and can run farther than me if that's the reason you're saying no. You win the running competition. Reconsider?"

She slows more and finally stops and bends forward to put her hands on her knees.

"Yeah, all right," she pants as she nods.

I grab my bag from the passenger seat and toss it in the back to make room and she climbs in, swinging the pack from her shoulder to the floor between her feet. I hold up the coffee thermos and offer it to her.

"It's hot, which is probably not what you're looking for, but you can have some if you want." She scrunches her face but takes the drink from my hand and indulges in a sip.

"Oh shit, that is hot!" She smacks her lips and puts the mug back in my center console as I drive us toward campus.

"Of all of the mugs in the cabinet, you chose the penis one, huh?"

My head swivels and my eyes rocket to hers, then down to the thermos. Once I reach the stoplight, I pick it up and rotate it in my hand until the golden, basically glittered, penis glints in the growing sunlight.

"Son of a bitch." I chuckle and glance back at Laney, who is now laughing heartily. I shrug and take another sip that burns the tip of my tongue.

"Ivy makes it hot and strong. She works a lot of graveyard shifts," Laney explains.

"Yeah, I may have insulted her coffee habit." I wince and give her a sideways look. She shakes a finger at me and chuckles as the light turns green.

"Never insult Ivy's coffee. I should have warned you."

We reach the edge of campus and I pull us into the Athletics lot near the gym and the infamous bank of locker rooms. Laney hops out and slings her bag onto her back so fast it's as if she's trying to cover the fact she was ever in my Jeep to begin with.

"If you're here late, I can give you a lift back to the house," I offer as I get out and grab my gear.

She glances around and turns to face me as she walks backward. "I think I'm good."

I give her a crooked smile and level her with a glare, my head leaned to the side.

"Nobody will accuse you of liking me just because I give you a ride," I call out after her.

She snaps and points at me then lets her arm drop to her side before she turns and jogs toward the practice gym, her braid swinging opposite of her hips like some devil's hypnosis. I hold in the tempting quip about offering other types of rides too. But I think about it. I think about it for the rest of the damn day.

I'M NOT sure whether it's because I was well-rested for once or Ivy's dangerously potent coffee, but I flew on the ice this morning. I'm not even gassed after breakouts and passing work. I'm literally whistling to myself as I lumber through the locker room on my skates when Coach calls me into his office.

I pull my skates off and slip out of my pads before popping my head around the half-open door.

"You wanted to see—" I catch my tongue when I spot the two men in the office with him, both wearing KC Spoilers branded polo shirts. "Sorry, I didn't realize you were with someone."

"No, come in Cutter. You're part of this." Coach Przynski is a big man, and he wears his white beard and mustache thick and rounded around his chin, which only adds to his girth. He skated for the Polish national team about three decades ago and apparently his temper is famous. He's an amazing coach, but my goal is to always be on his good side. Even though he's inviting me in, I can't tell for sure if he means it.

"Cutter, this is Duane Moore and Mark Shell from the Spoilers organization. They're going to be at a few of our games this season." Coach waves me toward them, probably because I'm still hanging by the door like a frozen child who caught Santa eating cookies. The Spoilers are a level below the league my brothers are in, but they're close to home.

I shake their hands and pray they can't feel the sweat on my palms.

"Sorry for the unprofessional look. I just got off the ice," I say, running my hand over my head and feeling what is probably a matted-down nightmare of hair.

"We're used to it, Cutter. Nice to meet you," the older one says. I think that's Duane. "Coach P. says you're quite the leader. You have this team in line for a title this season perhaps," he says through an expectant, toothy grin.

"Oh, well . . . ." I glance to Coach and his wide eyes signal me to go along with this. "That's the hope. It's for sure the plan. You get out of it what you put in, and this squad works hard. I try to lead by example, I guess."

The two men chuckle and exchange glances while my eyes dart from face to face to get a read on whether I said the right thing.

"You were right about his modesty. That's refreshing," the one I think is Mark says. He's shorter, and has an over-the-top mustache that twists up on the ends. If I were already signed or if he didn't have any power over my future, I'd tell him it isn't working for him.

"Thanks. I hope you get to see some good hockey. Our first series should be pretty intense." What I don't add is that I'm not sure we'll win it. We're still missing a few key guys from injuries, and Chuck hasn't been himself on goal.

"Good. We look forward to it. Well, you might see us around a lot, and we just wanted to make the official intro-duction and let you know. We're watching you." Heavy words from such a funny mustache. My stomach tightens and my throat dries. I try to swallow but it only makes me want to cough. I hold it in and press forward.

"That's great. I mean . . . great," I stammer in the voice of a junior high boy.

"Hit the showers," Coach says, ushering me out the door and saving my ass from ruining this whole thing.

Most of the guys have cleared out, so I take my time and really let the hot water pelt my skin. I feel almost manic, I'm so excited. I can't wait to call my mom and text my brothers, but I'm also freaking starving. I finish my shower and jog out to my Jeep to drop my gear off and grab my school bag before heading to the cafeteria for the all-you-can eat omelet station. I'm rounding the corner of the gym to head into the dining hall when the back door swings open wide and Laney storms out, her cheeks red and eyes puffy. I stop feet away from her, and her hands ball into fists at her sides when she turns to face me.

With teeth gritting and eyes burning into mine, she lunges into me and shoves my chest with open palms. I'm glad she relaxed the fists because fucking hell that was a lot of force.

"Whoa, Laney what's—"

I can't finish my words before her hands are on my chest again and I'm stumbling another few steps back to absorb the blow. She rears back and lunges at me again, and this time I catch her wrists and hold her back, her arms locked and muscles flexed in their effort to break through.

"What did I do? Where is this coming from?" I mentally catalogue our morning. We even had a decent night. I don't think I've ever uttered a bad word about her to the media, even the school papers and news sites. I'm at a loss.

"I need to go home. Take me home. Right now, please. Take me home." Her voice is a low growl, but I sense the emotion threatening to break out from inside.

"I was about to eat breakfast, but—"

"Please," she croaks, and the tiniest crack hits her voice, her eyes beading up with tears. She blinks them away quickly and runs her palms over her face as she sniffles. "Please, Cutter. I need to get out of here."

Her arms slacken, so I relax my hold on her wrists but don't let go of her. There's something incredibly broken about her right now, and I'm half afraid she'll fall over if I let go.

"Okay. Let's go," I say, dropping one wrist but sliding my other hand to grip hers. She indulges and clasps back for a few steps before jerking away and burying her hands under her crossed arms while we march toward my Jeep.

"Do you need me to grab your stuff?" I ask when I realize she doesn't have it.

"I'll get it later. I just can't be here now."

I open the passenger door for her and she closes it before I can. It's somehow a relief that her independent streak seems intact. I rush around to the driver's side and toss my school bag in the back as I hop in.

"I don't have class for two hours, so if you want, I can bring you back then. Or later. Whenever you want."

"Thanks," she says in a near whisper.

"Of course." I crank the Jeep and thank the battery gods when it starts right away. Whatever beef exists between Laney and me, it can wait until later. Seeing her like this sits heavy in my gut.

We ride back to the house in silence, and I pull up the driveway knowing we're the only people here. I saw Matt at the rink setting up for some interviews for our team socials. It looked like an all-day thing.

I kill the engine and open my door, but stop when I realize Laney is zoned out, staring straight ahead, the same puffy eyes treading on the edge of betraying her tough exterior.

"You wanna talk about it?" I brace myself because I'm not sure whether to expect more shoving or a complete breakdown.

Laney turns her head slowly, her eyes blinking as she focuses on me.

"They're starting Chelsea. And they gave her my fucking number."

I pull the door closed and fold my arms over the steering wheel. I shake my head as I process the feelings that come naturally to me as a competitive athlete. This is Laney's entire world—her identity. And in a blip—*poof!* Gone. Because of dumb luck.

"Damn, Laney. I'm so sorry." I lay my head on my hands and roll it to the side until my eyes meet her gaze.

She shrugs, but I know she doesn't mean *oh well*. I swear I know everything she's feeling without her putting a single word to it.

"We can sit right here as long as you want. And then, when you're ready, we'll go back to campus. And after class, I'm gonna let you hit some shit real hard. How's that?"

She blinks slowly, and for a few quiet seconds I don't think she's going to respond. But then her lip lifts ever so slightly on one side.

"That sounds . . . *nice*."

7 /
laney

I HATE that Cutter saw me that way. I hate that I'm letting everything with Chelsea and my injury bother me so much. I have never been the person to protest that something isn't fair. I know that's life's cruelest rule. The only thing a person can truly control is how hard they work. My mom spews a lot of crazy bits of life advice, and most I don't really take to heart. But that one piece has been embedded in my drive. It gives me power. *I can work hard.*

I have control over that. But I've *been* working *so hard.* And that's what's breaking me up so much. I've never been in a spot where working my ass off wasn't enough to get me what I want.

Yeah, yeah. Life isn't fair.

My marketing for non-profits class wrapped up early, so I'm making my way to the hockey arena for what Cutter promised would be a "transformational experience." I'm naturally skeptical of him, but hitting things hard really has an appeal right now.

I find the side door propped open with what looks like

one of Cutter's shoes. I pick it up as I open the door wide and take it inside the arena with me. The lights are dim, only a third of the rink lit up. And I wish like hell I was wearing more than a long-sleeved T-shirt and training shorts.

Cutter is weaving around the ice, working the puck in quick motions. It's like watching an intricate dance, and he's so focused that I stop at the top of the stands so I can watch a while. His eyes are zeroed in on every flick, never losing the puck when he maneuvers it around his body, as he changes direction. He's so fluid on the ice despite his massive frame. And when he shoots the puck to the back of the net as he circles the goal, it happens so fast I almost miss it in a blink.

He snags the puck with his blade and pushes it back to center ice, skating out to the dark half of the rink before his gaze lifts to me. He slides to a stop, that cool way hockey players do when they shift their skates to the side and kick up ice. I've tried it before. I fell on my ass.

"Like the view?" He pulls a glove off and runs his hand through his hair, leaning casually on his stick. The ego on this guy. I mean, yeah, he's hot, but seriously?

"I like viewing you from far away, if that's what you mean."

He bursts out a laugh and I make my way down to the ice.

"You keep me humble, Price. I'll give you that."

Well, crap. That goes against my ego theory. And his smile forms these extra lines around his mouth, lines that are somehow better than dimples.

"You should try being humble more. It suits you." My stomach flutters from my flirtatious banter. I don't want to think he's cute. Knowing he's hot is fine. But thinking someone is cute? That's somehow more intimate. That feels like a door to attachment.

"You're going to freeze your ass off. Here, let me give you something to wear. And I guessed on skates. I think you're a ten, right?" I nod as I sit down by his huge duffel bag and he skates off the ice and steps toward me.

"Try this," he says, tossing an enormous hoodie on my lap. I climb into it, drowning myself in his scent as I work my head through and leave the hood up to cover my ears. I stand and tug it down past the end of my shorts. The skin on my legs is beading with goose bumps, and my teeth chatter.

"That helps. Thanks," I say, the vibration in my voice betraying me.

Cutter laughs.

"Here, they'll be big. But just roll the top," he says, tossing a pair of gray sweatpants at me next. I clutch them against my body and sit down to slip my legs in. The fleece is soft and worn, and I recognize these as the same ones he wore last night. Being in his clothes sends an unexpected rush down my spine and into my core.

"Warm now?"

I nod. I'm definitely warm. I'm not sure whether it's the fact I'm in layers or in *his* layers, though. My God, does his sweatshirt smell amazing.

I retrain my focus and tug off my sneakers to put on the skates he's set aside for me. The laces are a little ragged so I do my best to tie them tight and support my ankles. I don't plan on trying anything fancy out here today, but the last thing I need is to snap an ankle while simply walking to the ice in these blades.

"Sorry they aren't the best. We have a few extras in the back for when the high school kids come for lessons or camps. They're all donated."

"They're fine." I hold my arms out and bring myself to a stand.

"I probably should have asked, but you can skate, right?"

I give him a sideways look. I may be awkward right now, but I spent my life on skates. "You don't grow up a Penguins fan and not pretend you're Mario Lemieux at least once. It's been a while, is all."

Cutter steps back and holds up his hands.

"Whoa, okay then. Also, you may have just gotten a smidge sexier throwing out the Lemieux reference."

I flit my eyes to him as I take a careful step forward.

"You should see me in his jersey."

His brow rises and a deep chuckle emanates from his chest. I flatten a palm on his bicep as I balance myself and work my way to the ice, stepping onto the slick surface with extra care. I feel a little like Bambi, my legs wanting to fly out from under me, so I clutch the wall until the balance on the ice becomes more natural. It takes a few minutes to reteach my body, but soon I'm able to push out into the center and even move backward, albeit not with the speed and ease Cutter does.

"Alright, Lemieux. Let's take some shots. How does that sound?" He hands me a stick and I grip it the way I used to when I was a kid, when I'd take my dad's stick out to the driveway and hit crushed soda cans at our tree.

"Okay, maybe let's make a little adjustment. May I?" Cutter skates close to me and hovers his hands over mine. I nod and he works his way behind me, then guides my hands into an adjusted grip. His chest presses against my back and his breath warms my neck. I'm grateful for the hoodie to hide my jawline from him because right now it's on fire sensing his closeness. I'm like a damn cat in heat.

"So, don't whack at it like a kid. You're going to want to be smooth, coming back like this . . ." He guides my arms and hands back with his, then pushes them through the swing. "Like that. Yeah."

He backs away after we take a few approaches together, and I nearly drop the stick when his hands leave mine. I'm rattled. But what straight woman wouldn't be? He's like cheesecake. Peanut-butter and chocolate. An indulgence. And I'm very much aware of the physical reaction I can't seem to help having around him.

He passes me a puck. I line it up and take a shot. I glance at him where he stands about a dozen feet away, weight resting on his stick, and he nods for me to shoot.

I take a deep breath before slapping the puck with everything I have, completely ignoring Cutter's whole "smooth" advice, and the puck sails about six feet wide and high, ricocheting off the glass.

"That wasn't very smooth," is his only response.

I look at him with a toothy, guilty grin.

"I maybe have more aggression than I thought I had."

"Ha! You think?" His eyes dazzle with his smile. I forgot how much fun flirting is.

"Okay, let me try this again, taking my coach's advice." I push my tongue in the corner of my mouth and really set my stance. I go with a less spastic shot this time, focusing more on aim than prowess, and the puck glides across the ice and into the back of the net.

"Boom, bitches!" I hold the stick up in one hand and make a fist with the other as I swerve on my skates as if I'm in an end zone on Super Bowl Sunday.

Cutter laughs hard, skating over to my stray puck from before and working it with his stick until he's a dozen or so feet farther from the goal than I was. He levels a swing that gets the puck airborne about a foot off the ice, sailing into the right corner of the net. He skates a wide loop, slowing as he crosses behind me just enough to whisper in my ear, "Boom bitches."

Shivers. More shivers than I have from this freezing place. Different shivers. Potentially dangerous shivers, though also —we-could-have-fun shivers.

"Oh, I see. You know, I could do it like that. If I wanted to." I'm blowing smoke because, while I can hit a puck hard, I'm not so keen with my aim.

"Is that right?" he laughs out, coming to an abrupt stop a few feet away.

I give a smug nod then sniffle like I'm about to start a street fight. For the record, if this were a street fight, I'd be more confident in my skills. Pittsburgh girls know how to throw a punch.

"Care to make a little side wager?" I lift a brow.

Cutter's stare lingers on me as he chews on the tip of his tongue and smiles.

"Maybe. What are your terms?" He skates closer, and I move one of the pucks from the line with my stick.

"I take a real shot, from wherever you say, and if I make it, you sleep on the couch for a week." I lift my chin in challenge as his eyes narrow. We're both smiling like villains.

"The floor, but not the couch. I can't handle any unexpected, lengthy conversations with Matt. And if Ivy finds me asleep, she'll shave my eyebrows off."

I laugh out hard. He's probably right.

"Okay, I'll compromise. The floor. Do we have a deal?" I pull my glove off and hold out my free hand, and Cutter's gaze drops down to my palm before flitting back up to meet my eyes.

"And if you miss?"

I don't plan on missing. But also, it was a lot easier to be bold and confident when I was going in with nothing to lose and a full bed all to myself to gain. I mash my lips and riffle through a zillion ideas I think he'd be willing to accept, and I settle on, "Dinner. Your choice. Any restaurant. Name your price." I have a lot of credit card points I can spare, and unless he plans on making me drive him into the city, I got it covered.

Cutter chuckles under his breath, then shakes his head slowly.

"A kiss. My choice. Anywhere I want."

There's a fire in his eyes, and I feel it crawl inside me and dive to the depths of my core. Oh, shit. I hold his gaze for several seconds, my pulse kicking up while my reason fights against base desires. There's a difference between falling for someone and wanting someone, and I'm not dead. I've never denied Cutter McCreary's appeal. Girls talk, and he earns a lot of praise for knowing how to treat women. He's never had a campus girlfriend, not that I know of. Despite the reputation for being a player, it's impossible to find a girl he's been with who speaks badly of him. It's what he does— builds an army of women ready and willing to take his call anytime. And he and I share a bed.

"Alright, hot stuff. If I somehow miss, which I won't, I doubt kissing you will do anything to me. I think I'm getting the better end of this deal."

Cutter slides his palm against mine, and the blood in my veins turns into lava. Kissing him will do things to me. Just nothing I can't snap out of after the rush passes. That much I'm confident of.

We shake.

"Alright, Laney Price. Let's see what you've got." Cutter drags a few of the pucks over to one of the red dots. It's not much farther than my last shot, but the angle is a bit tricky.

I steel myself as I trail behind him, then wave him out of my way so I can focus on my shot. I settle the puck where I want it and glance at Cutter for his approval. He gives me a thumbs up so I take a deep breath and exhale slowly, eyeing the goal and drawing an invisible line right to my stick. I visualize the shot a few times before finally I take it, and while it's not as hard as Cutter's shot was, it's got some zip to it. Puck flying across the ice, it feels like seconds pass before it ricochets off the left goal post and glides around the boards, along with my complete and utter disbelief.

"Fuuuuuuuck," I breathe out.

Cutter laughs and I jerk around to face him, holding up my pointer finger as my entire body vibrates with my overwhelming pulse. Turns out, I'm not all right with losing this bet. This was stupid. Bad idea, Laney. *Bad idea!*

"Two out of three!" It's a lame plea, and the minute I suggest it Cutter pauses his laughter to catch his breath and stares me right in the eyes.

"Oh, Laney. You were so close!" His boastful grin infuriates me.

"Yeah, I was. And I didn't get any practice. I don't play this sport and look how close I was. You wouldn't last a second on the other side of the net from me, and you know it. The least you can do is give me two out of three. That one was my practice shot."

A flash of my youth rushes through my mind. My dad

used to practice serving with me in our back yard, and he'd set up trash cans for me to try to get the ball into. I'd always beg for two out of three when I missed the first. And he always gave in. He used to show up for me. My lip sneers with my steaming emotions and from the memory and bad feelings I harbor.

"I'll tell you what. I'll let you have two out of three. But that's my final offer. And next bet is on your court. I bet I do better with your serve than you think." He leans on his stick and lifts one side of his perfectly handsome mouth, which morphs his square jaw that exposes the tendon along his neck. I may have stared at his profile while he slept and admired those sharp lines.

"Okay. Final terms. I agree. And you bet your ass we'll be taking things to my court." My nostrils flair with my fury. I feel the stretch. It's a characteristic I've had my entire life. My mom says I used to do it when I was a baby and she took away my pacifier.

I shut my eyes and take a cleansing breath, letting the air out slower this time, clearing away my fear and that little insult that Cutter could possibly live on my level in volleyball. When I open my eyes, I give him a sideways look and find him looking on with an amused smile.

"Why are you looking at me like that?"

His lopsided smile twitches as he rests his chin on his folded hands and leans into his hockey stick.

"You're cute when you're pissed off." He shrugs, which makes him look cute, too. But I keep that to myself.

"Careful, Cutter. Sounds like you might be catching feelings." I situate myself behind the puck to take a shot at the goal. When I glance back at him, he's still wearing the same wicked, crooked grin. I lift a questioning brow.

"There are many kinds of feelings, Laney. Go ahead and take your shot, then maybe I'll show you the kind I've got."

Oh.

I somehow manage to keep my mouth shut, though my jaw has mentally dropped. I'm definitely thrown, but I also don't want Cutter thinking he has *that* much power, so I roll my eyes at him and turn my focus on the puck. I visualize my attempt and even give myself a few slow-motion practice hits before nudging my way to line up for a less flashy wrist shot. I'm like a sniper, breathing only through my nose, then holding my breath completely. I let it all go . . . and send the puck to the same goddamned exact spot as last time. With the same fucking result.

"Oh, no." I'm left without more to say as I stare intently on the tiny one-inch-by-one-inch spot where my luck ran out. Why did I gamble this big? Why did I like it? Ugh, and I still kind of like the feeling in my tummy. Especially as Cutter skates closer and finally puts his hand on top of my stick.

"I can't believe I missed." *I totally can believe I missed.*

His mouth twitches, like it's aching to grin out an *I told you so.*

My eyelids flutter out of sheer panic, and my breath hitches as Cutter brings his other hand up toward the side of my face. My chin lifts, half in defiance and half in preparation. Cutter slips the hoodie from my head but his palm or fingers never graze my cheek. My skin rushes with the strangest sensation, almost as if my face wants to be touched—needs to be. Cutter leans in and drops his mouth to my ear, and again I suck in an audible breath.

"Oh, Laney. Don't you remember the terms? I get to kiss you anywhere I want. I don't want to kiss you here, Laney.

Not in this arena," he hums, edging back enough to look me in my eyes. I'm quivering. "And not on these lips."

He grazes his thumb across the bottom of my mouth before skating backward and dishing out a downright sinister laugh.

Sinister, and sexy as hell.

cutter

I'M NOT THINKING CLEARLY. Obviously. There are so many things that could go wrong with heading down this path. Laney and I could get messy. Not *feelings* kind of messy, but just . . . *messy.* I've got too much going on in my life to get into a relationship, which is why this stupid room bet was never an issue for me. But roommates with benefits is damn tempting. And more than that, it blurs the lines and seems to be warming Laney up to me. But really, if I can get through senior year—my last year on the ice before, hopefully, I go pro—without another firestorm of shade thrown my way from Laney Price, well, that's the best prize of all.

I don't really care if I win the bet and she moves out. She can stay here with me for the next eight months for all I care. If I have a roof over my head, I'm happy, and honestly, she's not a terrible roommate. She's definitely a neat freak, with maybe a thing or two to teach me in that department. We basically thrive on the same schedule and gym habits.

And as long as she isn't plotting to stab me in my sleep or pour bleach into my shampoo . . . which I don't think she would do, but then again? Maybe if she and Ivy were left alone? Drunk girls' night? I glance to my bottle in the shower. Shaking those thoughts off, I squeeze a small handful of shampoo into my palm and lather up my hair. No bleach smell. I sigh out in relief.

I'm not afraid of falling for her. But a distraction? Yeah, I can see myself getting awfully distracted. Laney Price is a beautiful woman. But it's that competitive fire that makes her sexy. And today, on the ice, that fire was fierce.

We didn't bring up the kiss again on the drive home. We hardly talked at all, and she sat on the couch in the living room with her big headphones on and her nose in a book for most of the night. I offered her some of the chicken I made for dinner, but she shook it off. The girl ate cereal instead, and I know it's because I threw her with that comment. I think she *wants* to be kissed. And something about that excites the hell out of me.

I rinse out my hair and shut the water off, then wrap a towel around my waist and head into our room to find Laney lying on the bed in those same mini shorts that got me going last night. Her ass is on full display, and the visual of my handprint on one of those cheeks perks up my dick. She's doing this on purpose, but you know what? Two can play at this game. And I have absolutely zero inhibitions.

Her book propped on her pillow and chin in her hands, Laney didn't hear me walk in thanks to the headphones she's still wearing. I'm able to cross right into her periphery, on her "half" of the room, where we agreed I was allowed to get inside the closet. It's where my laundry basket is.

I bend my body to the side to catch her view and she slides one of the earpieces away to hear me.

"Yes?" She's blinking more than normal, the way my mom does when she's telling a lie.

"Closet is neutral, right?" I grin and her eyes narrow on my gaze. I think she's suspicious.

"Uh, yeah." Skepticism colors her face, which I hope is about to blush a hard pink.

"Good," I say, dropping the towel and turning slowly, letting her get a full view of everything I've got. You walk around naked in enough locker rooms, you lose all modesty. And I've never gotten any complaints from women, so I must be doing something right in the gym. Plus, her short-shorts made me half hard, so I feel pretty good about her view of that too.

I grab my gray sweatpants from my basket, the same pair I let her wear earlier today, and step into them. I glance over my shoulder and catch her gaze, which she darts away in a flash, burying her very bright pink face in her book.

"You forgot your headphone," I say as I walk over to my side of the room. She pushes her earpiece back over her ear without blinking or looking away from the words I have serious doubts she is reading.

I flop into the bed with extra force to annoy her and get her attention. She squeezes her eyes shut but doesn't look my way. Amused by how hard she is trying to ignore me, I laugh to myself. I drag my school bag up from the floor beside the bed and pull out my laptop to check my emails. There's one from Coach suggesting I show up extra early for next week's games to put in more face time with the Spoilers guys I met this morning. I check the time, feeling good that it's only nine, so I grab my phone from the charger on my night table and give my mom a call. In the midst of everything, I never got a chance to tell her the news.

Glancing sideways at Laney, I let it ring, hoping my mom isn't asleep already. I'm overly sensitive to how she answers the phone, reading into the strength of her voice and letting my mind instantly go to the worst places. Allison McCreary is the family glue. She's always been the do-it-all, remember-it-all, know-the-answers and fix-the-problems parent. Which was good, because Patrick McCreary, Sr. was more of the fly-by-the-seat-of-his-pants parent. It was a good balance with the two, though my dad did make my mom crazy when he blew up family plans for one of his spontaneous family adventures. Those adventures were always so great, though, that they resulted in years' worth of stories, laughter, and all of us together.

When I hear the ring stop on the line and a shuffling sound, I sit up at the ready. My pulse is going to race like this until my mom gets that all-clear two years from now. Or maybe the next all-clear five years from now. Or maybe never.

"Cutter Ellison McCreary, if you are drunk dialing me during my program, we're going to have words."

I sink back against the headboard with relief and breathe out a laugh.

"If you used the on-demand feature I showed you, this wouldn't be a problem," I remind her.

"You know I like to watch it live so I can chat with the girls online. Besides, the commercials give me time to grab snacks."

We both laugh. My mom is obsessed with this hour-long murder show that they play once a week. The girls she's referring to use to pile into our home when I was a kid and all watch together. Chat rooms let them keep their hobby going while their families grew and they got busy with kids and the chaos of junior hockey.

"You at least know you can pause, right?"

"Yes, I do. But I don't want to get too far behind so get on with it. This call wouldn't have anything to do with the girl-friend you're hiding from me, would it?"

I flinch at her question and glance toward Laney, who is still locked into her book and wearing the headphones.

"There is no girlfriend, Ma."

"Then, what is this I hear about you shacking up with some *hot chick,* as your brothers put it?"

Ah, I see. Matt's post made its way to the twins, and Flynn and Todd love to throw me under a bus. Being the youngest is rough sometimes.

I pinch the bridge of my nose and quickly muster up the best way to explain this.

"It's not like that at all, Ma. Housing is really full, and I wanted to get out of the house sooner rather than later. It's literally a roommate situation until something better opens up. And you should be happy there's a woman around to smack some sense into me from time to time." My gaze flashes to Laney again to make sure she's still in her own world and not listening, which she doesn't seem to be.

"Well, that does sound like a benefit. Perhaps when I meet her I can show her the most effective place to smack you," my mom jokes. My parents weren't the spanking type. If anything, they let us get away with way too much. My mom used her Irish-American guilt to her advantage, playing the Catholic card on us when we got really out of hand. Other than that, we basically got away with anything we wanted to as long as we didn't burn the damn house down.

"I'm sure you two could exchange notes," I say. "But hey, I called to tell you some great news. I was so busy today I didn't get a chance until now."

"Okay, now I'm not even mad about pausing. Spill it, kid."

"Some guys from the Spoilers stopped by to talk with Coach today. I got to meet them, and they're looking at me pretty hard." I can't temper my massive grin as my mom literally screams into the phone. I'm not the natural that Flynn and Todd are, but what they have in talent I make up for with effort. My mom has always been my champion.

"Cutter, honey! Oh, that would be something. Your dad would be so proud."

I nod even though she can't see me.

"I think so. But listen, it's all still up in the air. I have to really kill it this year. Like, *really kill it*." I think about my sluggish start and wince. Maybe it is a blessing I'm stuck here with Laney. Early nights and focus are key right now.

"Cutter, I've been through this plenty. I know how it works. But that's great news. Really exciting news. Alright, I'm gonna let you go. I'm falling behind and the girls are starting to post spoilers. I can't have that."

"Yeah, okay, Ma. I love you. I'll see you Sunday."

My mom gets through half of her, "Goodbye, love you," before ending the call. I set the phone back on my charger and smile at it for a moment. When I turn back to finish going through emails, Laney's palm flattens my laptop screen. Her headphones are hugging her neck.

"Uh, can I help you?" I grimace as I set my computer to the side.

"What was that?" She points toward my phone.

"What was what? My conversation with my mom? You really seem to have it out for her, don't you?" I chuckle but Laney swats at my bicep and stops me. She sits up and snaps in my face, and I think for a brief second how pleased my mom would be with all this.

"No. Uh uh. I mean what was that about the Spoilers? Why didn't you say anything?" Her brow is low, and I honestly think she's upset that I didn't tell her.

"Uh, well . . ." I stammer for a moment, thrown by her reaction. "It's like I told my mom. Some guys from the Spoilers came by to meet me. They'll be around. I mean, I'm sure I'm not the only one they're looking at, but—"

"No, don't do that. Coach introduced you to them. I know how this stuff works, Cutter. Don't bullshit me. This is a big deal."

I can't tell if she's excited for me or angry. She's intense.

"Okay, yeah. It's good news. For sure. I didn't want to make you feel bad with my good news when you had a crappy day, so I put it on the back burner. But also, hey . . . how did you hear that through your music?" I reach toward her to snag her headphones but she backs away, sitting back on her heals. "Were you even listening to anything?"

She chews at her bottom lip and her eyes haze. I think she's deciding whether or not to lie to me.

"Laney?"

"What? Okay, fine. I wasn't listening to anything. I simply wanted you to leave me alone." She pulls her headphones from her neck and tosses them onto her night table.

"Wow, I mean. You could have just asked me for some space." I'm oddly a little hurt.

Laney's gaze hits mine and stalls. There's an obvious tension, one we both put there with our antics today. I'm still not sure it was a good idea.

"Why didn't you kiss me?"

I'm pretty sure I do a poor job of masking my shock. This

is not the route I thought this conversation was taking. But now that she's gone there . . .

"Do you *want* me to kiss you, Laney?"

"Why do you say my name? Don't do that. It's . . . it's . . ."

"Laney, Laney, Laney." I'm a child.

"Cutter, Cutter, Cutter," she mocks back.

I laugh hard and it cracks her armor, and she finally breaks into an embarrassed titter of her own.

"Stop it," she says, shoving my bicep again. I'm fast enough to grab her wrist, and she stops hard once she's in my hand, her gaze zipping to mine with that fiery intensity that has always made her so fucking hot.

I drag her to my lap, and her legs straddle me. I take her other wrist in my hand and hold them both between us while I force her to maintain eye contact. Her lips are trembling, and all I want to do is bite the top one and hold on to it. The way it curves up just a touch like it's volunteering for me. Jesus.

"Do you want to me to kiss you, Laney Price?" I let the soft *s* at the end of her name hiss as my tongue flirts with the edge of my teeth, and Laney's lips part with a tiny gasp. I tug her forward and bring her arms around my neck, then grab her ass and pull her into me to soothe the ache in my pants. There is no way she doesn't feel how hard I am against her.

"I don't *not* want you to kiss me," she teases. She's being coy, and it's infuriating. It's also turning me on.

I *tsk* and shake my head, leaning into her until my nose kisses the tip of hers.

"Come on, Laney. You're a confident woman. I'm no stranger to you saying what you think and asking for what you want. If you want to be kissed, all you have to do is ask. But this doesn't count, just so you know."

Her bottom lip juts out and her brow draws in.

"Excuse me? Why wouldn't it count?" Her hips rock slightly and the weight and rhythm of her on my cock makes it pulse. Fucking hell.

I squeeze her ass harder and pull her into me more. She rocks again, encouraging me to keep the friction going.

"I told you. I don't want to kiss you here," I say, flitting my gaze to her mouth. "I want to kiss you—" I drop my chin and look down to where her barely-covered pussy grinds on my hard-on. Goddamn, I bet she's wet. I curl my fingers against her ass to stem the craving to dive into her panties and sink my fingers inside of her.

"You should have made that clear in the terms," she says, her mouth by my ear. She's grabbed a fistful of my hair and is now circling her hips in my lap, pressing down so hard that I am seconds away from coming in my pants.

I drag one hand up her back and sink it into her hair, threading the strands around my fingers until I've got enough to pull her head back and force us face-to-face. My gaze swims around her features, from the heavy lids of her eyes to the way her tongue peeks out of her lips. I can smell how wet she is, and all I want to do is taste it.

"I see. Next time, I'll be sure to make it clear."

"As will I," she says, her mouth stretching into a devilish grin.

"I guess we know what the volleyball bet is, don't we?" I bring my mouth a fraction of an inch away from hers; our breaths mingle in the intimate space between us. I lift my palm from her ass for just a breath and bring it back with a light spank that makes her whimper. Her smile grows.

I nip at her bottom lip and suck it in hard while she rocks on my cock. I push up against her as my tongue dips into her mouth and tastes hers. She wriggles against me and pushes me back against the headboard, and I don't even care that I might get a concussion. All I can think about is how warm and soft her mouth is, how glorious she smells, how smooth her ass cheeks are, and how she seems to need this relief as much as I do.

"If you keep doing that, I'm going to soak these pants," I mumble against her. She nips at my top lip and I feel her mouth stretch into a smile a second before she rolls her hips even more.

"Good," she says, sinking down on me. I bend my knees for leverage so I can lift my hips and basically fuck her through our clothes as she pants and whimpers through our kissing. When her head falls back, exposing her neck, I bite at her skin and kiss my way up her jaw as she muffles her cries with her palm.

Seeing her explode in my hands—on my lap, in pure ecstasy—is too much to take and when her eyes finally open, I close mine and push up with a few forceful thrusts, spurting heat all over the inside of my sweats. She rocks on me a few more times, even after I come down from the high, then leans in to kiss me one more time, sweet and gentle.

Her lips are bright pink, her cheeks heated and red, and her body is covered in a sheen of sweat. If Ivy or Matt walked into this room right now, they'd shit themselves. There's no masking what just happened, and I wouldn't be able to get rid of the dumb smile I know I'm wearing if my life depended on it.

Laney crawls off of me and rolls to her stomach, picking up her book and flipping it open to a page she had dog-eared.

I feel euphoric, and my gaze drags up and down her body, inspecting her ass for evidence that my hands were there.

"You should shower, Cutter. You're a mess," she says, the faintest, sexiest smile playing at her lips. Her eyes linger on me for a few extra seconds before they dive right back into her book.

"Yeah, and whose fault is that?" I tease. She shifts her gaze to me for a breath, and for just a moment, something about the look in her eye pulls at something deep in the center of my chest. I don't dwell on it long. Dwelling is dangerous. Instead, I hop out of bed and head to the closet to grab the towel I left in there. Before I leave our bedroom, I glance over my shoulder to see if she's watching. She is.

"If you stay awake, I might give you another show," I say with a wink.

"Oh, my God. Just . . . go shower!" She shakes her head, the red on her cheeks shifting from heat to blushing, I think.

When I come back to bed, her book is tucked away and she's changed into a long T-shirt and leggings, her arms hugging a pillow to her chest and her eyes shut. I kill the light and quietly change from my towel to a pair of boxers in the closet, but I swear she's faking. I can feel her watching me. And I like it.

9 /
laney

I'M GOING to play like shit today at practice. I'm exhausted. I slept maybe a total of seven minutes last night. While I was busy faking sleep, I'm pretty sure Cutter's slumber was genuine. He passed out pretty much the moment he hit the bed, but not before dropping his towel in front of me one more time for good measure. I think he may have caught me with my eyes open, but I didn't move and snapped them shut to keep up the charade. Mostly because I didn't want to talk any more after . . . well, *after*.

Things are weird now. I knew they would be, but I also wanted every minute of what we did to happen. I think I needed it. A release. And there are things about Cutter that are so much *more* than Cam was.

I was with Cam for so long that I think I was complacent physically. We practically had a sex schedule, one that worked around his internship nights and my away games. There was never any heat, not like I felt last night. It was almost like we were in competition to see who could make the other person feel more. And it felt fucking amazing.

But now . . . it feels really weird. And my best friend is going to call me on it in exactly five, four, three, two—

"Why are you in my truck?" Ivy is standing by her open passenger door, hands on her hips and bent in half to look me in my eyes.

"I want to get to the gym early and I knew you had a shift this morning. Thought I could bum a ride?" I lift a shoulder and twist my lips, my acting skills all used up from pretending to sleep all night. Ivy must sense something is off because she hasn't budged. Or blinked.

"Hmm, while I love the morning company, you're lying." *Yeah, she knows.*

I sigh.

"Just, please can you give me a lift? Like, can we leave? I want to get there soon." *I want to leave this driveway before Cutter walks out of the house.*

Ivy's gaze drifts out the back window of her truck, over the bed, and to the Jeep parked along the curb near the end of the driveway. I hold my breath and make a silent wish for her intuition to suddenly break. *Fat chance.*

"You didn't!" She shoves her backpack into my lap and dives into the driver's seat, pulling her door shut, and immediately twisting to look me in the guilty fucking eyes.

"Can we please leave? I'm begging." I honestly consider sprinting at this point. The only problem with that is I'd have to change up my route so Cutter wouldn't see me, and then I'd be late instead of early to practice.

"Only if you promise to spill it," she says. I've never told my friend this, but in terms of bedside manner, I'm not so sure she has the gentle touch. I guess it's good she likes the emergency room side of things because sometimes she's downright scary. And right now, blazing eyes ready to break me with FBI-type interrogation skills, she's at the height of frightening.

"I promise. Now please, Ivy. Drive."

She slips back in her seat and cranks her engine, buckling up as she pulls out of the driveway and even squealing her tires a little as she shifts out of reverse and heads down the street. My stomach twists on itself and I flatten my forehead on the passenger window so I can look out for Cutter in the mirror.

"Did you need to make a scene?" I mutter.

"I'm sorry, but I'm not the one who slept with Cutter McCreary and regrets it," she fires back.

I sit upright, satisfied we have enough of a head start.

"I didn't sleep with him. We just . . . fooled around a little. It's been a rough few days, and he let me take some shots on the ice, and—"

"I'm sorry, but he took you down on the ice?" Ivy's looking at me and not at the road. I push my finger into the side of her chin and force her head to turn.

"Yeah. You've been working and school, but basically, my senior year on the team is falling to pieces. I'm still not fully cleared and Chelsea was given my number."

"Oh, shit!" Ivy isn't the world's biggest sports fan, though she does like athletes. She knows enough through our relationship to get how important this year is to me and how painful it is for my backup to steal my spot.

"Yeah. See? Now you understand why I wasn't in the right frame of mind. Cutter caught me when I was a little, well, emotional. And you know how much I hate it when people see me like that. He offered to let me hit things, and how could I turn that down? So, yeah, we were on the ice, and then there was a bet that I couldn't make a shot and if I missed he got to kiss me, and well—"

"Laney Price you have to stop making bets!" She laughs out her words, but she's being very serious. And I agree. If I keep this up, I'm going to be buried in trouble.

"So you kissed," she says.

I wiggle my head and she leans forward, eyes dancing from the roadway to me, then back again.

"Laney?"

"I mean, I maybe had an orgasm. And I may have made him—"

"Girl! Did you see it? What's he like down there? Are the rumors true?" She's only half joking. I look away and let out a breathy, embarrassed laugh.

"The rumors don't do it justice, okay? I mean, I only got a quick glance, but yeah. He's proportional." I shrug and my friend shrieks out a hysterical laugh.

We get to campus before my friend has a chance to really dissect things with me, something that I know is coming. I'm not ready to dissect them myself yet, so the longer I can postpone tag-teaming the topic with Ivy, the better.

I practically leap from her truck when she reaches the west end of campus. Snagging my bag from the floor and leaving her pack in my wake, I jog toward the gym, relieved to be the first person to duck into the makeshift locker room that doubles as the health studies classroom and first-year physical therapy lab. At least we benefit from the stretching tables parked in the back.

I change into my court shoes and slip on my compression sleeves before adding KT tape to my shoulder. I doubt it does anything for me at this point, but it's a mental comfort to have it there, so I'll die in this tape if it keeps me swinging hard. I expect the gym to be empty, maybe even dark, but Coach Kane must have been running from a bad decision too. She's trying to clip one of the antennas up as the door squeals to announce my entry.

"Ah, good. Height. Laney, give me a hand,.."

I drop my bag and jog over to her, taking the top clip in my hand and fixing it to the top of the net.

"I have good news," she says as I give the net a shake to make sure I've got things fastened. My gaze darts to hers and my breath pauses.

"Yes, you guessed it. You're cleared. We're still starting Chelsea this week, but work in at middle and outside today and the rest of the week. We'll get you going. I don't want the process to break you, though, okay?"

I nod, holding back the argument I'm dying to make that I'm not going to break, and that I've been working harder than Chelsea and am conditioned and ready. That's not how things work at this level, and if I'm going to move even higher, I better respect the ego. We all have one in sports— players *and* coaches. And Coach Kane was an Olympic setter so her ego is definitely not grounded on Earth.

"Hey, after practice today, I need you to go to the athletic director's office. He wants to get your media guide pieces going, and they're going to get an article out in the program for the first week of games. Something basic, but you can talk about your injury and adversity and coming back stronger. You know the drill."

I nod again. I know the dance well. My injury is a great marketing story. Even if I didn't make the full return I was planning, the team and Tiff University benefit from my mere presence. Donors love a good comeback story.

Wasting no time, I head right into my stretching and

warmups, throwing the ball against the wall so I don't have to wait for a partner. I'm ahead of the rest of my team, so while they're playing catchup, I get to take free swings from Coach at the net. I don't love that she wants me to try out middle, but I'm going to punish the ball no matter where she tells me to hit it from. After a few awkward swings to start, I get the hang of the position—which I played in high school—and start pounding the ball in all corners of the court. At one point, I hit one down with enough force that it bounds back up to the rafters and brushes a chunk of dust from the ceiling.

"That's my girl!" Coach holds up a hand and I slap it before ducking under the net to shag the balls I just sprayed around the gym. My gaze hits Chelsea's, and her eyes dim with threat that I put there. It fuels me for the rest of practice.

I HAVEN'T PICKED up my jerseys from the equipment room since Coach assigned our numbers, so I relent and stop there before heading up to the AD's office. Pete is the Tiff equipment manager. He handles everything from our hockey team's precious golden helmets to the spikes our track team wears in the spring. He's always watching some black-and-white TV show on the small set he keeps in the equipment room. It's some cop show with a guy who smokes a lot of cigars, and I kind of think it's the same episode on repeat.

"Well, there's my favorite player at Tiff. Miss Laney, I hear you got yourself a new number." Pete's in his seventies, and has a thick Brooklyn accent despite having lived in Iowa for the last thirty years. I'm not sure if he has his hair anymore other than the few white tufts that poke out of his Yankees ballcap.

"Oh, you know me, Pete. Keeping you on your toes." I have a feeling Pete knows the inner politics of this place better than anyone. But he's too nice to say it out loud.

"Well, for what it's worth, twenty-three was always my favorite number. It suits you." He hands me a stack of crisp uniforms.

Head leaned a little to my right, I give him an earnest smile and say, "Thanks, Pete. Now it's mine, too." And I mean it.

I slip out the back to avoid a run-in with Chelsea, and take the stairs two at a time to the third floor of the athletics building. The director's door is closed, so I take a seat across from his office and slip my arms out of my backpack so I can tuck my jerseys inside.

"You got called to the principal's office too, huh?"

My eyes bulge at the sound of Cutter's voice. I glance up as I zip my bag closed and our eyes lock for one long-ass awkward swallow.

"Let's not make it weird. It doesn't have to be weird," he says, slipping his bag from his shoulder and taking the seat one away from me. Thank God he did that. I'm not sure I need his thigh touching mine right now. Especially because he's in black joggers and this tight black T-shirt with his hair all combed back except for the perfect few pieces that have fallen over his forehead.

"It's not weird at all," I lie. He calls me on it with a hard, fast laugh.

"Yeah, it is. But let's pretend it's not. Then it won't be."

He pulls a stick of gum from a pack, then offers me one. My eyes squint as I focus on nothing but the silver foil.

"Sure. And yeah, pretend. *Poof!* All better." I smile as I pop the stick in my mouth and start to chew.

Cutter's chest puffs with a quiet laugh, then he reaches toward my knees. I jerk away and give him side eyes, and he halts for a split second before continuing his reach for my bag. He tugs it toward him and lifts a brow.

"*Poof*, all better, huh?" He sniggers.

"Shut up."

Cutter pulls the blue jersey out and unfolds it, holding it up at the shoulders. "Twenty-three, huh? You know, that's my brother Flynn's number."

"Cool," I say, snatching the jersey and bag from him. "If I ever meet him we'll have something in common. Maybe we can date."

A stunted laugh leaves his mouth.

"You guys wouldn't work." He's oddly quick to dismiss something I was clearly joking about. I stuff my jersey back into my bag, then sit back and cross my arms over my chest.

"And why's that?"

Cutter gnaws at his gum as he waggles his head. "It's hard to explain. You and Flynn are just way too different. He wouldn't be tough enough for you."

"Huh." I chew at the inside of my mouth as I look at him. My head tilts to the side.

"What? I'm being honest. You need a strong man. You're a lot, Laney Price." His lip ticks up in a short half-assed apology-type smile, and before I have time to think of the right thing to say, I flash my middle finger in his face.

Timing is everything, of course, and my attention is suddenly pulled toward a now-open office door as our athletic director clears his throat and drops his hands into the pockets of his slick gray dress pants.

"Always a pleasure to have you up here, Laney Price," he says.

My eyelids flutter shut and I shake my head.

"Sorry, Dr. James. Cutter McCreary does not bring out the best in me." I shoot a quick glare at my roommate, whose only reaction is to hold up two guilty open palms.

"Trust me, Miss Price. I'm well aware of your feelings for Mr. McCreary, and the Tiff hockey program for that matter. If you could do us all a favor this year and maybe not kick off the fall season with your usual anti-hockey talking points?"

I purse my lips and flutter my gaze from Cutter back to Mr. James.

"I'll do my best."

He laughs under his breath, but I don't. I redirect the conversation to my business so I can get out of here and away from Cutter and his stupid woodsy cologne.

"Coach said to get with you about my media shots and the program for this year?"

Mr. James nods and holds up a finger, ducking into his office to grab a yellow envelope. He hands it to me and I pull the small card and questionnaire out to give it a quick glance.

"We'll put together the piece based on your responses, so if you could fill it out and get it to my secretary by the end of the week, that'd be great. You'll need to set up your photo shoot too. The number's on that card."

I pull the card free of the paper clip and eye the number scribbled on top.

"No problem, sir. And I promise to be nothing but professional." I'm always professional, actually, but he and I have different definitions of that word. He means quiet and scripted—censored. For the sake of going pro, I'll repeat the university talking points this year. But when I'm on a professional women's team, you bet your ass I'm going to speak my mind about all the ways that Title Nine still misses the mark in making sports opportunities equal.

"Great," he says, giving me a timid nod. I have a feeling he has his doubts that I can keep my word.

"Cutter, nice to see you. Did you need something?" Mr. James asks.

I turn to leave the two men to whatever business they have, but then Cutter says, "Nope, I came up here for Laney."

I stop in my tracks and curl my fingers around the envelope and paper, stopping myself before I wad them into a ball. I glance over my shoulder to find Cutter's charming smile only a few steps behind me and Mr. James back inside his office.

"You followed me?" My eyes narrow on him.

"You ran away from me this morning."

I suck in a long breath and let it simmer in my chest as I continue my way to the elevator. My legs are spent from practice and the last thing I need to add to this day is falling down the stairs in front of him.

"Oh, wait . . . are you still running?" He jogs past me and turns to walk backward, forcing me to look him in his eyes.

"I'm not running away from you, Cutter. I had something to do. And I didn't want to wake you." We both know that's a load of crap, but he doesn't call me on it, thank God.

The elevator doors open and we both step inside. It's an odd time on campus, with all of the classes in session, so we end up in the tight space alone. Rather than enduring more of his teasing or pretending that we didn't do what we did last night, I turn my attention to the note card in my hand. I slip the form back into the envelope but leave the card clipped to the outside, then slip my phone from the side pocket of my workout shorts.

"Excuse me, but I have to set up my media photos." I clear my throat as I punch the number into my phone and press CALL.

The first ring I hear is in my ear, but the next one comes from somewhere else. The sounds aren't synced, the tone in my ear and the faint ding that sounds in the elevator. I turn slowly to follow the sound of the noise as Cutter pulls his phone from his pocket and answers his call.

"This is Cutter. How can I help you?" His voice is both in my face and in my ear.

"God dammit." I end the call and stuff my phone back in my pocket just as the elevator door opens and my pesky roommate begins to cackle.

"This is not happening. How are *you* the person taking my photos?" I scowl at him as I step out of the elevator and double time it to my first class, which doesn't start for an hour.

Cutter keeps up.

"I needed an art credit. And I'm actually a great photographer."

"I don't need a mug shot. So if it's all the same, I'd like to request someone else."

"Hey." His hand lands on my arm so I stop in the middle of the main campus walkway and with a heavy sigh let my shoulders drop.

I lift my chin to find his waiting stare, his head cocked to one side, hands in his pockets as he gives his shoulders a quick raise.

"Look, this is part of my grade. And I'm not screwing with you. Well, I mean—"

I swat at him and he takes a step back, laughing me off,.

"Okay, okay. Seriously, Laney, I'm pretty good at this. When is your last class today?"

My chest tightens. I don't want to do this, but at the same time a pulsing hunger inside my body pushes me to give in. More time doing things other than sitting in our shared room and fighting our physical attraction isn't a bad thing.

"I'm done at four."

Cutter holds up his phone, his lips curving up on one side as he squints under the glare of the sun.

"Well, now I've got your number. Call me as soon as you're done and I'll come pick you up. I have some ideas."

That twist in my gut is still there, but I agree anyway. We shake on it, and even though his hand is hot against mine, and it reminds me of how it felt on the rest of my body, I force myself to imagine that my palm is numb and unaffected. I pretend nothing's weird. Even though literally *everything* is now weird.

10 /
cutter

EASY FOR ME TO criticize Laney for taking off this morning when I watched her go and didn't say a damn word.

I don't know what's wrong with me. I've done the mutual hook-up thing and been absolutely fine the next day. Hell, Addison Cage, the Tiff student body president, and I had a pretty hot moment after she won the election last year, and she still called me last week and asked if I'd be a personal reference for the internship she's applying for. And when I got the call, I gave her a glowing recommendation—professional, of course—never once feeling anything weird even though the last time we hooked up we inadvertently made sex shadow puppets on the backyard wall at the Omega house thanks to a fire pit.

But Laney and I hump each other like sixteen-year-olds, with our clothes on, and I feel this knot in my stomach over it. It almost feels like guilt. Like I crossed some line my conscience knows I shouldn't have. I spent the morning on the ice dissecting it, and I decided to rule out regret when I asked myself whether I'd take the opportunity again if presented with it. I would. In a blink.

That's when I started plotting how to make it happen again. And when Pete told me I'd just missed her after I picked up my new helmet from him, I took it as a sign. One that was confirmed when I spotted her long legs trekking across the main lawn toward the athletics offices.

I went home at lunch and grabbed my photography gear out of the storage bin that's been living under my half of our bed. I haven't used my kit in a while, so I cleaned things up and spent the afternoon taking practice shots of the crazy cross-country runners who I swear never get tired. Some of my shots of them are pretty sweet so I might send them in to the coach and see if she wants to use them for anything.

This session with Laney has to be special, though. And I need it to be different. Which is the *only* damn reason I called Matt in to help. I'm rethinking how badly I thought I needed help now that he's here with about a dozen tripods, light stands, and whatever the hell else he's pulling out of that rolling case he dragged into the gymnasium.

"Where do you want to set up?" He's wearing sunglasses again. I mean, they're barely tinted, but still. He's ridiculous.

"I'm not sure we're going to do all the shots here, man. Why did you haul all that in?" I scowl at his setup and take in deep breath.

"Oh, this isn't for you. I'm gonna get some shots too, maybe go live with some of this." He surveys his pile of phone adaptors as he scratches his head.

"I'm not sure Laney's on board with that, man. Just stand over here and take these chalk blocks." He jogs over to me and does as I ask, thank God, and I position him out of the frame of the shot I've lined up so I can take a few test shots with the spotlight on. I borrowed the light from my teacher, whom I now realize I should have asked to help instead of Matt.

I take a few practice shots as Matt claps the blocks together to give me the foggy effect I need to pull this off, and I'm just finishing sweeping up the thin layer of dust we left on the floor when Laney cracks open the door.

"I got done early," she says.

"It's fine. I'm about ready," I say, my pulse suddenly racing. I think I'm nervous. I want her to trust me to do this, but more than that, I want her to like it.

Laney walks toward my setup near the net, dragging her feet and scanning the scene—I think a little put off by all of Matt's extra shit.

"Ignore that," I say, waving at Matt's setup.

"Hey, Laney. Cool if I get some socials on this? I'll tag you!" Matt interjects.

I grit my teeth and smile through my irritation while Laney looks back at his gear.

"Yeah, uh. Sure, fine. Tag me. I should get better at that stuff." She shakes her head, maybe a little overwhelmed as Matt snags his phone-tripod combo to talk over a livestream he started.

Laney's panicked gaze meets mine, and once Matt's gotten the camera out of our faces I whisper to her, "You can say no to him."

"I know, but he's good at that stuff," she mumbles. "And I need to up my brand."

"Okay," I say, shaking my head. I guess having Matt around hockey all the time has gotten me used to all things social buzz, and I've seen enough of the negatives to not care about the attention as much as I used to.

"Can I tell you what I'm thinking?"

Laney nods as she sits down to pull out her jerseys and her court shoes.

"I want to make it look like you're sort of frozen in motion. I saw this hack where we use chalk dust to make it really smoky, and I think it could create a pretty cool mood. Might get a lot of dust on the dark blue though, so maybe let's start in white?" I point to the last jersey she pulled out and she nods in agreement. She glances over her shoulder at me with an uncertain expression as she heads into the equipment room to change. I'm going to need to prove my skills with her on this first set of shots.

When Laney comes out, Matt picks back up with his filming, making commentary on her new number, which I can tell gets under her skin by the way her eyes instantly dim as she shoots him a sharp look.

"New number, new season. Laney is back," I say, my messaging skills on point. Her gaze drifts back to me and a faint smile plays at her lips.

"I am back," she utters, that fire rekindle. This is the Laney who gets me into trouble.

"Okay, so once Matt stops dicking around—"

"Sorry, sorry. I'm here." Matt sets up his phone tripod, which I'm sure is still filming, and sprints into position. I've affixed a handle made of athletic tape to one side of the volleyball that I hand to Laney to make it easier for her to palm it through our action shots. This way we don't need to keep chasing down the prop after every shot.

"You just want me to swing then? But not hit it?" She practices the motion and the ball stays in her hand, which is a relief because I didn't test the physics.

"Yeah, like that." I move back into position and get low to the ground to make her height and jump seem exaggerated.

"Go as many times as you can," I command. "I'll just keep shooting, and Matt, you keep clapping that chalk, dude."

Laney's face turns serious, shifting into competitive mode, and I flip the spotlight on to capture the lines of her body and the flicker I anticipate will be in her eyes. When I say, "Go," Laney makes an approach and Matt fills the air with dust. I slide around the gym floor to capture various angles from below as she goes through maybe a dozen jumps toward the net, and when I get the one I have a feeling will be the winner, I tell her to take a break.

The air is thick with dust. That was a lot more chalk than we practiced with, so Laney coughs her way to the side door to prop it open and get fresh air while I cup the screen on my camera and sort through the shots I was able to get.

"Amazing!" My enthusiasm gets her attention, drawing her back inside.

Matt, not interested in cleaning, instead circles us as Laney sits on the floor next to me and hunches close so we can both look at my camera screen.

"Oh!" Her surprised response perks my lips into a bit of a smug grin, and when she glances at me and catches it, she leans into my shoulder and topples me over so I'm lying on my side. She snags my camera from my hands and leaves me to fend for myself as she continues to flip through my shots.

"I have to admit it. These are really good, Cutter."

I roll to my back and tuck my hands behind my neck and smile.

"I know."

Laney gives me a sideways glance before groaning and getting to her feet. She steps above me and reaches out her free hand to pull me up. I take my camera back and flip through the rest of the images on my own. The effect came out better than I expected.

"Hey, Matt. Nice work on the chalk. Thanks for helping," I say, partly to segue into me being done with his services for now. He's reviewing his own footage, though, and barely registers me with a nod.

"Right, well. Unless you want to try something more traditional—"

"No, I love these. I mean, these will work." She clears her throat as if she's trying to bury giving me too enthusiastic a compliment.

"Cool, well, let me sweep this mess then pack up. I can give you a lift." I raise a brow at her while I squat and pack my camera into its bag. She gives me a relenting smile.

"Fine, you can drive me home." She adds a *humph*, I think to show off for Matt that she's begrudgingly letting me be nice to her.

I'm glad to see she's getting over making things weird. I'm also glad she's happy with the photos I took. It's been a while since I did any editing, but I think when I pull them into my computer and play with the color a little, I can really create something special for her.

I finish packing up my gear, then run the broom over the entire floor twice. Laney wheels the ball rack back into the storage room but stops at the edge of the court, glancing at me over her shoulder.

"You know, you still owe me a little bet of my own." Her smirk is defined enough that I can see it across the court. I can feel it. She's back to being willing to play.

"I'm pretty sure you just want to hit balls at me. But if you really want to go, let's go. What are your terms?" I set my camera bag and backpack on the floor, then crack my knuckles as if that will somehow help protect my face from getting smacked by a Laney Price serve.

Laney glances to her right, where Matt is still very much interested in us. My stomach sinks with disappointment because Matt being here is definitely going to take a lot I would *like* Laney to propose off the table. Still, I can find a way to work this into spending time with her. And time turns into affection, and then maybe more of me making her come.

"I have an idea. I'm starving, so how about this? If I can return just one of your serves, drinks and food at Patty's is on you. If I can't, then I'll buy." I cross my arms and mentally cross my fingers that she'll take this offer.

She pulls one of the balls from the bin and begins to bounce it on the floor, smacking it lightly at first with her palm but gradually working it into a more forceful slap as she edges toward the back line of the court.

"You're on, McCreary. You get ten serves. If you can get under one of them and pass it so it stays even remotely gettable by a setter, I'll give you the point." She holds the ball at her hip and lowers her chin.

"Ha, you're on!" I nudge my bags to the side with my foot and stretch my arms across my body, again pretending this will somehow help. I bounce on my toes as I make my way to the center of my side of the court, then I lock my hands together and bend my knees.

Laney shakes once and breathes out a condescending laugh.

"That's how you're going to get ready?"

I stand up straight and glance to Matt at my right. He simply shrugs, then moves his tripod and phone out of the danger zone—aka he stands in the far corner of the gym.

"Yeah, this is how I get ready." I try to sound sure of myself as I shake my arms out then lock my hands together again. I haven't played serious volleyball since high school, and by serious, I mean me and my brothers at the family picnic. Laney's going to kick my ass. I'm certain of it. But either way, she and I are getting dinner and drinks.

"Okay. Here goes."

She shakes her head, amused by me, I'm sure, then takes several steps backward before bending forward and dribbling the ball with both hands. She snaps up straight, holding the ball out in front with one hand, and the moment she makes her first step, I know I'm in serious trouble.

Laney almost looks like she's moving in slow motion, though I know that's not what's happening at all. I'm taken by the power in her jump, the distance she flies in the air, and the strength in that arm that smashes the ball at me. I don't even have time to blink before the ball hammers me in the center of the chest, a hollow thud literally echoing in the gym.

"Oh, damn!" Matt's laughter is mixed with my cough from getting some of my wind knocked out of me. I hold out a hand for a timeout while I walk in a slow circle to reset for another pummeling.

"Okay, now I know. I'll see it coming now. One second." I jog in place, knowing that's all bullshit. I'm merely hyping myself up to get smacked somewhere else this time.

Laney's laughter is silent, but the way it paints her face with self-satisfaction doesn't require sound. I do my best to stand on my toes this time, ready to move into the ball, only to take the impact directly in my Adam's apple. I cough more this time, and glare at Matt who has now moved out of his safe corner to make sure he captures every sound I make. I flip off the camera and he flips his screen to show his face.

"Someone is having a bad day," he says.

"Nah, it's a great day! I'm just warming up. I'm ready now. Laney who?" I'm purposely getting under her skin. The more she's playing rival, the less she's playing the ignoring game with me, and if I want any more of the perks of being roommates, I can't have her pretending I don't exist.

Laney pounds me in the chest two more times, but on her fifth serve, I finally get the feel somewhat and manage to get my arms under the ball in the right spot. Of course, I have absolutely zero control and send the ball off into the duct work on her side of the court. Definitely not a pass she would consider receivable, but getting a taste of nearly doing things right sparks my competitive side.

"Oh, I'm getting it now. I feel it," I razz her.

Laney pauses bouncing the ball and walks across the court to meet me at the net. Our gazes fix and there's almost a snap to the connection. It's the same way she looked at me before we made each other come last night, a devilish haze mixed with confidence. Perhaps a touch of dominance, which surprises me how much I like it.

"You getting scared?" I tease.

She scoffs.

"No, dumbass. I don't want you to break your fingers or thumbs, so I'm going to show you what you're doing wrong. Hold out your hands in ready position."

I give her a skeptical look but do what she asks, linking my fingers and putting my arms straight out. Laney places the ball on the ground and dips under the net to push my hands down but stops right when I feel the tension where my fingers intertwine.

"Yeah, okay. I see," I say.

"Your fingers don't like it when that happens, so you bend your elbow to compensate, thus sending the ball to Illinois."

Matt snorts out a laugh and I shoot him a glare.

"Sorry, boss," he says. *Boss. Can this fucker ever just call me by my name?*

"Hold your hands like this." Laney crosses her palms and wraps them together without linking her fingers. Then she bends her knees and sways side to side. "See how you're more mobile?"

She's right. And it's a lot like working on the ice. Not getting locked into one position lets you sprint and redirect. I nod as she picks up the ball and walks back to the serving position.

"I don't know why you showed me that. I'm definitely getting underneath one now," I brag.

Laney's head snaps up as she holds the ball out to serve again.

"Cutter, you aren't going to come close."

Rather than using a high toss and leaping at the ball this time, her serve is soft, and the ball crawls inches over the net as I stumble forward into a slide, feet away from where it hits the floor. *Damn, I had no shot at that.*

"That's a foul!" I make that up. I'm sure it's not.

Laney laughs, then slaps the top of the ball, holding her hand there as I regroup and ready myself for more embarrassment. Serve after serve dives onto different pockets of the court, and other than punching the ball once as I fling my body out of bounds, I don't come close. Just like she said.

I lay flat on my back with my arms out at my sides as Laney wheels the ball cart into the storage room and Matt finally packs up his crap and leaves. Laney's shadow casts over me as she blocks the light hanging high above my head. Her hands land on her hips.

"So, it's my call, right? Anything I want on the menu?" She reaches down a hand and I take it, letting her help me up for a second time.

"I mean, I've had the lobster at Patty's and I am pretty sure it's not really lobster, but if you want that then go for it," I joke.

I snag my bags and the two of us head toward the parking lot, testing the gym door to make it's locked behind us before we go.

"I want take-out and a six-pack."

I chuckle as I give the door one last tug then turn to meet her gaze. Her lopsided smile is genuine.

"All right, we can order to go. We don't really need to eat at Patty's if that's what you prefer. We can order a pizza and beer from Razzo's and grab it on the way back."

Her head falls back as she sighs, "Yesssss." The braid that practically lives on top of her head dangles along her spine. I picture wrapping it around my fist but shake that thought off when her head snaps back upright and her eyes are on me. I think I might have been too late, because there's a coyness playing at her lips. Those damn dark lashes of hers always look like they're seducing me, though, so it's hard to tell.

"I'm dying to shower. It's been a day. No, it's been a week!"

I smirk as we walk toward my Jeep together then I reach into my pocket and pull out my wallet. I hand it to her.

"You call the order in and put it on the Express."

She blinks at me a few times, then shrugs.

"Okay, if you insist."

We pile into the Jeep and Laney dials Razzo's, putting

them on speaker as she riffles through my wallet. She orders the protein pizza, which is basically Razzo's excuse to serve people a shit-ton of sausage. She reads off my card after ordering the beer, then gives them my name for the pick-up. She eyes me as they confirm the order, then ends the call and tucks my card back into its place.

"This is quite an overpacked wallet you have here," she teases, purposely holding my wallet to her right and out of my reach as we drive. I swat at it, not because I'm embarrassed of anything I have in there but because I know she's going to see some things that are a little more private, like the photo I have of my mom and me when I was six.

She sifts through my cards first, noting how cute it is that I have three different library cards.

"I told you I could read," I retort.

"*Hmm*, we'll see," she teases, sliding the last of my cards back into place. She pulls out a twenty and two ones next and rolls them up to tuck inside her shirt. I pull to a stop at a red light and roll my head to the side to give her a daring stare.

"I'm going to have to get those back, you know."

She shrugs.

"We'll see."

Oh, this is the Laney I wanted to bring back. Now we're talking.

She pulls out a folded receipt that can't even be read anymore so I tell her to toss it in the cupholder. I think I'm just about to survive her invasion of privacy when she feels inside the last pocket on the back side of my wallet and slides out the photo of me and my mom. I'm missing a tooth in the shot, which I guess some people might find embarrassing, but I don't really care about that stuff. I was a cute kid, and Laney seems to think so too.

"Aww, is this really little you?"

I nod and smile on the side closest to her. My mom was young in that shot, sure, but the last year has really aged her. Her hair is thin, though she covers it with various hats her girlfriends have given her as gifts. I can see the wear of losing my dad and fighting cancer in her face. Her eyes aren't the bright orbs they were in this photo.

"You look just like your mom," Laney says, perhaps sensing that this photo isn't something to joke about.

"I get that a lot. Thanks. I think she's beautiful." I glance to Laney as I smile, then hold out my palm. Hopeful she'll give me my wallet back now. She holds on to the photo for a few seconds, a puzzling look to her eyes as her gaze moves from the picture to me.

The light turns green so I cross the intersection, then pull into the shopping center where Razzo's is.

"You and your mom are close. You talk a lot, I mean. And Sunday—I know all about Sunday."

We both laugh softly at her call-back joke.

She holds my wallet out for me as I shift into park and I take it and grip it tightly as I nod.

"All of us are close. But yeah, my mom and I probably more than any of the others. She's my rock." I stop short of filling Laney in on the rest. Before I climb out of the Jeep to grab our order, her hand wraps around my wrist. My eyes dart to her face, but her gaze is on the wallet still in my hand.

"You're lucky that you have that. Maybe I'll get to meet her sometime." There's a tinge of melancholy in Laney's voice all of a sudden, and she lets go of my wrist as quickly as she grabbed it.

I pause half in, half out of the Jeep and survey her as she quickly retrains her focus out the other window. She bites down on her thumbnail and her jaw flexes the way mine does when I'm holding something in.

"Maybe if we survive a week together you can meet her at my game. She'd like you. She'd *really* like that you kicked my ass."

Laney shakes with a laugh and her head swivels my way.

"She would, huh?" Her eyes squint.

"Oh, without a doubt."

We hold on to this sweet moment for a breath, and somehow it doesn't feel awkward. It does, however, feel heavy, so before it leads to either of us speaking more, I hop out of the cab and jog into the restaurant to grab our order.

By the time I get back behind the wheel, Laney's turned her attention to her phone, and we finish the drive home in silence.

11 /
laney

WHAT AM I DOING?

I showered ten minutes ago and have done nothing but change from sleep shorts to night shirt to sweats, and back to the night shirt.

The pizza is probably cold by now. I knew Ivy was working an overnight tonight and that Matt was heading to Chicago for some invite he got from the Blackhawks thanks to his social coverage. I woke up this morning swearing I would never let what happened between us last night happen again. And yet the first thing I do when presented with an opportunity is go full vixen.

It's not that I like Cutter. I mean, I'm softening on him a little. I don't necessarily want to wish never-ending jock-itch on him anymore, but I also don't fully trust him to not throw me under the bus in favor of his hockey team. I do like the attention, though. I like getting his attention, and having him look at me like someone other than the girl who can't stand him. I like the way he makes me feel, and looking at him. Touching him.

"Screw it," I mutter under my breath, spraying my hair

with a few spritzes of the coconut oil that Cutter commented on liking when he gave me a ride the other morning.

I march out to the kitchen wearing my white cotton night shirt that buttons down the front. I haven't worn this since Cam and I first started dating. That was back when things were new and exciting. Even then, he never commented on it. I always felt like he preferred me to be less promiscuous. Maybe less dominant. That's not who I am, though. And if Cutter can handle sharing space with me being me, without crossing into that *feelings* territory, then this roommate situation might turn out all right.

"You missed most of the pizza. There are still two sli—" He stops mid-chew, practically choking on his bite as I step around him and pull out a chair at the table. I know how short this shirt is. I'm aware of everything I came out here wearing—and not wearing.

"I had a nice shower," I say, reaching toward him and dragging the open pizza box toward me with my index finger. I grab one of the two remaining slices and prop it up on my fingertips before taking a careful bite. No need blowing my sex appeal by spilling a marinara-soaked sausage slice down my chin.

Cutter swallows and sits back in his chair, spreading his legs out wide. He's still wearing his black joggers and that tight black shirt that he should probably just make his uniform because it literally contours to every muscle on his body.

"You uh . . . you have not been sleeping in that at night." He raises his half-eaten slice. "I would have noticed." He takes a bite, smiling through his chewing as his eyes rake over me.

"*Mmm,* yeah. I wasn't sure how you'd take it. I wouldn't

want to make you fall in love with me or anything." I shoot him a devious grin, then take another bite.

Cutter leans in and drops the rest of his slice in the open box before standing and moving inches from where I've propped one leg up in my chair. His gaze snakes down my thigh to where the tails of my cotton shirt tuck between my legs. His tongue peeks through his front teeth and he smiles.

"I think you know exactly what you want me to feel right now, and it's not love, Laney." He winks, then walks to the fridge to grab two beers. He pops the cap off each bottle, then hands me one. I finish off my slice of pizza, then take a long sip while my gaze remains glued to his. I pull the bottle from my lips with a slight suction, letting my lower lip linger against the smooth glass for a few seconds.

"You said we shouldn't let this get weird, right?" It's easy for me to be bold when my body is buzzing with need.

"I don't find anything weird. Do you?" He slides back in his chair again and moves his hand over the growing bulge in his pants. I breathe out a quiet laugh but also instantly swell between my legs.

"No, I don't. If you can handle this . . . *arrangement*, so can I." I take another drink from my beer, then set it on the table before slouching in my seat to mimic him. I leave my palms flat on my thighs as my legs part slightly, and Cutter's gaze heats as his head falls to one side in an attempt to see more.

"Oh, I can handle this. I promise you." His eyes flit to mine at the last second and his lip ticks up to form a dimple. "Why don't we play a little game?"

My gaze narrows on him and for some reason I study his lips as I consider his proposition. His smirk is a little cunning, but that's also what seems to cut to my core. I think it's what I'm attracted to most.

"Like what? Monopoly?" I set my beer on the table and match his scheming expression.

"Truth or dare, Laney?"

"Dare," I answer instantly. Truth is a far more vulnerable choice. Always. Only fools choose truth.

"I dare you to unbutton that night shirt right here, right now."

My mouth buzzes with nervous energy, but I stand from my chair and bring my trembling fingers to the top button and push it through the hole. My nipples harden against the cotton as I work my way down the center of my chest until the sides of my shirt hang open, held in place by luck and the natural curves of my breasts.

"My turn," I say, letting my hands rest at my sides so Cutter isn't only being taunted by my nearly exposed tits, but by the white lace front of my panties too.

Cutter shifts in his seat, clearly affected by seeing more of me than before. Standing in front of him like this, exposed and just out of reach, is sending a current through my body and I'm practically buzzing in anticipation.

"Truth," Cutter says, and I blink a few times, surprised that he's playing this way. My eyes dim and I study his face, the slight curl at the edges of his tight-lipped mouth, the sharp line of his jaw and days' old stubble. There are so many ways I could go with this question, but also, there's an opportunity I have never had before. Not that he will play fair and be honest. But I think I'll be able to read him.

"Okay, Cutter McCreary." I step toward him to put him on edge, and perhaps a little to make him regret not choosing my dare.

I bend down, resting one palm on the table and letting my shirt open enough that I feel the hard peaks of my breasts peer out from the edge of the fabric. Cutter's tongue passes over his bottom lip as he adjusts himself. *Should have picked dare.*

My lips part and I'm about to ask him point-blank if he supported the locker room takeover when my brain suddenly flips a switch and forces me to change gears.

"Why did you hit on me freshman year?"

Cutter's eyes widen and his body makes the tiniest flinch as he swallows. Yeah, I wasn't expecting that to be my question, either. But now that I've said it, I realize it's the thing that's always truly bothered me. Why was he so persistent? Why was he so drunk? Why did he pick me out of the hundreds of girls who came in and out of the frat house that night? And at the root—was it part of another bet, the one I know all of the freshmen male athletes are pushed to accept? It's a not-so-secret tradition at Tiff that the freshmen are all given a target, and if they close the deal with the girl the upperclassmen choose, they're given special status at parties and let out of having to buy kegs and rounds for the year. I went to enough parties to know that Cutter was almost always buying, hauling, and cleaning up.

"Why do you think?" He sits up and slides his hands over mine, so I pull my hands away and stand tall.

"That's not how this game is played. If you're going to cheat, I get to give you two dares." The thought of daring him to take my nipple in his mouth is awfully inviting, but my insides are conflicted now that he's being evasive. More than ever, I want to know.

"You know why, Laney." He blinks slowly, his heated gaze glued to mine.

"And you lost." I wait for him to react to my assumption,

and it takes him a few seconds before he finally leans back in his seat again and breaths out a heavy sigh.

"You could say that. Though, it was my own fault."

I tilt my head slightly.

"How's that?"

A soft, seductive chuckle parts his lips as his gaze dips toward my navel then trails slowly back up my body to my face.

"I was supposed to hit on Ivy, but she just didn't do it for me. I wanted a challenge." His brow lifts a hint, and a rush of heat dives down my body and pools between my legs.

"And you failed," I respond, suddenly prouder of myself for turning him down three years ago. I was admittedly a lot stronger then at resisting him. Or maybe I'm old enough now to get the rules, and to make games of my own.

"I not only failed, but I also went down in flames in front of everyone. 'The worst rejection in Tiff history,' I believe one of the hockey captains said that year." He chuckles and I lift my chin, a bit proud of helping him earn that title.

My memory of that night is incredibly vivid. I'd just been stood up by my dad, who was supposed to be at the parent orientation dinner for my first year. My mom didn't bother coming for fear of running into him. Ivy was my roommate by chance, and we clicked right away. She dragged me to the party, and the minute she saw Cutter walking my way with two drinks in his hands she told me to cheer myself up with a hot jock. In that instant, I decided to cheer myself up by shooting one down, repeatedly.

"Do you regret it?" I ask.

Cutter quivers with a quick smirk, then shakes his head.

"You asked your question. That's all you get, Price. My turn." His lip sneers in satisfaction, and though my gut knots with a touch of uncertainty, something tells me this whole situation we're in now is his big re-do. And this time, I plan on taking Ivy's advice and making myself feel better with a hot jock.

"Fine. I choose dare," I say, resting one palm on the table and leaning my weight into it to force myself to relax despite the constant vibrations thrumming through me.

"Lay on the table." He nods toward the table, then stands and removes the pizza box and our two beers, discarding them on the kitchen counter. He turns his chair around and slides it between us to give me a step, then offers his hand to help me.

I freeze and give him a sideways look.

"We eat here."

His smirk grows.

"Yes, we do."

Fuck me. My center throbs at his suggestive reply, and as he licks his lips I can't help but imagine that tongue trailing up and down my pussy.

I take his hand and step up on the chair, then turn to sit on the table. I hope this isn't some family heirloom or a piece that Matt or Ivy plans on keeping for years to come because I have a feeling—a very hopeful feeling—that Cutter and I are about to ruin it.

I lean back on my palms and arch my back slightly so my tits are on full display. My knees bent, I slide my feet down the top of the table as I lower myself until I'm lying flat, like a feast ready to be eaten. Cutter slides his chair out of the way and steps up to the table's edge as if he's the doctor and I'm his patient. He opens my shirt wide and lowers himself until his mouth is less than an inch away from my pebbled nipple. He blows cool air against my tender skin and I writhe at the sensation. He stands back then and drops his hands in his pockets before staring at me with this satisfied expression, one earned by leaving me on the verge of begging. That's what I get for saying no all those years ago.

"Your turn," he pronounces, meeting my heated gaze with his own. I see what he's doing. He wants me to ask for it. But if I ask, then in a way, he wins.

"Truth or dare, Cutter." My voice comes out raspy, and his face betrays him with the tiniest wince in reaction. He likes it.

"Truth, Laney. Ask me anything." His hand moves to cover his very obvious hard-on, and he strokes himself slowly through his joggers. My memory of how hot he felt through our clothes sends a shockwave through me and makes me even wetter between my legs. I let my knees part a little for relief and to draw his eyes to where I desperately want him.

"Do you want to fuck me, Cutter McCreary?"

Without hesitation, Cutter groans and grabs himself more forcefully, running his hand over his hard cock while his eyes bore into the lace trim of my panties and the insides of my thighs.

"Yes. Very much," he says, moving back to the edge of the table. He walks to the end, where my feet play against the woodgrain. His palms flatten against my shins then drag down to my ankles where he grips me tightly before shifting his gaze to mine. He lifts a brow.

"Dare," I say for the third time.

"Lie perfectly still. And if you move, everything will take longer." His voice comes out almost possessive, dark and heavy, and I shift my hips just from the sound of it. "Ah, bad girl."

"Oh," I whimper before bringing the back of my hand to

my mouth to muffle the sounds I fear I'm about to make. Cutter leaves my ankles and steps to where my head rests flat on the table, my hair fanned out to match the walnut wood. He peels my hand away from my lips and stretches both of my arms above my head, layering my wrists one over the another before looking straight down into my eyes.

"Do not move," he commands. I blink, and he smirks. "I'll allow that, but that's it."

Cutter leans down again, hovering an inch away from my mouth, then moving down the length of my neck to my clavicle and then my other nipple, once again hitting it with cool air blown through his puckered lips. I tuck my chin slowly as I bite my bottom lip, not wanting to get caught but desperate to know what's coming next. Where he's moving.

He trails his soft breath down the center of my body, over my stomach and over the wet cotton strip of my panties. Soon, he's back at the foot of the table, and his hands are creeping up the sides of my legs, flat palms sliding along my calves, then my hips, and soon, his fingers are playing at the thin straps holding my panties in place.

His fingers curl around the strings and slowly drag the material down my hips, tugging to not make me move to assist him. He drags the garment down my legs until its free from me. He tosses it to the floor before returning his hands to the insides of my legs this time.

I can feel the needy cry begging to leave my chest, but I mask it under my heavy pants. Cutter meticulously curls his fingers around my ankles again, squeezing tightly then pulling my body down the length of the table until my knees meet the edge and my legs dangle over the side. He pushes my legs apart and drops to one knee so his mouth is inches from my swollen pussy. Once again he blows, and rather than cry out, I lean my head back as far as I can and take in the sensation.

I never knew how hot not being touched could be. I'm about to be undone completely, just from anticipation. In fact, I hope his touch never comes. I'd rather see how long this feeling can last.

I get my wish as Cutter spends the next several minutes almost touching my most sensitive skin—my aching center, my raw and hard nipples, even my mouth. Through it all, I nearly obey his dare, barely moving an inch except when his tongue finally reaches a fraction too far and tickles the inside of my thigh close to where I want him to devour me.

"Truth or dare, Cutter," I finally say, unable to handle much more. My body is on the verge of exploding, and from what I've been able to see, Cutter isn't too far behind.

"Dare," he growls, pouncing over me and caging me between his palms as he stares down at my tits.

"Own me." I say the words loud and slow, and his eyes drift up to meet mine, I think to be sure he heard me right. I lift my chin and arch my back, which gives him what he needs to break his own leash and drop his mouth over my breast, suckling my nipple and swirling his tongue around the hard peak until it's numb.

I hiss, arching my back more and coaxing his hands to move around my back. They do, and he pulls me into his mouth, moving from breast to breast, biting my nipples softly and holding them hostage one at a time with his teeth while his tongue flicks the tip. I cry out the sound I've been holding back and finally Cutter pushes me to my back, flattening me on the table with a hand over my breasts as he drops back down to a knee and licks my pussy in one long, tortuous stroke before sucking the raw, swollen center so hard it makes a pop when his mouth breaks free.

"Oh, fuck!" I bring my wrist back to my mouth and bite my own skin to temper my sounds as Cutter does it again, this time flicking his tongue up and down my clit before sucking it in once more. His tongue dips inside me after that and he pulses in and out, pushing me toward climax until I'm completely out of control. Just as I'm about to fall over the edge, he pushes his finger into me and curls it to put pressure against the most sensitive spots as his tongue flicks and his mouth sucks. I arch my back hard, lifting half my body from the table. Cutter pummels me with his hand and draws the orgasm from me, holding me to the table and forcing me to take every single lick until the waves stop and I can breathe again.

I lift my head, dizzy from the sweet torture he put me through, and find him getting to his feet and pulling his cock from his pants. He holds himself in one hand and grabs my hip with the other, his fingers digging into my skin as he strokes himself three times before coming on my stomach and letting out a deep growl.

"Fucking hell, Laney. Next time, we start with my dick inside you," he pants out, stroking himself a few more times to empty his cock on my body. I want to tell him that I'm ready for next time now, but also, I don't know if I could handle more. Every cell of my body is on fire, and I think every touch he gives me for the next twenty-four hours is going to send me tumbling over the edge.

This is now my favorite game.

THANK God Laney doesn't talk to the other guys on the team. We travel tomorrow so we didn't have skating or breakouts this morning. I packed up early, though, and pretended we did because I wanted to drive her to campus. I probably could have just told her the truth and offered to be a nice guy, but I'm afraid she'll take me being nice as a step too far.

It's one thing what we do in the bedroom—or on the kitchen table, apparently—but being anything but semi-cordial in front of other people seems to make her uncomfortable. It's fine by me. I'm not looking to get pegged as Laney's boyfriend, but also, I sort of like spending time with her. She gets the pressure of being a college athlete, and not many people understand that. Plus, she gives me shit, the way my brothers always do. Most girls want to talk about my great game or how hard I get hit, but Laney asks questions about my workout routine and whether our coach ever has one-on-one meetings with us. I know she's looking for tips she can use or trying to make sense of the situation she's in with playing time, but it's refreshing not to talk about the flashy parts of my game all the time.

That's what makes the shit Matt posted in his Hot Campus Minute social show this morning so damn bad. I figured something was up when a few of Laney's teammates stared at us when I pulled into a spot near the gym and let her out. I hopped onto my apps after she headed inside and there it was: "Tiff's Hot New Couple Does It All Together."

The post is mostly footage from our photo session. I'm a little annoyed Matt took screenshots of some of the outtakes before I got to touch them up and they were published, but whatever. Matt didn't outright *say* we were a couple in his commentary, but he sure danced around it with lots of insin-uation. I counted the times he said, "Seemed awfully friend-ly," and "Lots of long stares." Five, for the record. He said those things five times. And yeah, we stared a lot—she was posing and I was taking photos. I stared at Matt too, but he didn't mention that. What started as a bet less than a week ago is turning into a collegiate gossip-fest, and the second Laney sees it she's going to want to murder Matt and prob-ably toss my shit into the yard and force me to sleep in a tent. It's basically her worst nightmare, having headlines that talk about her supposed love life and not her skills. And even though Matt took the video, I'm the guy in the pictures. She'll pin this all on me.

Maybe these shots will change her mind, though. Or at least soften her knee-jerk reaction before it hits me in the balls.

I've been working in the editing lab for the last two hours while pretending to be at practice, and I think I have two winning shots for the school to use for Laney's media piece. I'm not sure whether I should show them to her or simply let her be surprised. While I dig the shot I took with the chalk in the air and her palming the ball, my favorite is the outtake I took when she wasn't even looking at me. Her mind was elsewhere, probably on how she was going to get her starting spot back. She's standing in the shot and looking toward the spotlight, which forms a warm, glowing profile of her face. Her eyes almost seem golden from being lit up, and the determined expression that sharpens her jaw and weighs on her brow is not just intimidating, it's also the perfect representation of what I think Laney is.

Focused.

Driven.

Unstoppable.

She's not wrong when she talks about the funding and attention our men's teams get. And yeah, our hockey team is ranked and all that, and football makes the money. But Laney Price might just be the most dominant athlete Tiff University has ever had in a uniform. She knows it, too. And she's going to put Chelsea back on the bench in no time.

"Whoa, are you going to make me look like that?"

I jerk around at the sound of my teammate Max Syme's voice. I forgot I told him to meet me here after eight. Unfortunately, I'm not slick enough to minimize Laney's image so he slaps my shoulder as he leans in next to me to get a better look. He takes control of the mouse and zooms in on the curve of her ass, and I'm tempted to punch him. No idea why I'm instantly possessive over her, but something about the way he's grossly going about objectifying her sort of pisses me off.

"Yeah, I'm not going to be able to make you look that good. You don't have much to work with," I tease, taking the mouse back and minimizing Laney's image. I'm glad he can't see the other shot with the chalk. I don't feel like putting that much time into working with Max. Honestly, he has plenty of shots already, ones that the press has taken of him literally flattening our opponents on the ice. Max gets *a lot* of penalty time.

"Yeah, well, I don't know if there's room for me in the whole Caney-ship thing."

My face bunches up at his absurd mashup.

"I'm sorry, did you just say . . . *Caney-ship?*"

I twist in my chair and look up at him as he pulls his phone from his pocket and shows me a meme of Laney and me, and the term CANEYSHIP. *All those letters between our two names and all I get is the fucking C?*

"Seriously? This shit is going to get old." I push his phone from my view and turn my attention to my student drive so I can save my work and head out with Max to get his shots taken care of. Max knows why Laney and I are living together, and I seriously doubt anyone can tell we've added benefits to the roommate part in the last couple days. Other than the shit Matt puts out on social, we're rarely seen together.

"I don't know, man. I think hooking up with Laney Price sounds pretty fucking amazing. Can you imagine those legs wrapped around—"

"You ready?" I thrust my camera bag into his chest before he has a chance to finish that fantasy out loud. Not my most subtle move.

"Dude, maybe *you* can imagine that." He snickers as he walks behind me through the long corridor that leads to the dining hall and the back half of campus.

"Sorry, brother. I've got nothing for you there, I'm afraid," I say over my shoulder. I'd feel smug about the fact I'm lying except something about Max talking about Laney's body sparks some possessive caveman ego crap deep inside my chest. I'm not sure what I'm angrier about—what he said or that I give a shit what he said.

Instead of giving Max a chance to grill me more and pick apart my façade, I ask him what he thinks about a few photo ideas I've been kicking around. Rather than getting more images of him on the ice, I decided to try something a little different and take some shots in the Tiff Hall of Fame room by the football stadium. They have an actual knight helmet on display that I got permission for us to use, and I talk Max into putting it on in front of the hockey trophy case that shows our years of awards. It takes us a few minutes to get the glass open and slid out of the way to avoid reflection, then we spend a little time checking out the team photos from my brothers' freshman year along with the last big title run twenty years ago when my uncle played here. He was a goalie. Now he mans shipping equipment outside Boston, moving freight from boats to rail and trucks. I don't get to see him much, and it's hard to feel upbeat about bonding when the family get together is your own father's funeral.

"Look at that beard, Cutter," Max says, poking a finger at my uncle's chin. He still sports the same thick-ass beard today. "Skipped a generation, huh?"

"What do you mean?" I run my hand over my scruff and laugh. He's not wrong—rather than growing a beard, it's more like my beard grows a face. Patchy is only the start of it. But my two-day-old shave seems to be a sweet spot, at least that's what Laney said last night.

Laney. I'm thinking about her again.

"Okay, so maybe try this on first and see how heavy it feels." I hand Max the helmet and tuck Laney's opinion on facial hair back into the *non-essential* file in my brain. Max works the mask up and down a few times to ease the hinges after years of sitting in a display case, untouched. He gives me a thumbs up after he flips the mask back down for the final time.

Max plays along, crossing his arms in his jersey and propping the iron up on his forehead for a few shots, and then looking through the mask for a few more. I get a great closeup of his eyes through the helmet that I think the marketing guys are going to want to use for the season and we call it a wrap.

We're walking back to campus across the giant parking lot between the school and the stadium when my phone starts to ring nonstop. I'm sure it's Laney wanting to chew my ass out for somehow making Matt stir up controversy, so I ignore the first two calls, but when the third vibrates in my pocket I pull my phone out to answer. I glance at the screen and see Flynn's name and number, and my stomach drops.

My mom.

"Flynn, what's up?" I naturally pick up my pace and Max asks what's going on as he tries to keep up. I hold up a finger and focus on my brother.

"Mom drove herself to the ER, so she's okay, but—"

I don't hear the rest of what my brother says. Once he uttered *ER* I shot into panic mode and handed over my camera and schoolbag to Max. I'm running through the lot now and panting into the phone. I take a shortcut through mid-campus to get to where I parked by the gym and put my phone on speaker before I toss it into the cupholder.

"Cutter, I said she's okay. You don't have to freak out, man." The problem I have with what Flynn is saying is that nobody freaks out over mom going through any of this, and that means nobody shows up for her when she hits rough patches. If mom needs me, I want to be there.

"Tell me what's happening again. I'm heading to Mercy." I shift into reverse and peel out of the lot.

"It's just a cold, and with the chemo they want to have her stay overnight. She's not going to want you dropping everything to come sit in a hospital with her, Cutter." Flynn lecturing me is like being told what to do by a Muppet. Of all my brothers, he's the most irresponsible and reckless.

"Yeah, well, I'd rather her be mad having to put up with my company than wondering why she's eating green Jell-O in a hospital room alone because her five kids are too busy warming benches in Bakersfield or playing some board game, counting down for bath time."

"Wow, man. Cheap shots. You can rip on me and Todd all you want, but don't give Pat and Andrew crap for having families, dude."

I pull up hard at the stoplight and pinch the bridge of my nose.

"Sorry, Flynn. I didn't mean to be a dick. I worry about her, is all." My heart is racing and my leg teems with energy, ready to push the pedal through the floor when the light turns green.

"I know. That's why I said don't worry. Mom told me not to bother you. That's why she called me instead, to make sure someone knew. But I knew you'd want to know. Try to take a breath, though, yeah? She's really all right."

I do my best to take Flynn's advice, drawing in a long breath through my nose while my eyes zero in on the flaming red LED lights above the road. They switch to green and I give the Jeep gas as I blow out through my mouth.

"Call me when you know more," Flynn says.

"I will," I say before ending the call.

It takes me about ten minutes to carve through what should be a twenty-minute drive, and once I get inside and get her room number from the main desk, I dash to her wing. I slow to a walk before I make it to the nurses' station and spend a few seconds checking my phone while I catch my breath. The only message is from Max who says he'll drop my bags off at my house and to keep him posted.

With a cooler head and a slower heart rate, I round the nurse's station and head to room four seventeen. The sound of true crime TV has never soothed my soul more.

"Now, why would you go and call Flynn instead of me, Ma?" I plop down in the chair by her bed and she doesn't even look in my direction.

"Damn him. I told him not to tell you," she gripes, picking up the remote from the folds in her blanket and muting the TV. She tosses the remote on the rolling tray table, then picks up a cup and shakes it.

"Since you're here, can you get me more ice?" She has some liquids going through her IV, so I glance over the chart to get a handle on what's going on with her.

"I'm allowed to have ice!" She shakes the cup again, more vigorously this time, and hits me with a tight-lipped glare.

"Fine, I was just making sure. You're getting some vitamins, it looks like. What did the doctor say?" I step one foot into the hallway, flag down one of the attendants and mouth, "Ice." She nods so I head back into the room.

"It's just your average cold bug, but my immune system is working at a two, so they're adding some more defense." She holds up the drip line and gives a soft laugh. My mom and dad always talked about our game play on a scale of one to ten. They both knew the game well, and since my dad quit playing because my grandfather was apparently a real hard-ass about winning, my parents never wanted to put negative words in any of our heads after a bad loss. Still, when mom says I looked like a two out on the ice, it feels pretty damn bad. Which means she's probably not feeling so hot.

"Well, you came to the right place. Thank you for not being stubborn and trying to tough this out at home. However, if you could just get over this idea that I don't have time to help and call me, that would be great." A nurse steps into the room with a small bucket of ice and a new pitcher of water. She pours a fresh cupful for my mom and checks her line before leaving.

"Well, it's because you *don't* have time. I know you head out tomorrow for the season opener. You think I'm not following every game like usual?" She takes a long sip of water, then plunks the cup back on the table like it's a punctuation mark to her response.

I shake my head and breathe out a soft laugh before taking her hand and sitting down by her again.

"You're stubborn," I say.

"And how the hell do you think you got the way you did?" She squeezes my hand back, then pats the top of it with her free hand.

"I'm probably going to be on the bus when they discharge you, so I expect you'll at least text me updates. I mean, how am I going to know who killed that blonde lady they keep showing pictures of on the screen if you don't?" I gesture to the TV and my mom smirks.

"Neither of us will find out if you don't let me turn the volume back on." She quirks a brow and I chuckle, shaking my head.

"Go ahead. I'll stick around for the end," I say, turning my chair and pushing it right up next to the bed so I can sit with her and watch a seventeen-year-old murder case come down to a fingerprint on a jar of peanut butter.

I MISSED MY MARKETING CLASS, but my professor knows about my situation, so I send him a text from my Jeep after sticking around long enough to talk to my mom's oncol-ogist. The fact he didn't seem worried definitely helped take my anxiety down a notch or two. And over-caution is better than being reckless, so I'm glad she's here, even for just a cold.

I call Flynn during my drive home to update him and Todd, and they promise to fill in our older brothers so I don't have to. I may be the one here and doing the hands-on care-taking, but my brothers are very much locked in with every-thing that happens. We all share with each other, something Mom hasn't seemed to find a way around for, well, I guess twenty-eight years since that's how old Andrew is. I'm pretty sure when he was born, Patrick invested the brother code with him, and the two of them simply passed it on with each new McCreary.

By the time I pull up to the house, it's late afternoon and my stomach is growling. Ivy's truck is in the driveway and the garage is shut, which I think means Matt's car is probably tucked inside. I'm not really in the mood for a full house, but I'm also kind of glad it's not just going to be me and Laney alone right away. I don't feel like talking about my day. I'd rather blend in and simply pick up on what the rest of the housemates are doing.

When I walk into the house, I'm hit with some serious grilled onion aroma. My mouth waters so much that I'm practically drooling, so I follow the scent to the kitchen where Laney is working a skillet on the stove while Ivy sits across from her on one of the stools.

"What's cooking?" I take the other stool and twist to look for Matt. I find him wearing some headset game that has him karate chopping around the living room. When my gaze meets Ivy's she rolls her eyes and shrugs about her brother.

"He's ridiculous," she explains. "And homemade pasta and sauce. Laney's brilliant in the kitchen. Five bucks if you want in." She holds out a palm and I immediately glance to Laney as if she'll tell me whether her friend is taking me for a ride or not.

"Pay up, buddy," Laney says. "When we make meals for everyone, we all chip in. I've been coming over here to eat for a year. That's the rule."

I look back to Ivy, whose open palm is still waiting.

"Okay, I'm in." I fish out my wallet and stretch it open in hopes of a stray five. I rarely have cash, though, and all I have in there now is an old dime I think is probably stuck to the lining with syrup and the receipt for the pizza and beer Laney and I picked up last night.

"We accept Venmo," Ivy says. By the time my wallet is tucked away and my phone is out, she's already got hers ready to scan.

"Wow, you run an efficient business," I say, scanning her code with my phone and sending her five dollars.

"I'm going to be an ER nurse. I better run a tight ship." She winks at me, then snags her purse from the end of the counter and pulls a five-dollar bill from her wallet. She hands it to Laney who stuffs it into a jar by the sink, where it joins more cash.

"You could maybe get a ship a little tighter than an open jar," I joke.

Ivy leans toward me and smacks the back of my neck lightly, but with enough snap to it that I get the point. *Do not pick apart Ivy or any of her systems. Noted.* I hold up my palms.

"My bad."

While Ivy recounts stories about the various patients and other nurses she saw today, my mind keeps bouncing back to my mom. I probably could have easily run into her today, though I know she's not on my mom's floor. I wonder what I would have done. I almost want to ask Ivy some questions about the hospital, to get a feel for when my mom will be discharged so I can check on her before the game tomorrow. I decide against it when Matt finally takes his headset off and joins our conversation.

"Hospitals are gross."

Ivy smacks him on the back of the neck, and I see the difference between when she really means it.

"Don't be a dick," she says, giving him a glare.

"What? I mean, everyone there is sick. And you know how it is—the first six months you did an internship you were sick all the time, picking up stuff there. Plus there's the creepy factor of, I don't know, death and all that."

My stomach fills with lead and suddenly the thought of eating anything makes me want to vomit. "You know what? Keep my five, but I'm actually exhausted. We travel early tomorrow, so I'm just gonna—" I point over my shoulder to my room. Laney's the only one who notices, though, and her brow draws in.

"You okay?" she mouths.

The lead in my stomach tumbles.

I give her a small nod and head toward our room while Ivy rattles off a dozen reasons why Matt is a dumbass. She's spot on with every single one of them.

I grab some clean sweats and an old T-shirt and hit the shower, letting the water pound my face and chest until I've drained it of hot. I feel bad because Laney won't have any for a while now, but I couldn't seem to pry myself out.

The living room and kitchen are quiet by the time I crack open the door and let a puff of steam out with me. When I get back into our room, I toss my dirty clothes into my laundry basket in the corner, then fall face-first into my pillow. I don't sleep, but I lay like that for several minutes simply listening to the various sounds in the house. The stairs creak when Matt and Ivy go up them, and Matt's not gentle with his door, but his sister is, which isn't really that surprising. Laney seems to be cleaning up in the kitchen, and the fact that nobody is helping her kind of ticks me off a little, but not enough to drag my ass out there and help.

When our bedroom door creaks, I roll to my side to find Laney walking in with a small bowl, a fork, and a potholder.

"I saved you some. Literally nobody turns down my pasta." She flops into the bed next to me and hands me the potholder first, then sets the bowl onto it before twisting the fork prongs into the noodles.

"The bowl gets hot," she explains.

I give her a crooked smile, then take the fork in my hand and twist some more. I breathe in the scent and fill my mouth with a way-too-big bite. The tangy sauce hits my tongue and the sharp contrasts of the seasoning and peppers literally coats my mouth in savory goodness. I practically swallow without chewing and go in for a follow-up.

"Damn," I mutter through chewing.

"I told you."

Laney gets up and steps into the closet, taking off her shirt and tossing it into her clothes bin, then putting on an extra-long T-shirt. She wriggles out of her sweatpants then climbs back in bed next to me. I do my best to ignore how tempting her body is, instead allowing myself to be taken in by the temptations of her cooking. I scrape the bowl practically clean and Laney takes it from me, then sets it on her night table.

"I'll deal with it in the morning."

I grimace, and her face contorts with a question.

"You don't have to deal with it. You did the cooking, so I do the cleaning."

She leans close, smiling, then taps her fingertip to my nose twice.

"You travel tomorrow, which means you get up at four a.m. Why don't you let me take this one?" Her lips tug into a half smile and I relent, holding up a palm.

"Fair enough."

I have a marketing paper to write, but it's not due until Monday, and I don't think my mind can switch into the right gear now. I'm not worried about my mom, but I'm not exactly *not* worried either.

"One of your teammates gave me a ride home today. Max? He seems nice. He said he had to drop your bags by the house because you had an emergency." Laney sinks down to lay on her side, propping her head on her hand.

I'm not sure what to react to first. Max taking her home.

Max being nice. My emergency. I choose option four—none of the above.

"Thanks." I blink through our stare until I realize she hasn't blinked once and I look away. Maybe I'll work on that paper after all.

"You want to talk about it?"

No.

I focus on nothing in particular straight in front of me and consider her offer again, and decide that either way my stomach is going to twist on itself until I get the text from Ma that she's heading home. I shift my gaze to her and try to read her eyes to get a sense of whether she really wants to hear about my problems or is just being polite since I'm in her way. The longer I look at her, though, the more I want to kiss her, and it takes about ten seconds of silence for me to decide I'm going to.

Shifting my body lower in the bed, I roll toward her until my right hand is cupping her face and she's caged between my arms.

"No. I don't want to talk," I say before dropping my mouth on hers and sucking in her bottom lip. My tongue tastes her skin, coaxing her to open more for me. Within seconds, her hands are on my face and neither of us is breathing—we're just kissing. Tongues exploring and teeth nipping at each other's skin, we take turns peppering one another's lips, jawlines, and necks with hungry kisses.

We never take it further, but we kiss until I can tell I've made her lips raw with my scruff. I have to shave. Kissing Laney is good motivation to keep up with it, too. Not ready to let her go completely but too distracted to sleep or hint that I want more, I settle into the center of our bed and hold her at my side. I run my hand through her long, soft hair, over and over, counting at first then simply making it a permanent routine as she drifts to sleep with her head on my chest and her leg slung over mine.

I lie awake knowing my mom is probably being checked on every hour. I try to guess when, and a few times consider texting her to check whether she's awake too. At some point, I'll either drift off or get out of bed and pack for a bus ride to Wisconsin. With my luck, the guys from the Spoilers will somehow hitch a ride with us and want to talk, and then I'll have to pull some energy out of my ass so I can perform on the ice. I guess at this point I'll be pulling out magic energy, regardless.

I can do this all.

I can do it all.

I can handle it.

I match a thought with each pass of my hand through Laney's hair. And finally my eyes close.

13 /
laney

IT'S hard to get pumped up for the bench. I have a new respect for our players who don't get much time on the court. They're always with us, cheering and hyping. They grab towels and wipe sweat from the floor, grab water, and scream for our success.

I'm one of them now.

Early warmups were solid. I hit the ball with extra muscle, and even though Coach kept pushing me to the middle, I slipped out and took a few outside sets too, just to show the contrast between Chelsea and me.

"You're looking great out there. I wish it were you I was setting high and out today," our setter Kiera says. She's been setting high and outside to me for six years. We played club together during high school, and she's half the reason I committed to Tiff. We're a killer combo, and it does ease the sting of being replaced a little knowing she'd rather I were out there instead of Chelsea.

"Thanks for saying that. It's not easy." I wince as we head into the makeshift locker room to hydrate and cool down before pre-game really begins.

"I can imagine. And with your dad here today."

My jaw slackens and the skin on my face suddenly feels heavy.

"Oh, shit," Kiera says. "You didn't know? Did you not see the program?"

"Uh, no!" My wide eyes scan the room in search of a loose copy. The last thing I want to do is ask a teammate for one and get more pity glares.

This cannot be happening!

Kiera saves me and pulls a copy from her bag. I turn my back to everyone and hunch over so I can flip to the page and read. I quickly find the photo Cutter took, and I probably would have been proud of it if I knew it was being published today, and if I knew what the story on me said. I don't even remember getting an interview.

"The first part is all the same as usual. Your bio and background stuff. Read a couple of paragraphs down." Kiera points over my shoulder and my eyes follow her guide.

Price was a lock to go top five in the first pro draft after her senior season, but an unfortunate shoulder injury left her sidelined for most of her junior year. Now her future is hazy. It all comes down to one season.

Her dad, famous beach baller Bobby Price, knows a thing or two about working through injuries. His college career was cut short after a similar injury. But he says his daughter is built on the same foundation he was, and like him, she'll fight her way back and dominate.

"Beach opened up a whole other world for me, and I'm not saying that's where Laney is headed, but I know my daughter and I know her determination. She'll be a force on whatever type of court she chooses," the senior Price says. "I'll see it firsthand at the opening game of the season. I can't wait."

"Well, fucking hell!" I toss the program on the floor and drop my head in my hands, my temples pulsing with anger.

"I thought he said nice things," Kiera utters behind me. She's trying to make this better, but she's the only player on this team who knows what bullshit that all is.

I pop my head up and twist to meet her eyes.

"He said he knows his daughter, Kiera. I bet if I quizzed him on the color of my eyes, he'd get it wrong while staring me in the face." I shake my head and breathe out a heavy gush of air before glancing to the other side of the room where Chelsea is wrapping her ankles and retying her shoes.

"And he's going to see me sit on the bench and cheer like a good sport. He's missed countless games. I've asked him to show up so many times. He didn't mention my injury in texts once, but he knows how I am going to overcome adversity. Kiera, I haven't responded to him in years."

"Maybe he won't show," she offers.

My shoulders drop as I consider that option. It's likely. She's right. I nod.

"You're right. I'm probably worrying about nothing." I turn my attention to adjusting my socks and pulling them up tight over my calves.

"Besides, you're going to have so many fans out there because of the whole Caney-ship thing." Kiera giggles, amused that I'm now some gimmick because of my housing situation with Cutter. I've tried to ignore the posts that Matt lit a fire under, but by the time I walked to campus today for the game, they were too numerous to ignore.

"Ugh, don't remind me. It's a nothing burger, the Cutter stuff. We're stuck in the same house, and that's all." My lips literally burn from kissing him last night. In fact, they flare up right now like some Pavlovian liar test, which I of course fail.

"Girl, you don't have to feed me anything. You're living with the hottest guy on campus, and we all know it's more than sharing a house." She shoots me a knowing glare that literally sends bile up my esophagus. I don't want to be some gossip topic. And I don't want people knowing what Cutter and I are and aren't.

"He sleeps on the couch," I sigh out.

He slept there once.

"Okay. But all I'm saying is if that man were sleeping on my couch, I would have a damn hard time concentrating on sleep." She titters, then pulls her hair loose to re-form her ponytail. "Maybe you should introduce me to your *housemate*."

I roll my eyes and turn my attention to stretching out my already well-stretched arms. "Yeah, maybe I will. Careful what you wish for."

Kiera laughs off my offer and heads back to the hallway leading into the gym so we can make our entrance for the announcers. My eyes scan her body and the long silky blonde ponytail that sways as she jogs away. I bet Cutter would be into her. The thought makes my throat tighten so I look away and refocus my thoughts on my biggest problem. What if my dad shows?

I line up with my teammates last, taking a spot near the back, not feeling the usual hype I do when we wait for the introductions and the sound of thunder that the announcer plays for our entrance. We're a ranked squad, and I usually eat up the fanfare that goes with that. Today though, I feel empty. I'm going to have to fake it.

The rumble of the crowd shakes the doors and the lights dim on the other side.

"Let's hear it for your Lady Knights!" The announcer's voice booms as Kiera pushes open the doors and leads us out to the court to run our laps and take a few final swings at the net before game time.

I jog by the line of coaches, training my eyes straight ahead so I don't accidentally connect with Coach or anyone in the stands. I don't need Coach filling my head with false hope or trying to coax me into leading from the sidelines. I'll do my job, begrudgingly but well.

We meet in the center of the court and all start to clap until our hands meet in the middle and we shout, "Win!" Everyone takes a ball from the rack and splits into specialties on the court while Kiera sets us. I make my way to the outside position as someone calls my name. I know better than to look, but today's weird—my life is weird. I turn my head without thinking and come face-to-face with the man I haven't seen in real life in years. His smile is for everyone else, but the fire in his eyes is for me. He's a competitor. And he's going to be so disappointed.

"Laney! Shift middle!" Coach Kane's orders break through the noise and stab me in the chest. I nod at her while my insides start to crumble.

I don't want to hit middle. That's not where I'm strongest. It's not my position. Of course, I don't have a position.

I wait my turn and get a total of three swings in at middle, only cleanly attacking once and putting the ball down hard. My gaze is like a magnet for my father's approval, which makes me sick. I haven't needed his approval for years. I haven't had it in years. Why I keep looking to him now baffles me. It's like I'm trying to telepathically explain the situation to him and defend myself for not being the amazing offspring he thinks he deserves.

I am amazing! I'm better than he is!

I take a spot in the middle of the row of seats and we all listen while Coach walks us through the sequence she'd like us to work on with our offense and what to guard on defense. We're playing Lincoln, and they like to tip. A lot. Our libero is going to look like a stud today.

The game starts, and when I don't take the floor when the starters are announced, my father shifts his weight back and crosses his arms. The visual tugs at the nine-year-old who still lives inside me somewhere and much prefers seeing her father nod with approval.

"Let's go, ladies! Watch the short serve!" I shout, redirecting my focus to the court and my team. I get to my feet and stand in a cluster with the rest of the bench players, ignoring the pang of jealousy I feel when a few of them get to sub in to serve. Through it all, I'm poised. Or at least, I think I am. I high five every single player as they exit and enter the court. I shout tips to Chelsea while secretly wishing her shoelaces would disintegrate. I celebrate the points, and even go as far as getting on the floor to pound my palms on the wood when we manage a pancake.

I'm the perfect example of team player and sportsmanship. And I ache not getting to be the one hearing the encouragement instead of giving it.

We cruise to victory in three sets. It was an easier matchup than Coach predicted. Lincoln graduated their power hitter last year, and it seems they haven't done much to fill the role. Too bad it's too late for me to transfer.

I avoid the student reporter after the game, not feeling up to mentally riffling through my talking points. *I can't wait to get back out there, and I'm proud of our team. I played a role in the background, and it's not about me, it's about the team. Blah, blah, blah.*

I get a "good job" from Coach Kane, but nothing more than that.

The only interaction I can't find a way to avoid is waiting for me by the exit. I catch him signing an autograph for a woman his age. They take a selfie together and I get caught in my father's gaze as he fakes a smile.

I draw in a deep breath through my nose and ready myself for whatever the next ten minutes hold. I'll do my best to control what comes out of my mouth, but there are a lot of years of anger brewing in my chest right now. It's blanketed with disappointment from not playing, though, so maybe I'll be able to leave this gym without making a scene.

"Yes, nice to meet you," my father says to the woman as I walk up. He turns in my direction and lifts his brows. I'm not sure if he's expecting a hug or an explanation.

"What are you doing here?" Yeah, that's the best I'm going to do.

My father steps back, feigning offense.

"Laney, you know I love watching you play." He glances around to see if anyone's within earshot but I don't care. I roll my eyes and huff out a laugh.

"I mean, I was a pretty solid nine-year-old server. I guess you could say I've grown since you saw me last." I pull my bag strap up on my shoulder and shift my weight, jutting out a hip and catching a few stares from some of my teammates as they maneuver around us to leave the gym.

My cheeks are burning. I hate that people are seeing this. They've never seen my father at a game, and I'm sure they read the program piece and figured I'd be excited. Or maybe they pieced our shitty relationship together. It's not a new story. A lot of people have fucked-up relationships with their parents.

"Laney, don't make this about me," my dad says in a hushed tone, leaning toward me.

I breathe out a short titter and my mouth tugs up on one side.

"It's always about you, isn't it?"

Our eyes lock for several seconds, and my nostrils stretch wide with my breath. My dad's gaze is simply unfamiliar. I know his face. I've seen it in photos and in video. I just haven't seen it in person in a very long time. There's nothing to hold on to behind his eyes. No warmth or understanding. We have no backstory.

"I'm guessing Coach is still working you in after your injury?" Finally, something he's familiar with.

"Yes." I don't elaborate.

He nods. Dropping his hands in the pockets of his high-end jeans, he scans the gym some more. Nobody really left for him to show off for.

"Thanks for coming, I guess. I should go." I move to push past him, but he places his palm on my arm.

"Laney, I—"

My eyelids flutter as my gaze shifts to his touch. I don't recoil, but I want to. My stare climbs to his face and I shake my head.

"What?"

He takes a deep breath, and for a sliver of a second, I swear his lips start to form the words *I'm sorry.* But his mouth quickly closes as his shoulders roll back.

"You know, now is the time to focus. You're in a fight for your life, and you really shouldn't be letting yourself get distracted with . . . what, hockey players?" He waves a hand dismissively as my stomach churns.

"I am focused. And you're too old to be stalking college kids on social apps." A repulsed sneer forms on my mouth.

"Well, my brand sort of requires I pay attention to things. And it's hard not to notice your daughter being linked to some showy romance bet or something. He sounds like a loser, you know. This boy? His brothers barely made the draft and his numbers are nowhere near theirs."

He seriously researched Cutter.

"Good to know. Also, he's twenty-two. So, probably not a boy. And we're not anything. We are housemates, and people like to gossip. Now, if you'll excuse me—"

"Your mother said you turned down a proposal from Cam?"

I stop mid-step, my back to the man, and drop my chin to my chest. Since when do he and Mom talk? And how would he know about Cam? I didn't think he knew I dated.

"I can't do this right now," I say, refusing to look him in the eyes one more time. "Just, I don't know. Text me or something. Send a birthday card. You know the drill."

My stride is long and quick. I can't get away from my father fast enough, and my insides are literally boiling with a mix of emotions. Part of me wants to cry, but those tears will only be hot lava because I'm also so angry I could punch someone.

I march home alone, and the weather is starting to turn. The days are getting shorter, and it's pitch black outside by the time I reach our street. I could shower and change and head to Patty's to celebrate with a few of the girls, but I don't fit in. Not now. At least, not in my head. There's so much noise bouncing between my ears—this voice that sounds like mine only slightly more commanding—and it keeps telling me I'm a failure and not good enough. I know it's lying to me, but for the first time in my life, I'm giving it space. I'm letting it win.

Ivy's working and Matt isn't home, which I'm oddly disappointed about. I don't even have the energy to shower, so instead, I toss my bags at the foot of the bed, kick off my shoes, and crawl into the blankets. I roll to my side and look at the plump pillow and open space where Cutter should be. He'll be home tomorrow sometime, after dinner with his mom, I suppose. It feels as if someone is pressing a thumb into the center of my chest, just where my ribs part. I feel helpless. I feel lonely.

I bury my face in my pillow and scream loud, letting my voice crack and gurgle since nobody is home to hear me. I do it three times, until my throat hurts and my head feels dizzy. I swivel my head to look the other way and spot my laptop charging on the night table. Unplugging it, I drag it to my pillow and flip it open, checking the time—six p.m. Cutter's game should still be going.

I log in to the division website and pull up the stream for his game in time to see the start of the third period. It's tied one to one, which is strange to see for our men's hockey team. We tend to score a lot, and there is no mercy for the weak.

"There you are," I mutter to myself when I spot Cutter hopping over the boards and onto the ice. I smile at the visual. It's such a stereotype, but something about seeing him do it makes my stomach settle and my chest warm.

"Let's go," I whisper, nestling in and propping my head on my hands.

I've watched a few of their games, though usually I'm

only there to put in my hours. Every athlete has to help out other teams—selling snacks, working as security. I like to help people find their seats; I get to watch the games that way.

I've never felt invested before. Now, however, I feel that same fire I get when I play. Watching Cutter check guys into the glass and skate away with the puck has me sitting tall, and when he gets undercut, I grit my teeth.

"Come on, Cutter. You got this." The room is dark, except for the glow from my screen. I feel like a pre-teen watching rated R movies under her blanket.

When Cutter takes a shot, I hold my breath. The puck soars off of the goalie's stick and wraps around the goal.

"Damn it!"

Cutter chases it down, in a race with some guy who is about his size and has the speed advantage. When his opponent gets to the puck first, I will Cutter on. My mouth keeps silently uttering *come on, come on* as Cutter regroups and more Tiff players spill onto the ice while others leave. Our goalie makes three massive saves in a row, finally getting one into Cutter's control.

A million calculations happen at once as I watch him work our team into position before attacking. I want to be inside his head to tell him what I see, but it's almost as if he reads me anyhow. They've been double-teaming Cutter the entire period, but he's managed to lose one of the defenders, and he takes a pass from the right of the goal in time to flip it into the net so fast I'm not sure whether it went in or not.

I pile my hands on top of my head as I sit up and stare at the screen, feeling pretty good as Cutter and a few of the guys huddle in celebration before skating back to center ice. The student broadcasting seems as unsure as I am, but eventually he gets confirmation from the refs and Cutter raises his stick in the air while pumping his other fist.

I hold my hands up and grin, and I don't lay down again until time runs out and we come away with the win. I'm so fired up from the game that I think I could run a mile without breathing hard. The invisible weighted blanket I was carrying around before seems to be gone, too. My father, the Caney-ship posts, Chelsea—it's all a haze in the past. I know this feeling won't last, but for now, it feels nice to be distracted. Maybe what I need is the opposite of my father's advice. More distractions. Less focus.

I pull my phone out and send Cutter a text.

ME: Great game! Congrats!

I close my laptop and fall back onto the bed, smiling at the ceiling. The euphoria sticks with me for about twenty minutes. Maybe thirty. Like alcohol, though, it wears off. And now, not only am I the girl whose deadbeat dad is disappointed in her and who lost her starting spot on the team, I'm also the girl who is desperately checking her phone every two minutes to see if the guy she supposedly doesn't have a thing for has texted her back.

I drown my repetitive nonsensical thoughts in a hot shower, pulling a Cutter and using up every last drop since I'm here alone and got to the shower first. Too lazy to dry my hair, I leave it wrapped in a towel as I tuck myself back into bed to scroll on my phone.

I start at a few of the Caney-ship posts on some of Matt's pages, and mistakenly peruse a few of the comments, some nice, most not. Apparently, being with Cutter is a coveted honor that I don't deserve, according to—pick any female name out of the Tiff directory. A few male names, too. I stop short of fully wishing those other girls or guys could have him. I stop short because I don't really want them to.

That thought sends me down a new rabbit hole, and before long I'm on Cutter's profile, scrolling through every post he's put up over the last year. I start to get into some of the comments on his photos, which are usually of him playing hockey or holding a beer up while standing with some girl under his arm. His smile is always the same in the couple photos. And his fierce eyes are always dialed in when he's playing, at least when it's a close-up and I can make out his expression. There are two Cutters according to his page, and maybe a week ago, I would have bought that to be true. But now? I'm not so sure. I've seen glimpses of another guy. He's pulled that mask away long enough for me to see other sides. Like yesterday, for example, when he was clearly upset about something. Or when he woke up early to take me to practice and pretended he had practice too. I let him think he got away with that. But also, I like his kindness.

Under every photo are dozens of comments, some from people congratulating him on a good game, others from girls asking him to hook up. He almost always hearts the response, and often flirts right out in the open, basically calling their bluff and telling them where to find him if they ever want to experience Cutter McCreary for themselves. The whole thing amuses me and also clears out some of the confusing thoughts I've had about Cutter in the last couple days. But then something strange stands out.

Cutter and I have been sharing a space for a little more than a week. And if I look at the photo he posted from practice the day he moved in, I see the same fifty comments as usual from his fan club, but zero responses from Cutter. The next day is the same. And the post of him and the guys on the bus this morning? It's filled with well wishes and propositions. Cutter thanks everyone who wished him luck, but the girls basically throwing themselves at him digitally have zero engagement. He hasn't even as much as liked one of those *you're so hot* comments in nine days. Sure, that's no record or anything, but it is obvious and it is strange. And I maybe, kind of, like it.

My phone buzzes in my hand, and when I see it's a text from Cutter, my heart swings into my throat and I roll to my side, pulling my blanket over me so I can hide. It's not like there are ghosts floating around waiting to taunt me, but somehow, it feels safer to be unsure of things under here. To smile when I see his name. To swallow hard at his words.

> CUTTER: Hey! You saw? Wow! Thanks! You guys swept them. I checked. I also saw the box score, and I know. I know and I understand. And if you want, when I get home, we can hit things hard some more.

I drop my chin to my fist and reread his message a few times, my mouth caught somewhere between a smile and the quivering frown that usually precedes one of my very rare but quite potent crying fests.

The blinking dots have me glued to the screen, waiting for more. Maybe I'm waiting on his permission to cry over the shitty day I had. To mourn the loss of always being on top. So I can feel sorry for myself and know it's okay that it hurts to step backward, even a little.

> CUTTER: I hope you're out celebrating at Patty's. But if you're not, it's ok. I wouldn't be able to either, and it doesn't mean we're shitty teammates. It means we care about our passions more than others, and we take our business personally.

Yeah, that was the permission slip I needed. A single tear escapes my right eye and slides down my cheek, stopping at the curve of my lip. I swipe the back of my hand over my face to erase it, letting the salty taste seep into my mouth just a little. Then I write him back.

> ME: Thanks. I needed that.

His response is immediate.

> CUTTER: I know. I'll see you soon.

I roll to my right and stare at the screen for nearly a minute before pulling his pillow to my chest and wrapping his blanket around my body. I imagine it's a hug, and it soothes me. But I refuse to think beyond that.

14 /
cutter

MY BROTHER'S text hit my phone seconds before I had to put it away for game time. It was like I had wings. Coach said it was my best game, and it couldn't have come at a better time. The Spoilers guys weren't there, but two other team scouts were—Ice Devils and the Vagrants. Two more minor organizations all within driving distance of Ma's place. It felt like destiny. And I can't wait to tell my mother about it when I get to the house.

I came home first, hoping to maybe see Laney before taking off, but she was at practice. The women have another game on Tuesday. They play pretty much nonstop for the next three months. I'm sure Laney is anxious for the next game, hoping the coach finally cuts her loose and lets her play.

She didn't text much last night, but I could read her pain in the brevity of her words. Being at the top of your game and getting knocked back down to start the climb all over again is hard physically, but emotionally it's worse. I was

171

hoping her coach would change her mind and start Laney, but when I saw the box score after my game, my gut sank for her.

Thing is, I can't imagine a Tiff volleyball match in which she isn't the dominant force. She belongs out there, and I know that the coach and the school are simply saving her ass by A, not bringing her back too quickly and risking injury, and B, not upsetting the other players putting in the work. There's a C situation too, that I'm not sure Laney knows about. Chelsea's parents own a software company, more of a corporation really. Well, it's listed on the stock exchange frequently, so however big that is—maybe that's a dynasty.

That corporation pretty much bankrolls Tiff athletics. So Chelsea is going to get her time one way or another. But the team can't afford to keep Laney on the bench, so she'll get back into the starting six. Might not be in the spot she wants, though, and that—that's not right. I can't decide whether it's better she knows before the system screws her over or after. The system will do its thing regardless.

I pull into the familiar driveway that's permanently stained with various paints and chalk lines my brothers and I have drawn over the years to make our own rink. Plenty of McCreary-family defenses were hatched on this makeshift goal. We had just enough space to draw out the house, including two face-off circles that bled into the sidewalk and street. Our neighbors put up with it because we cleaned their lawns on weekends. My dad made the trade and to me and my brothers, it always felt like a fair deal.

My mom hits the garage button to bring up the door just as I get out of my Jeep. I crouch down to spot her feet shuffling toward the opening, and when it's clear enough for me to pass through, I rush at her and sweep her into a hug.

"Oh, all right. I said I was fine." She plays it off but I can feel in her hug that she's happy to see me.

"I didn't make dinner like I was supposed to. I think maybe a hospital stay is a good excuse?" She pulls back to look me in the eyes, and I grin.

"You know I don't come here for the food."

She waggles her head.

"*Sometimes* you come here for the food."

I laugh and relent. She's partly right.

I follow my mom inside and immediately go to work tidying up. She keeps a neat house, but some things she struggles with, like putting the big pots away after the dishwasher. She lectures me about coming in and visiting first, but it doesn't stop me from coaxing her honey-do list out within a few minutes. By the time I'm sitting on the porch with her and drinking some of her diabetes-causing sweet tea, I've changed out four light bulbs, two smoke detector batteries, checked the pilot light, and run a broom over her back patio. I was always the best at chores. I sometimes bribed my brothers into paying me to do theirs. I worked faster than they did, so they split their allowance with me if I did the things they hated. I have toilet cleaning down to a science. Four minutes flat.

"If you're hungry, I can make you a sandwich."

She leans forward, about to get up, but I wave her back down.

"Stop, you do not have to feed me. Besides, my roommate happens to be an amazing cook. She made homemade pasta sauce the other night and I'm hoping there might still be leftovers." My mouth actually waters a little at the thought of Laney's pasta. Even at my lowest her food was amazing. Right now? I could probably finish a full pot all on my own.

"So she cooks, huh?" My mom lifts the brim of the hat she's been wearing since I got here so she can eye me. Her hair is thinning, something I know makes her self-conscious. She's always had thick hair that she had to braid or wear in clips. She cut it to her shoulders when she got the diagnosis, and though it stuck around for the first few rounds, it's starting to change.

"Yeah, she cooks. I know where you're going with this, though. Don't start doing that mom thing." I waggle a finger at her and gulp down the rest of my tea. My brain buzzes from the massive dose of sugar.

"What mom thing? Oh, do you mean the whole 'stick your nose into your son's love life and hope like hell he doesn't pick an asshole' thing?"

I laugh out hard.

"Yeah, that's the one." I stand up to take my glass back inside before I leave, but my mom stands and rips it from my hand.

"At least let me handle one damn dish," she grumbles. I relent and let her take the glass.

She has some antibiotics to finish out this week, but she's already sounding better than she did when I visited the hospital. If it weren't for the small subtleties—the dark circles under her eyes and the thin nature of her face—I don't know that anyone would suspect she had cancer, either. Strangers probably don't. But around here, in Springs, her world knows what she's supposed to look like. Her sheen is off. But it's only temporary.

"Patrick is coming to town," she says, following behind me toward my Jeep.

"Oh, yeah? For work?" My oldest brother is on the road a lot, something I know he hates about his job. But he makes great money consulting with companies on new payment systems, so he tolerates the travel to keep his wife and daughter in a seriously killer house in Boulder.

"He'll be here for three days, and Flynn and Todd are off for rookie camp, so they're flying in too. Andrew can't get off from school, but the rest of us are coming for the Saturday game."

A satisfied grin takes over half my face as I climb into my Jeep and shut the door. I hang on the window as my mom steps up to the side.

"That sounds really nice. I can't think of the last time all of us were in the same building," I say, instantly souring my face when I realize what the last time was. It was Dad's funeral.

Mom lays her hand on my arm and squeezes.

"It's all right. It's how he would have wanted us there. All loud and hungry and bossy." We both chuckle at the memory. Even for Dad's funeral, my brothers and I couldn't simply be chill. After I spilled the punch all over one of the cousins I didn't know existed, Flynn and Todd slipped in it and fell on their asses, but not before clinging to the table-cloth Ma put over the counter on their way down. They took out at least a dozen pasta salads and a whole tray of cookies.

"I should have known better than to throw a nice party in his memory with you all in the house. This is why we never got a dog." My mom leans in through the window and tugs the sleeve of my shirt to urge me closer. I give her my cheek and she kisses it, then pats it twice with her hand.

"You drive safe. And I expect I'll get to meet this mystery chef-roommate of yours who is nothing more than splitting bills with you and that's all." I think she lets out a smug *mmm-hmm* before backing away, or maybe it was simply implied in her tight-lipped smile.

"I'll get right on it," I say through a puckered smile. I shake my head then shift into reverse, leaving her to stare at me with crossed arms and her *I know better than you do* stare.

Maybe she does know me better. Because I sure am thinking about Laney a lot more than I expected to a week ago. And it's more than just thinking about touching her or getting her naked. It's bet-losing kind of thinking, but really, is that bet even still a thing? Have we moved past that?

As I hit the highway, I crank up my stereo to clear my head, but somehow, Laney's playlist is permanently burned into my system. She did something the last time she was in the Jeep to sync her phone, and we somehow synced music too. Now here I am, rocking out to everything from Paramore to Sharon Van Etten to Carrie Underwood. The only common theme for a Laney Price playlist, it seems, is a bad-ass female singer.

"Fuck it," I say, turning the music up and singing along with Carrie about digging keys into the paint job of some poor asshole's expensive car. As much as I want to avoid thinking about all the ways Laney and I are right together during my drive home, fate seems to kick my ass right back to the center of my feelings for her.

Feelings. I have fucking feelings for Laney Price.

It's the one thought I keep coming back to, and no matter how many times I try to convince myself that it's all physical with us, I know it's not. Hell, I was stuck on her the minute she first shot me down. Her tough interior only made me want her more. Sure, maybe at first it was about the chase, but even after four years of her avoiding me during media days, of taking little digs whenever she could and shooting cold-dagger stares at me at sporting events, I always admired her. Even now, I know that version of Laney, she's a front. Oh, there's a lot of truth to her sharp edges, but also, she never hated me the way she pretended. She simply never wanted to be in a position to like me.

Too late now.

I find myself hitting ninety on the highway with about five minutes to go before my exit when my phone buzzes with a message. I give the command for my phone to read the message, which it understands on my third attempt after first directing me to the nearest gas station and then offering me reviews on the best insoles.

CHUCK: Party at your place, I guess. Help with keg?

Crap. How is there a party at my place? I still don't even really feel like it's my place. Unless . . . *Matt.*

I hit the call button to get Chuck on the line.

"Yo, so is that a yes on the keg? I paid for it, but I can't get it to fit in my trunk."

If Chuck has a keg, that means it's a team party with lots of guests. Probably the Greek houses, and as annoying as Matt is, he seems to have this huge following of people who gravitate to him. They want to be around him, I suppose hoping his weird fame will rub off or something.

"Yeah, sure. I'm by your exit now. I stopped to see my ma. I'll be right there." I end the call and take the exit for Chuck's. He's in the driveway waiting for me when I get there, and judging by the gaseous waves of cologne coming off him, I'd say he's planning to hook up with someone tonight, which means, yeah . . . big party. No matter how many times I tell the dude less is more when it comes to scents, he keeps doubling down with that rainwater fragrance he bought last year. He smells like a storm drain.

I cough.

"What?" He glares at me and I simply laugh. *He knows what.*

I drive him to the liquor store and we haul the keg into the back of the Jeep and head to the house. All I can do is think about Laney and this serious talk I was planning for us to have, but instead, the house is going to be full of people, half of whom I won't recognize.

The street is packed when Chuck and I pull up, so I end up parking at the top of the hill after dropping Chuck off with the keg. I hover by my Jeep for a few seconds, the pulsing music hitting my ears from a quarter mile away. Our neighbors are going to break this up soon, I'm sure. The sun went down thirty minutes ago, so at least it's early yet. But if this drags on, people are going to be pissed. It's a Sunday, for fuck's sake.

Ivy's got to be mad, unless she's working. For Matt's sake, I hope she is. If she comes home and walks in on this, he's likely dead. And that's just me basing things off her reaction to me asking once for coffee. And Laney—I don't know what her feelings are on parties like this. I know this weekend wasn't her favorite pair of days, so maybe she'll revel at the distraction.

I head down the hill and get my answer to most questions the second I walk through the door. Ivy and Laney are being held upside down by a few of my teammates and they're chugging more than their weight in beer. Ivy's the first to give in, and she taps out while Laney, who is holding a short shirt against her chest with one hand, goes for five more seconds. I can tell the second the guys help her back to her feet that she's tipsy but not totally tanked.

It's Sunday. I'm sure she has practice tomorrow.

"Aww, I hear you helped bring us more beer," Ivy slurs as she falls into me, one hand on my chest and the other arm hooked around my neck.

"Oh, wow. Okay, I'm not used to you being affectionate, so how about we go sit down, huh?" She bobs her head up and down, then laughs hysterically. I guide my roommate and Laney's best friend to the sofa, where she immediately starts kissing our backup goalie. I shake my head and hold out my palms when my gaze meets Laney's from across the room.

She shrugs. Her eyes haze as she hooks a finger in front of her body, calling me to her. I step over the coffee table to get to her.

"That was impressive, I think?" I quirk a brow.

"Maybe, but I can only do that once." She folds her hands on my shoulder then leans close, bringing her lips to my ear. "I'm pretty drunk."

I laugh lightly and put a hand on her back to make sure she stays close to me and away from alcohol for the rest of the night. In fact, when some frat guy walks over with two red cups I tell him to go fuck himself before he has a chance to open his mouth.

"*Ohh*, Cutter's getting protective," Laney teases.

I purse my lips and bite my tongue as I lead her into the kitchen. I pull out one of my super-hydrating waters with alkaline and force it into her hands.

"Drink."

She meets my stare with a hard one of her own. I tilt my head slightly to the right in challenge, and she shakes me off finally and gives in.

"Fine. But we're playing a drinking game after this," she demands. "Me and you." She takes a big gulp, then hands the bottle back to me. She thinks she's done but she's not. She has practice tomorrow. And my gut tells me she's acting out right now.

"Come on, Cutter. Play a game. For me?" She puckers her lips, and while she's rather adorable in her short red shorts and cropped white tee-shirt, she's also trying to tank herself.

"No games tonight, Laney. I have a job to do." *Watching you and making sure you get your ass up in the morning, which you are not going to want to do.*

"Party pooper." She stammers on that word, and it makes her giggle. Or maybe she's drunk enough to find poop funny.

"Why don't we get some air and bring the water with us, huh?" I thread our hands together so she doesn't have much of a choice. But Laney is still Laney, and true to her core, she decides now is the time she's going to make a stand. At my expense. Always at my expense.

"Cutter, do you have feelings for me? Do you love me? Because you're sure acting like you love me. And you know what that means." Her red lips spread into a massive grin as she raises her hands and starts to sway her hips, taunting me along with every other person attracted to females in this house as her cropped shirt flirts with the bottom curve of her breasts. She's not wearing a fucking bra.

"Laney, come on," I reach toward her, sucking in my lips as I feel the heat of more and more people staring at us.

She shakes her head and licks her lips, then turns to her right and takes a red cup that's maybe half-full from the counter.

"Come on, Cutter. It's not like I *have* to get up early. I could always call in sick." She snickers at her lame joke. Sick time is not a thing for college athletes unless you want to find yourself off the roster and out of a scholarship.

Her lips soften into a cunning smirk as she brings the cup to her mouth. I knock it from her hand before she has a chance to take a drink, spraying beer on anyone within a five-foot radius and sending the cup somewhere on the other side of the kitchen counter.

"This is not you, Laney. Come on."

She lifts her chin as her top lip sneers.

"Oh, it's me, Cutter. And you should quit while you're ahead."

We hold this absurd standoff for several seconds, and it grows eerily quiet in the area immediately around us. A few people push their way out of the kitchen, clearly not here for the awkward tension that gets thicker by the second. Matt, however, is not one of those people. He worms his way in, putting an arm around the both of us as if he's our agent and he has any right to touch me right now. I'm ready to swing fists.

"Guys, guys. Come on, what's with my happy couple? Caney-ship lives!" Matt's drunk but he's always this stupid. I shirk his arm off me when he tries to coax us to the back yard.

"Let him go, Matt. He's in love with me and afraid to admit he lost the bet. And he doesn't want to play a drinking game with me. But you will, right?" She puts a hand on the center of Matt's chest and his eyes drop. I don't think he knows what to do when a girl like Laney gets aggressive. Normally, I think he'd give in and let her be the boss, but he also is sober enough to know this is his sister's best friend, his roommate, and my . . . my problem.

"I don't play drinking games, Laney. On account of my

dad having been an alcoholic and all." I level her with a hard glare and her fingertips slide down Matt's chest until her hand drops off completely. Her eyes flinch along with the corners of her mouth. Matt backs away a step and Laney grabs the bottle of water from the counter, never breaking our eye contact.

"Fine. Let's go to bed."

She whips around with the bottle in one hand while she uses her free hand to shove people out of the way. I trail behind her, waving off offers of help from a few of my team-mates, including Chuck. If I were more established in this house, I'd tell everyone to get the fuck out, but I don't need that rap being laid on me for the rest of our senior year. I've got enough bullshit to wade through, including a five-eleven drunk one who's seriously got me stuck right now. I'm so pissed at her yet so fucking worried. *Gah!*

Laney marches through our door, and I pull it shut behind me as she climbs onto the bed and folds her legs up as she sits staring at me. She makes a production of pulling the cap from the bottle then taking a long drink that sends some of the water dribbling down her chin and onto her white shirt. If she weren't angry and drunk, this would be one of the hottest moments of my life. Not now, though. Not like this. This Laney, she's sad. She's broken.

I lock the door behind me to keep unwanted visitors out of our room for the rest of the night.

"I'm right, though, aren't I?" she says, pulling the bottle from her lips and letting it suction the bottom one just a little. I wish it were time to kiss it. It's not. My eyes flit back up to hers.

"Right about what?" I lean against the dresser and fold my arms.

"You might not love me but you like me. You're falling first. You lose." Her eyes narrow on me and dance with her competitive fire. There's a nastiness to this, though.

"I admire you, Laney."

And yeah, I feel plenty of other confusing things, but damn, is now not the time.

"Ha. Whatever." She pulls her shirt off and tosses it at me. I swallow hard because whether she's acting out or not, she's fucking gorgeous and nearly naked.

"Laney, stop." She sits up on her knees and hooks her thumbs in her shorts, teasing to pull them down. I throw her shirt back at her before she has a chance, then open my top drawer and get out my hockey sweatshirt and add that to the clothes in her lap. "Put it on. And sober up."

She falls back on her heels and swallows hard, instant hurt pulling her eyes down.

I turn my back to her, half to get my head right because goddamn, is she sexy, and half to take away her power. I glance briefly to make sure she's getting dressed, and when she has my sweatshirt on fully, I turn back around and move toward her. She scoots back until her shoulders reach the headboard. I take the cue, stop at the foot of the bed, and sit with my feet on the floor. Our eyes lock for a few hard seconds, and there's a palpable ache. It's there because I get it. I know how she feels. I know what disappointment feels like when you set unfathomable standards for yourself and work your ass off. But I also know that Laney, she's not going to fail.

I take a deep breath and look down at my thighs and the small hole forming on the knee of my jeans. I have to get her off of this stupid bet thing so she'll hear what I have to say. I have to take away her excuse, even if it means going back on all the hard conversations I'd hoped to have instead tonight. The *feelings* talk.

"We're not in love, Laney. We both know that." I meet her gaze, and her eyes widen for a breath at my words. That tiny flinch, I'll come back to that. Tomorrow. In a few days. Sometime. I saw it, and it meant something.

"That doesn't mean I'm some asshole who doesn't care about you," I continue. "Because I do care about you. And you have practice in the morning. And some work to do. And if you leave this room and go back to that bad idea Matt brought into our house, you're going to hate yourself tomorrow. Maybe not right away, but eventually, you'll snap out of this anger fog and sober up, and then you'll realize you made a mess out of your dreams. Don't do that. You don't want to do that."

Her eyes don't blink for several seconds. Eventually, they flit to the bottle she's clutching in her hands and she fidgets with it a little, rotating it while her fingernails pick at the plastic wrapping.

"My dad showed up to the game." Her head snaps up to meet my gaze again and she blinks a few times.

That's what this is about.

"He showed up to see me play. But, well—"

"You didn't," I finish for her. I toe my shoes off and make my way closer to her, slow and steady. She might want space, and if that's the case, she can have it.

"I haven't seen him in person in . . ." She looks up at the ceiling with glassy eyes and her shoulders drop. "Ten years? Maybe? I don't even know." Her voice cracks.

"That's a lot. I didn't know that. I'm sorry." I scoot so I'm next to her and swing my arm up to rest on the headboard.

She turns and eyes my chest, then moves her gaze up to my eyes.

"Come here," I offer. She pauses, biting her bottom lip, I think in an attempt to stop it from quivering, then gives in and falls into my side. I put my palm on her back and rub in slow circles while she sniffles.

"They quoted him in my profile story in the program."

I shift and dip my head to meet her eyes.

"They printed the program?" I didn't even sign off on the photos yet, not that I have a say, but I'd like to know what they used.

Laney nods, then runs her sleeve—well, *my sleeve*—along her nose.

"I'm kind of glad you didn't know about it. Now I don't have to be mad at you for not warning me." She flashes a short-lived smile and I breathe out a soft laugh.

"I'm sure you can find something else to be mad at me over."

She shakes her head and smiles more, which makes it worth it.

"He said all these things in the article that made it sound like he was there—*present*—for my life. And then I found out he talks to my mom sometimes, about me. And he thinks I'm not focused. That was the best part. He said I was too distracted by hockey players."

I shake with silent laughter at her final point.

"All I know is you said I was the best part."

Her palm pushes hard against my ribs as she sits up only to shove me in the ribs again. I wince, but also laugh.

"Baby," she grumbles.

I lift up my shirt to show her the marbling bruise that

spans my hip to my armpit and she slaps her palm over her mouth.

"Oh, shit." She reaches for the bottom of my shirt and tugs it down, perhaps the first time she's put clothes back on me since we started this shacking up business.

"That was the one against the glass," I say.

She snuggles back into my side, a little more strategic about where she rests her palm.

"You scored the game winner off that, though."

The grin is automatic and I tuck my chin to make sure she can't see it. She watched my game intently.

"I sure did."

15 /
laney

"ATTA GIRL. YOU CAN DO IT."

Cutter is being obnoxiously cheery, which I suppose I deserve. Or maybe I don't. Maybe I only deserve the obnoxious part. I was an asshole last night. My worst self. I'm embarrassed, but also, the thought of admitting that makes me want to throw up. Or maybe that's the alcohol.

"Did I really do a keg stand?" I arch a brow at Cutter as I climb into the passenger seat of his Jeep.

He laughs and winces at the same time.

"In a crop top."

"Oh, Jesus." My eyelids flutter shut and my face is instantly hot.

"Don't worry. You were impressive holding it down. Or I guess holding it up, considering your position."

I groan at his cleverness and my reality, then bury my face in my palm.

"Thank you for rescuing me from myself." I can only say that to him without facing him. And for some reason, he doesn't seem eager to throw an *I told you so* at me this morning. He'd have every right. Especially after that remark I made about pushing him to play drinking games. I don't even like drinking games. That was not cool of me. Not at all.

Cutter turns the music on, and when I hear Pink coming out of his speakers, I give him a sideways grin.

"You do that for me?" I ask.

"Uh, sorta?"

I quirk a brow.

"You synced our playlists. No, scratch that. You commandeered my playlists, which are now yours. So pretty much this is all I've got." His lip curls up and he does his best to match Pink's pitch. He's not even close, but it's kind of cute to watch him try.

He entertains me with his terrible voice but odd knowledge of female power lyrics all the way to campus. I hop out near the gym door, thirty minutes early. I hold on to the Jeep door for a few extra seconds and muster the courage to look him in the eyes. When I lift my gaze, he's casually resting on his steering wheel, arms crossed, hat backward, wet strands of hair dripping down his neck from his rushed shower. The back of his T-shirt is soaked.

"Cutter, I—"

"Don't mention it," he breaks in. He gives me a wink then drives away, and I let myself have this tiny moment of weakness and admit that yeah, I like him more than a little.

I'm first to practice, arriving a few minutes before Coach, so I get some good face time with her to prove I'm a team player. That I'm willing to be a middle if that's what it takes.

"It's been a while since I've blocked here, and I'm not the tallest on our team, so what can I do to maximize what I've got?" I step to the center of the net and hold my arms up, then glance over my shoulder where Coach Kane is watching with the clipboard held to her chest.

"Laney, you know you're the most talented even if you're not the tallest, right? Using you here, it's not about you."

My lips buzz with adrenaline. I wasn't expecting to hear her say that, but I needed it more than I realized. And I knew I needed it bad.

"I know," I say, and we both know that's as close to *thank you* as I'm going to give.

Coach lets out a breathy laugh, then steps to my side and nudges the toe of my shoe with hers, pinching my feet a little inward. "I want you to feel uncomfortable for a minute. Find your balance, even like this. You have to be ready to pivot and jump at all times. You're used to blocking in two spots. Now you have three. And inches or not, your reach wins every time. I've watched the video. You have the highest vertical on the team. We don't block with our heads while we stand still, Laney. We block with these."

She squeezes my wrist with a bit of force, then wraps her other hand around my bicep, showing me how to keep my arm firm. Our eyes meet, and I search behind hers for any hint of whether she's feeding me a line or being straight. Her hard expression doesn't mince meaning. This is my position now, and she intends to have me win every battle here.

"Let's run a few blocking drills before everyone gets here. What do you say?"

"Yes, Coach."

And suddenly my head isn't throbbing as much as it was a minute ago.

THREE HOURS of non-stop blocking and practicing slides and quicks has depleted me of all liquid. I bailed on my constitutional law class because the professor posts the lectures after she's done. I would have been useless anyhow because the minute I stepped into the bedroom after walking home, I lost all awareness of the world at large. I don't even remember my face hitting the pillow, but apparently I made it to the bed. And now, six hours later, there's a definite layer of crust on my face from sleeping hard.

I shower to force myself to reset mentally and physically, even though the sun is about to set. I'm going to have to listen to the class I missed, so I need to be as alert as possible. I texted Cutter that I was heading home while I was walking so he wouldn't worry about giving me a lift after classes.

So he wouldn't worry.

Now rested, I read the message I sent him and feel an anxious twist in the center of my chest. It's as if a bowling ball is sitting right between my ribs making it hard to breathe and uncomfortable to swallow. Cutter simply sent a thumbs up back. And that should be fine with me. Yet, I wish he had said more. I think I'm caring too much about what Cutter McCreary thinks, and I don't like how vulnerable that makes me feel.

I never would have cared if Cam responded that way to a status update. However, Cam was an over-responder. He would have called to check on me. But it was never quite actually to make sure *I* was all right. It would have been to make sure I wasn't sick, that he shouldn't sleep on the couch, or more likely, move *me* to the couch. No spreading of the germs and all that. Practical Cam.

It's as if my mom has a neuron alert for my brain because

the moment I mentally compare Cutter to Cam, she calls. I consider for a brief few seconds letting her go to voicemail, but that won't stop her from calling a second or third time. And if I skip those, she'll move right to the video call feature. I should have never let her know that those come to both my phone and computer.

I close my eyes and let out a heavy breath, imagining all toxic feelings flying away from me.

"Hi, Mom." I sit on the edge of the bed and hold the phone between my shoulder and ear while I rub lotion into my legs.

"Hi, Honey. I was just calling to see how you were doing."

My brow pinches as I try to work out her angle. It's never a well check. It's an agenda.

"I'm fine. A little tired. I had a hard practice today, and I have some homework to catch up on, so—"

"Oh, good. You're fine," she interrupts.

"Yup. Fine." I drop my feet to the floor and hold my phone in my hand, pinching the bridge of my nose with the other. I'm not hydrated enough for this phone call.

"Good. Glad to hear that. I was worried since you didn't play. It seems like maybe the team doesn't have a place for you this year. And I was thinking, if you made a phone call to the dean at Chicago, maybe—"

"I am not going to law school, Mother." I break her off this time. We aren't doing this routine again. It's old.

"Honey, you have to be realistic. I know you wanted to play a game for a living and all, but some of us have to grow up and get big girl jobs." Now she's just being outright aggressive. Skipped right over the passive part.

Well, two of us can act that way.

"This an argument you hashed out with Dad already?" Her brief silence is satisfying.

"I don't talk to your father, Laney. You know that." Her ability to lie is impressive.

"That's not what he said." My response gets another, longer silence. And my pulse is picking up with my ire. This isn't a good state for me. I don't want to be in this conversation.

I can actually hear her swallow.

"We talk occasionally. Fine. But we're adults, Laney."

"I'm an adult too," I sigh out, reminding her.

In some ways, I think I may be more adult than she is. Although, I doubt my mother would do a keg stand in a half shirt on a Sunday night, so perhaps she's got me there.

"We're trying to be cordial. Friendly and professional," she continues.

"Yeah? In Dad's professional opinion, then, should I try to become a professional athlete?" I know how she's going to respond to this. Her laugh comes right on cue.

"Well, we both think you're losing focus. And what's this business about you moving in with another man already? So soon after Cam? And he's a hockey player? Honey, if you miss Cam, I know he wants you back."

I shoot to my feet and slap my palm on the side of my face.

"Are you still talking to Cam?" I'm incredulous.

"Only in emails. I was worried about you and wanted his take on things. He's still very hurt, Laney."

I start to laugh, quietly at first, but it grows into an uncontrollable hysteria that has me leaning my weight on the door jamb while hot tears form in my eyes. I'm not sad, though I am pretty pissed. And I find all of this incredibly funny.

"You know what? I need you to stop. I need you to stop emailing Cam because he's not *your* ex. And it's weird. And I need you and Dad to stop making me an agenda. I know you think you're protecting me. I get it, Mom. You're worried that I am going to make the same mistakes you did somehow and then end up alone. If I end up alone, though, Mom, it's going to be because that's what I choose. And I choose not to be with Cam. He's not for me. We aren't good together. He made me miserable. I'm too independent. And I want to make my own choices. The fact I'm not choosing to drop out and open a marijuana bar should make you happy. I could actually fuck up, but instead I'm driven and committed. At some point, you're going to have to get that. I have to go."

I end the call before she has a chance to respond, and we've done this enough that she knows now is not the time to call back. Even if she were to apologize, I'm not in the headspace to believe it. I need to be distracted. Also, I need to fucking eat.

I poke my head out my door and hear the murmur of the television.

"Ivy?"

I'm relieved when she hollers back, "Yeah?"

I don't think I'm in the headspace for Matt either. Maybe I should hand my mom's phone calls to him. The two of them can make each other dizzy with nonsensical logic.

Reaching back into my room, I snag my phone and wallet from the top of the dresser, then head into the living room to join Ivy on the couch. She had the day off today, from class and work, which is why she cut loose last night. I glance around the house and notice it's free of cups and trash from the party. It's basically as if the party never happened.

"Did you clean all day?" I ask.

She rolls her head to me slowly, her eyes puffy and still fairly red.

"God, no." She leans forward and picks up a water bottle and guzzles down half of it.

I know Matt didn't do this. I've been to enough of his parties to know cleanup is not his forte. He's more of a "vibe man," or so he says. The only other answer is Cutter. I wish I had been in a better state of mind this morning to have noticed for certain, but I'm pretty sure I woke up to a clean house. Which means he took care of things while I was sleeping.

"I'm starving," Ivy announces, and my stomach literally growls in response.

"Oh, thank God. Burgers at Patty's? There's no way I'm cooking." Ivy nods and gets to her feet, offering me a hand up from the couch. At this point, I should probably be helping her, but I take her hand and snag her keys from the coffee table as we head out.

It's definitely a no-alcohol night for me, and Ivy seems game too. We order two waters and Cokes because sometimes carbonated caffeine just hits the spot.

It's a Monday, so Patty's isn't very crowded, which means our food comes out fast. The two of us scarf down half a burger in record time, and I'm working on shoveling a mouthful of what I've got left when Patty's doors swing open with a gush of cold air and about a dozen Tiff hockey players.

"Was there a game tonight?" Ivy asks.

I shrug while I chew, acutely aware of my chipmunk cheeks and the fact Cutter has spotted me and is coming over to our table. I hurry and swallow, chasing it with a gulp of water that makes everything sort of clump in my esophagus. I cough and Cutter rushes behind me and starts patting my back. Thankfully, the bite goes down before he has to administer the Heimlich.

"You really like to bite off more than you can chew, don't you?" he teases.

I scowl at him.

"Good to see the old Laney back," he adds before dragging a stool out and taking a seat with us. He parks himself on the other side of the table, and I find myself a little disappointed that he's not closer to me. And that he thinks the old Laney is nothing but grumpy and mean. *Shit, am I?*

"Did you clean the house?" Ivy points at him, talking with a full mouth.

Cutter leans back on his stool and gives us both a closed-lipped smile, his eyes shifting between us.

"Dude, I'm not mad about it. I was going to thank you, but if you're going to be all coy and shit, fuck off." Ivy dives right back into her burger and Cutter's gaze drifts to me as he laughs.

Well, I'm not that grumpy.

My eyes narrow on him while my friend ravages what's left of her dinner.

"When did you even do that?" I'm not sure how aware Ivy is of my night and that Cutter pulled me out of the party scene and locked me in our room. From best recall, she was a little distracted making out with one of his teammates.

Cutter shrugs one shoulder and smiles on the same side. I hold his gaze while I do some quick yet messy math. I'm pretty sure he was in the room with me until I fell asleep around ten or eleven, and the party was still going then. We got up at five. So the odds that he slept any, if at all, are slim.

"Right, well. I'm gonna order some food. We had a scrimmage and I skipped lunch, so . . ." He stands and clutches his stomach before letting out a corny, "Rawr."

"No fish fry! You'll stink." I point at him as he backs away.

He makes an *aww shucks* kind of face and snaps his fingers, then spins around to head to the bar. I pick at what's left of my burger, my brain finally catching up with my stomach and that famished feeling shifting over to the side of stuffed stupid. I swirl a fry in the cup of ranch I snagged from the salad bar then push my plate toward my friend.

"Rest are yours if you want 'em."

"God, yes," Ivy says, scooting my ranch closer. She dunks a few fries into the dressing at once and stuffs them in her mouth, propping her head on her fist as she stares at me with a quizzical look. She takes another bite the same way, all the while staring, and I start to feel the heat of it.

"What?" I squirm in my seat and shimmy my arms out of the flannel shirt I put on. I roll it into a ball and set it on the table by my wallet and phone. I'm suddenly hot, and I'm not sure whether it's the growing crowd in Patty's or my friend's interrogating stare.

"He likes you a lot. You see that, right?" Ivy points from Cutter to me with the end of a fry before popping it in her mouth. Her frankness is sometimes exhausting.

"He tolerates me. And we definitely have chemistry, but that's it." I don't fully believe the words I'm saying, but also, I don't want to open up this enigma right now. I'm still mentally debating whether or not to reply to the text my mom sent a few minutes ago. My words must have really cut her this time because it's unlike her to apologize. But that's literally all she said this time. One word. *Sorry.*

I keep subtle tabs on Cutter's movements, following him with my gaze after he places his order then takes a pitcher to the back table where some of his teammates have settled in near the pool tables. Our eyes meet a few times, and whenever Cutter gets caught, a faint but sexy smile tugs at the corner of his lip.

"You're not freezing?" Ivy redirects my attention, pointing at my bare shoulders. I'm wearing a white tank top and jeans, but now that I look around the joint I realize that most people are in sweatshirts and jackets.

I shrug.

"I'm probably still sweating out alcohol." I tuck my chin when my friend looks away to see if Cutter is still watching me. He's telling a story to a rapt table filled with teammates and a few of his "fan girls," so I drop my smile and swivel my attention back to our table. Ivy snags my flannel and quirks a brow.

"If you're not going to wear it, you mind?"

I shake my head and my friend slips her arms into the sleeves over her long-sleeved Tiff Nursing T-shirt. The music kicks in a few seconds later, so I spin on my stool to face the dance floor and Ivy scoots closer to me. One of our favorite activities is watching college dudes try to learn line dancing. There are always a few pros hanging around Patty's, and being in Iowa means country music is on heavy rotation at just about every bar. Tonight's spectacle starts with two very cute blondes in boots, frayed denim shorts and pink hockey jerseys. Their steps are complex and the routine is one of the faster ones I've seen. As they spin and tap their heels and toes, a few of Cutter's teammates migrate from the pool tables to join them. And as I hoped, things get hilarious.

"Why do they insist on even trying," Ivy says, leaning into me.

"Because they think this is the key to getting in those girls' pants. If only they could spin and step and slide in the right order, their nights would be made."

We both laugh at my assessment and don't bother with the unsaid reality. Those girls are doing this to get eyeballs on them. They're already in hockey jerseys. Those dudes would be better off never getting on the floor and making jackasses out of themselves. They're sexy enough simply being hockey players.

When one of the guys finally breaks the sympathy bubble, which is when the girl showing off finally feels bad and offers to teach him a few steps off to the side, Ivy and I turn around. I refill our waters with the pitcher that was dropped off, then slip from my stool to take the empty back to the bar and hit the restroom. I must finally be catching up because this is the first time I've had to pee all day.

The ladies room is empty when I go in, but I hear the door whoosh open along with giggling when I'm in the stall. I lean forward to spy through the crack in the door and recognize one of the dancers right away.

"Why do you think Cutter never dances?" she says to whoever is with her and out of my sightline.

"Girl, I don't know. But I bet he'd know what he was doing if he did. He's the kind of guy who just knows how to do *everything*. Know what I mean?"

I roll my eyes and hold my tongue. And Cutter wonders why I give him such a hard time. I guess this reputation isn't all his fault, but it had to start somewhere. He certainly feeds it.

"I would give anything for him to walk up to me and ask me to dance. His hands on me, *ooooh!*" They both giggle and I let my head fall forward into my palm while I squat out of sight with my jeans around my ankles.

After eavesdropping on that, I can't bring myself to leave my stall until they leave. After a makeup reapplication and a short phone call with one of their friends who apparently went to the wrong Patty's first—*there is no other Patty's*—I finally break free. I wash my hands and flip my head upside down to run my fingers through my post-practice hair. I didn't wash it because I was feeling lazy, but that means the weird kinks and waves that form after a day or two are at their most mischievous.

When I flip back upright, I'm hit with a wildness of hair that leaves me with no other choice but to laugh. I feel in my back pocket with a silent wish and am rewarded with two hair ties. I almost always have one around somewhere. I twist the mess up into something semi-human-looking on top of my head and work the band around it to form a bun. The blessing of the curls is that I can tuck and pull just about any piece to form some sort of style.

I walk back out into the bar just as the music turns over into something a little more R&B, and I see quickly that one of the dancing hockey players has scored himself a slow dance with his very pretty instructor.

"Good for him," I say, sliding back into my seat.

"I'd toast to him, but it's not the same with water," Ivy teases.

I decide to do it anyway and grab our glasses, handing one to her so we can clink. We gulp down several more ounces, then fish out our credit cards as the waitress delivers our check. Ivy snags my card and forces it back on me.

"This one's on me," she says, ushering the waitress away with only her card and the bill.

"Ivy, you don't have to do that."

My friend clears her throat and nods over my shoulder.

"Yeah, I know, but you're about to have company and I think you might be too busy to settle up."

I spin back toward the dance floor in time to catch Cutter's last few strides toward me. He's wearing the same jeans he wore last night, the small hole on his knee a tiny bit bigger. Probably because I picked at it while trying to fall asleep. His hair is a bit messy, but intentionally so, a few pieces flopped over one eye, giving him something to push back with his hand like a freaking *Esquire* model. There's a definite difference between him in a jersey and the average fan wearing one. Cutter's shoulders and chest fill out *everything*.

"Isn't this on your playlist?" He points his thumb over his shoulder toward the dance floor. I know this song, but it's definitely not on my playlist. This is a line.

I sit back and rest my elbows on the table behind me.

"Don't think so." My lips tighten into a smug smile and I let my head fall a little to one side.

Cutter's gaze sticks to mine as his tongue pushes behind his teeth and flustered smile.

"You're really gonna make this hard on me, huh?" he says, eyes squinted.

I shrug, ignoring my best friend's foot kicking mine.

"I don't know. Am I?"

We lock gazes for a few more seconds before he finally breaks contact and quietly laughs as he looks down at his feet. I start to turn back toward the table as the waitress comes back with the check for Ivy to sign, but Cutter pauses me with a soft touch to my bicep. I was warm before, but now I'm burning.

"Dance with me."

My eyes flit from his touch to his face, his mouth a resolute and gentle smile, crinkles formed at the sides of his eyes.

"Cutter, I don't really dance. We're about ready to go, so . . ." I glance to Ivy, who gives me side eyes as she finishes signing her name on the bill.

I sigh and roll my head back to face him. He hasn't budged, the only change a sense of hope tugging at the corners of his eyes. His hand slips from my arm and he takes a step back, dropping his hands in his pockets as he shakes his head.

"I'm going to stand out there and dance with myself, like a fool, until you come out there and dance with me. If this means I lose my status as campus hot boy, I want you to know that's on you, Laney Price." He nods at me, the playfulness of his smirk making it hard for me not to smile back at him.

I let him make it all the way to the dance floor, where he holds out both palms and tilts his head, silently calling me to him. I suck in my lips and fight with myself internally. If this weren't at Patty's in front of people, I'd be there in a heartbeat. But if I go, it's going to become one more thing. A story about *Caney-ship*. A distraction.

Cutter drops his arms to his side and mouths, "Come on." After a few more seconds, he folds his arms around himself and slowly starts to rock side-to-side, backed by the catcalls and cheers of his teammates who are now overly invested in his attempt to get me out there.

"Go dance with him, you jackass," Ivy says.

I turn my attention to her and she shrugs.

"There's nothing wrong with actually liking someone, Laney. With actually *liking* Cutter McCreary. Hell, I like him. Fucker grows on you."

I shudder with a laugh and slide off my stool, turning my attention to the hot hockey player dancing with himself to a song all about making love to a woman. The moment I begin moving toward him, his teammates erupt into cheers. The attention almost convinces me to turn and run out the door, but I don't. I cross through the few high top tables between us and stop a foot away from him.

"Can I cut in?" I half expect him to turn me down to prove a point, but instead he drops the act and moves his hands to my hips, tugging me close.

I grab the center of his jersey with both hands and let my forehead fall to his chin. He kisses it and I glance up at him as he rocks us back and forth.

"Was that so hard?"

Whistles blare from behind him, the kind made with fingers in mouths, like how you call a dog or celebrate a Super Bowl. I glance around his bicep then pop my gaze back up to his.

"It was kinda hard for me, yeah," I admit.

The tender smile that got me out here in the first place spreads, dimpling his cheeks, and he drops a hand from my waist to signal to his friends to cut it out. A few of them wave him off, but within seconds they're back to playing pool and trying to hook up with someone of their own. The only onlookers left are the pair I overheard in the bathroom, and while they don't look jealous exactly, they also don't look like they want to become my friend.

Cutter reaches up to smooth a few stray hairs from my face and his thumb trails along my cheek. His eyes scan my face, and his mouth hangs open as if he's trying to find the right words.

"Post practice hair. Well, post-practice-nap-partial-shower hair."

He chuckles at my self-assessment and tucks one more strand behind my ear before moving his hand back to my hip. I fold into him and link my hands behind his neck, resting my head on his shoulder.

"You know, I didn't go to prom or homecoming or anything like that. This is nice."

"Good. I'm glad you like it. And for the record, I would have taken you." His head leans into mine, making our space more intimate.

"It's not that I didn't have boyfriends or opportunities, but I was usually traveling for volleyball. My mom ran me all over the Northeast." My chest burns at that out-loud realization. For all her faults, which are plentiful, my mom always said yes. Every request I made to do a camp, to try out for a higher level, to go to an open gym in the city that required her to drive me and sit there while I played. She always said yes.

"Oh, crap." I bury my face in the crook of Cutter's neck and he runs a hand up my back to my bare shoulder blade where he pauses to stroke my skin with his fingertips. It's intoxicating and comforting all at once.

"What's wrong?"

I shift to meet his eyes, but his hands remain on me, comforting me, drugging me.

"I really let my mom have it today. And while we don't get along super well, I maybe took it too far. I owe her . . ." I stop there because it hits me that an apology is not quite enough. I owe her for a lot of things. She did her best, and my dad leaving us the way he did really messed her up.

"Okay, so tomorrow you make a phone call. It starts there."

I stare into his eyes and choke down my natural instinct to scoff as if it's that simple. He's actually right, and it really is that easy.

"Hold me to it," I request, falling back into his chest.

He strokes my back with both hands, and if we weren't in the middle of Patty's I'd be working his jersey off and running my hands up his chest.

"You think you can handle me kissing you in front of all these people?"

His question darts through my chest and pierces my insides, my arms growing hotter, face burning, and lips numbing. I shift to look at the crowd around us, my bathroom friends still looking on at one side and our roommate and my best friend at the other. Cutter's hand finds my chin and he lifts it until our eyes meet. He shakes his head with tiny movements.

"I didn't ask them. I asked you."

I blink twice. The first time to make sure my eyelids still work and the second time out of panic.

"I can handle it," I say, despite the inner voice telling me to stop crossing lines.

Cutter's palms glide over my shoulders and up my neck, snaking into my hair as he closes the few inches between us and takes my mouth with his. His kiss is soft and sensual and slow, his teeth grazing against my top lip. His thumbs caress my cheeks and he somehow steps in closer, practically towering over me, which is not an easy feat. I let my hands slide into his hair, grabbing at the strands as I open my mouth to let him deepen the kiss. By the time our lips part, he's left me raw and completely high on him.

When the music changes to a slightly faster tune, I begin to pull away. He tugs me back to him and cups my face again, forcing me to look him in the eyes. His perfect freaking face, and toxic dimples, and mix of green and gold that swirl around his pupils. His scent. The warmth of him. The words he always somehow knows to say.

I'm falling. Little by little. I am. And I'm so fucking scared.

**16 /
cutter**

EVEN THROUGH OUR kiss I could feel the tension in her body. I was so afraid I was pushing her to do something she didn't want, even though I felt her kissing back. I never want to be that guy, the one who assumes all women must want him and what he's got. Those guys are dicks. And while my mom doesn't use foul language often, that's one term she isn't shy about with me and my brothers.

"Just don't be a dick," she says any time we come to her with girl trouble. And she's always right. Her advice has never steered us boys wrong. When I had to break up with a girl my sophomore year, I followed Mom's advice and made sure to be thoughtful but direct. And when karma made that same girl a teaching assistant in charge of grading algebra tests my junior year, keeping her respect meant not failing when my answers were *kinda* right.

Ivy got tired of waiting for Laney, so I promised to drive her home. Now in the quiet of the Jeep, that tension I sensed before feels more prominent. And as much as I've learned Laney doesn't love to be prodded into talking, I've also learned that sometimes it's required.

"Hey, you all right?"

She breathes out a heavy sigh and rolls her head on the seat rest until she's facing me.

"Yeah, I'm fine."

She's not fine. I can tell.

I trap her gaze for a beat but let go when I realize she's holding her breath. I shift into drive and pull us out of the parking lot to head to the house. About halfway there, I have an idea that might just get my ass in trouble. I do it anyway. I turn onto the main drive toward campus and Laney shifts in her seat. I glance to my right to catch her concerned glare.

"I'm not kidnapping you. Well, I'm sort of kidnapping you. I just need to make a quick stop. Trust me?"

She doesn't answer right away, and when I glance back at her, her expression seems caught, as if she's uncertain how to answer.

"Okay, so maybe you don't have to trust me. How about we negotiate for a ten-minute detour?"

"I trust you," she whispers.

A stupid, crooked smile melts on my face, so I look straight ahead to at least hide half of it from her.

"Good. Because you can. I hope you know that."

I pull around to the back of the athletics building and kill the lights as we drive up so I don't draw extra attention. There are a few cars in the faculty lot so we blend in, though most people in this building know what I drive thanks to being campus hot boy. Football staff is always in this building until late at night when they're in season, so I find the unlocked door and prop it open as I convince Laney to follow me inside.

"Are we supposed to be in here?" she whispers as I tug her along, our fingers threaded together.

"It's a public university. And we pay taxes." She tugs my arm and I stop, turn, and look at her tight lips and dented forehead.

"It's fine. It's only football here this late, and they're clueless." We both laugh at that and I convince her to stick with me as we walk down the long hallway past a handful of open office doors, a few with players inside watching game film.

We get to the end of the hall and I fish out my keys from my pocket, locating the small silver one that I've had since freshman year. This key opens a few closets in this building. It was passed down to my brothers from someone on the hockey team, and they passed it down to me. I haven't decided for sure yet, but I think I'll hand it off to Gavin. He'll be a sophomore next year and a real grinder on the ice. The key might give him the confidence to grow into a leader.

"What is this place?" Laney asks as I work the key in and push the door open. I pull her inside and flip on the light after shutting the door behind us.

"This place is where Pete keeps literally everything," I say, walking backward through one of the rows of shelving stacked with bins. "And I mean literally everything."

I stop at a bin marked 1978 FOOTBALL and crack the lid open. The musty smell makes me take a step back, but I wave my hand and pull the lid off completely then snag the jersey on top. I hand it to Laney.

"Oh, my God! This was back when they put the names on the back. I would have thought those guys got to keep these!" She unfurls a jersey that's probably meant for a lineman and holds it against her chest, wrapping the leftover garment around her like a towel.

"That's a blanket on you," I laugh out.

"They should go back to this look." She runs her hands

over the detailed stitching and the dark gray material high-lighted with blue and gold.

"I bet that was sewn by hand, like by one woman who spent all day working on that jersey." Laney hands it to me and I do my best to refold it and tuck it back into the bin.

"No doubt," she responds.

I guide her deeper into the room and we spend an hour revisiting Tiff University sports history through Pete's carefully documented storage system.

"I asked Pete about this place when he first showed it to me, and he said the school won't give him permission to give anything away and he doesn't have the heart to destroy it, so he started stockpiling." I toss a forty-year-old tennis racket to her and she takes a few practice swings before strumming the strings.

"I can't believe these strings held up," she says, moving in next to me and hanging the racket on the wall of honor Pete built. "Does he know you come in here?"

I shake my head vehemently.

"I get the feeling Pete likes to keep things a certain way and wouldn't want anyone messing with his system, even if nobody at this school knows about this treasure trove."

Laney chuckles and nods in agreement.

While she spends time with a box filled with bowling shirts, I sift my way through some of the bins stored on the top shelf near the very back of the room. I have to step on the second shelf to reach it when I see it, and thankfully my weight doesn't send everything into a domino chain around the room. I come down with the reason I brought her here and kneel in front of the box on the floor.

"Okay, here it is. This is what I wanted you to see." I open the bin and sift through the first few sets of warmups until I find twenty-three. I pull it out of the mix and close the box back up before handing it to Laney. Her eyes light up as she reads the embroidered slogan on the back of the jacket.

"Tiff Volleyball is Tiff Tuff." She lets out a snort-laugh and covers her mouth when she looks at me. Embarrassed, I think.

"No, it's that funny. But also . . . pretty cool." I hold the pants up between us so she can see the gold stripes down the sides of the dark blue satin. The entire outfit is quilted, made to withstand the Iowa winter. It's hideous, yet somehow awesome.

"You want it?"

Her eyes flash to mine.

"I can't take something out of here. I don't think I could do that. Steal?" She whispers that last word even though we're alone in a locked room far from anyone's ears.

"I figured you'd say that. Hand it over."

Laney jerks her head around to look over her shoulder, then comes back to me, clutching the jacket to her chest.

"I don't know. It feels wrong."

"That's because it's probably a petty theft misdemeanor and it is wrong, but also . . . fuck it."

She chortles at my cavalier attitude, then checks over her shoulder again.

"Laney, we're all alone."

"I know, but I'm just . . . nervous," she leans in and whispers.

My lips form a puckered smile as I hold in my laugh. She's really adorable, and while I was a tad nervous about coming in here and doing this, I'm nowhere near as terrified as she is. But I can tell she wants it.

"I'll tell you what." I lean to one side and pull my wallet

from my front pocket. I crack it open and pull out the forty bucks I took off of Chuck playing pool tonight, then set it on top of the old uniforms still inside the bin. "What if I pay for it? Make a donation. And maybe one day Pete, who we both know is the only person who knows these exist, will clean house and find himself a tip. Which we both know he deserves."

She blinks a few times, I hope considering it. She gives one more glance over her shoulder, which sets my laugh free, and when she looks back at me she flails her hand at the open bin and says, "Do it!"

I grin, proud of her for giving in to something she wants even when it means breaking a rule. I kind of hope she pieces that together a little and applies it to other things in her life. Like me.

I drop the cash under the lid and snap it closed. It's a little harder to put it back and it takes me a few missed attempts before I balance it in my palm and step on the shelf to slip it back in place. I take the jacket from Laney and roll it up with the pants, then tuck it under my jersey. Laney isn't quite convinced it's concealed enough so she convinces me to tuck in my jersey so it looks like I have a lumpy beer belly. If it makes her feel better, fine. But there's no way this is less suspicious.

We slip out of the room and I lock it up swiftly, stuffing my keys into my pocket and grabbing hold of Laney's hand. She squeezes my palm and picks up the pace, which again seems more suspicious to me, but I let her have this. We're nearly free when one of the football players I shoot hoops with sometimes pops out of the men's room and basically runs into us.

"Hey, Cutter. Good to see you. What's up?" Darren and

I lived on the same floor freshman year and he was one of the few guys willing to put in extra lifting time. We bonded.

"Nothing much, man. You know, start of the season and I'm exhausted."

We both nod and his gaze drifts to Laney, who I know he knows because *everybody* knows Laney. She doesn't realize how big her star is around this place. But maybe I can show her otherwise, if she gives me time.

"Hey, I'm Darren," he says, and I sense his game shifting. He's trying to be suave and I admire his effort, but he doesn't have a 1995 track suit stuffed in his shirt so he can game all he wants; I still win this round.

"Nice to meet you. Laney," she says, taking his hand.

"Yeah, I know. You're pretty badass. How's the shoulder?" Darren rolls his arm in a circle to emphasize his obvious question. He's crashing and burning, and I can't help but chuckle.

"What? She hurt her shoulder. I was just—"

"Illustrating?" Laney adds.

Darren sucks his lips into a tight, straight line.

"I'm cleared to play. I'm at middle this year. Oh, I forgot to tell you, I'm starting Thursday." Laney hugs my bicep when she breaks the news to me. Darren's eyes zero in on the intimate touch, then he nods.

"Nice. I don't know what middle is but I know you hit the ball hard," he responds, his eyes lingering on Laney's connection to me for an extra beat before his gaze shifts back to her face.

"Well, I'll catch you later. Maybe after the bowl games we can pick up some more hoops." He moves past me and glances down at my gut. "You're putting on a few."

I shake with a nervous laugh, then flatten my free hand on my contraband.

"Hey, in-season athletes have to eat."

He points at me as he walks backward a few steps, then turns to head back into the film meeting.

"Let's go!" I whisper shout, suddenly a little less confident about this whole plan.

We speed walk the rest of the way and sprint when we hit the main doors, not stopping until we're climbing into my Jeep. I rip the pants and jacket roll out from under my jersey and toss it on Laney's lap.

"He thought that was your belly!" she teases.

"Yeah, well, he also thought you were into him for about ten seconds, so let's not split hairs." I roll my eyes and roar the engine to life, shifting into reverse then driving like I'm in an actual getaway situation. When I realize it's been more than a minute of silence, I glance to Laney and catch her staring at me with a smug bend to her lips.

That sounded jealous. Because it was.

Rather than get into it, I flash my gaze to the rearview mirror, then quickly adjust my hands to a perfect ten and two and sit up tall.

"Oh, shit!" I say.

Laney twists in her seat and scans the road behind us, and after a few seconds I laugh. She turns her attention back to me and that smug grin has been replaced with an *I'm-about-to-punch-you* glare.

"Just kidding," I say, pulling up to the red light before our street. Laney smacks my arm with a little bit of muscle and I wince, even though it didn't really hurt.

"That wasn't nice," she says, falling back into her seat and crossing her arms.

"I'm sorry." I mean it. But what I'm sorry about is that I didn't have the balls to segue being jealous into a talk about my feelings for her.

"Do you like it?" I tug on the sleeve of the jacket that she unfolded and laid across her lap. She flattens her palms over it and runs her hands along the silky tufts.

"I do. I really do." She lifts her gaze to me and for a split second, I swear she's admitting something. The light turns green, though, and just as quickly, that feeling is gone.

laney

IVY AND MATT are playing a video game when we get home, so Cutter and I hang out in the big sitting chair while they battle it out. When I went to sit on the couch by our roommates, he tugged the loop of my jeans and offered his lap instead. I felt weird being so out in the open like this in front of our roommates, but now that his arms are around me and I can feel his chest crackle with laughter, I'm glad he made the move. Besides, Ivy saw us make out at Patty's, so there's not much of a secret left.

Caney-ship is on.

I love watching Ivy and Matt interact. They're so obviously siblings, even though they're massively different. They're playing some tennis game and things are getting heated to the point that Ivy is physically pushing her brother into the bean bag chair in order to catch him off guard and score points. She's pint-sized in comparison, but like a rabid animal when she's competitive. She would have been a great athlete if she had any sort of skill. We've tried. She subbed on a rec softball team with me once and we spent the night at the ER getting stitches on her chin from where she was tagged by the ball when it completely missed her glove. A glove she had on the wrong hand.

"You should see me and my brothers play games. You think this is intense," Cutter says at my ear.

"I'd love to meet them."

His arms snake around me tighter and his lips press to the back of my head. This is nice. What we're doing, what we've fallen into here in this house. It's easy. But is that because of the rules we put in place? We're pretending, like Cutter said, to not make things weird. But there's a lot about this that doesn't feel like roommates with benefits anymore. What he did for me tonight, the way he held me when we danced . . . those things feel. *They feel.*

"What's with the vintage track suit, Laney?" Matt picks up my stolen treasure that I'd set on the table and holds the jacket up to inspect it. "Oh, this is sweet! You've gotta let me make a post with you in this."

Before I can advise against the idea, Cutter lifts me from his lap and jets toward Matt, snagging the garment from one hand and Matt's phone from the other.

"This does not get posted anywhere, you got me?" Cutter drops his chin and holds Matt's phone hostage against his chest, and Matt's eyes dart to me for some sort of explanation. I draw a line across my closed mouth as if I'm zipping it, then pretend to throw away a key.

"Okay, so the track suit is off limits. Kinda weird, but whatever," Matt says, shaking his head and clearly thrown by our overreaction. If he only knew. I rather like that Cutter and I have a secret.

Cutter hands over Matt's phone but keeps his eyes on him as he walks back to me and retakes his spot in the chair, promptly pulling me back to his lap. "That phone better go in your pocket and not come out," he warns.

"Dude, it's in my pocket. Look, see?" Matt spins around and pats the block in his ass pocket.

"Man, Cutter, if I knew that worked I would have talked him into shoving that phone up his ass a long time ago," Ivy says, pressing pause on the game to take it live again so she can score the winning point while her brother is controllerless.

"Aw, damn! Ivy, that's cheating!" He picks up his controller from the sofa and presses a few buttons in some last ditch attempt to stop the tallying of the score, but it's useless. We laugh as a cartoon version of his sister dances around the screen and taunts him before Matt presses the power on the TV and pouts his way upstairs.

"Hard to believe he's twenty-three," his sister says.

She grabs a stack of books from the side of the couch and tucks them under her arm before heading upstairs too. Cutter and I are left alone in the chair, the room barely lit by the light spilling over from the kitchen. It's quiet and peaceful, and I could sit here with his arms around me, his chin resting on my head, for hours.

"Do you really want to meet my brothers?"

His question fires up my chest. Family is definitely not something you throw into the mix when you're simply hooking up. Family is a step. It took a year before I met Cam's family. I've been with Cutter—if we can even call this being together—for not quite three weeks.

"Hey, if it makes you uncomfortable, never mind."

"No, I want to," I interject, the thought of him backtracking on the idea giving me a sharp pang in the chest.

He nudges my chin so we're eye-to-eye.

"Are you sure?" His fingertips hover below my chin, and when I nod, his touch returns.

Cutter drops his forehead to mine as his thumb caresses its way to my bottom lip.

"They're coming up for my game Saturday, along with my mom."

I breathe in sharply, and Cutter's soft laugh tickles against my cheeks.

"Yeah, my mom too. You can still back out if you want to," he offers. I roll my head against his to signal no.

"I'm in," I assure him.

The pad of his thumb runs along my bottom lip again. I open my mouth and he slips it between my teeth. I bite down softly and close my lips around the tip, sucking as my eyelids flutter shut.

"Good." I'm not sure whether he means that in response to me being all in or to my not-so-subtle hint that I'd like him to touch me now.

His hand falls from my face and I lift my chin until our mouths meet. I take his bottom lip between my teeth and tug lightly as my tongue paints across his skin. He lets a deep moan hum in his chest and I feel his dick growing hard under the pressure of my thigh.

I shift to sit on his lap and face forward, centering his hard-on against my ass. Within seconds, his hands claw up my stomach, bunching my tank top and bra over my breasts. His lips suck at my neck as his thumbs rub against my hard nipples, and when he rolls them between his thumbs and index fingers it sends a bolt of need between my legs. I sink into him, wanting to feel his hard cock against my ass. It flexes against my weight and the sensation makes me wet.

"Touch me," I whisper, turning my head enough to catch

his mouth with mine. He nips at my bottom lip as a smile grows on his mouth and a gravelly, sinister laugh leaves him.

"I am," he reminds me, pinching the hard peaks of my breasts with more force, sending more waves of pleasure through my body. I'm pooling between my legs, desperate for him to ease the growing ache.

"Not there," I plead in a soft moan.

"Tell me where. Show me." His dominant dirty mouth turns me on even more, and I clutch at his wrists and guide his hands down my body until they land on my button and zipper.

"Say it," he growls at my ear.

My breath shudders and chills run along my bare, exposed skin. I undo the button of my jeans for him, and he takes over, slowly dragging the zipper down. He tugs my jeans a few inches lower on my hips as I grind my ass against his hardness. When his fingers pause at the lace trim on my panties, I squirm, desperate for his touch.

"You have to say it, Laney. Tell me what you want."

I groan and rock my hips before giving in.

"Touch my wet pussy, Cutter. Please."

He wastes no time sliding a hand beneath my panties and cupping my swollen center. His fingers splay out over my wet skin and he slides them over the most sensitive spots again and again until I'm writhing. That's when he dips a finger inside and I arch my back against his chest and whimper.

"Fuck, are you wet."

I nod. "Uh huh."

He works me with one hand while his other pinches then flicks the raw tips of my breasts. One finger becomes two, and I welcome the stretch as he pushes inside me then presses a thumb to my clit. I'm on the verge of coming when his mouth clamps down on my neck and his teeth tease at my skin. If he were a vampire I would willingly let him drink right now. I want to feel him everywhere. I want the sweet ache, and I never want it to end, but I'm going to have to come now. I'm too far gone to stop it.

I writhe on his lap as he pummels me with his fingers and licks at my neck. His hand claws at my breast, holding it with a possessive touch that locks me against his touch. I fall over the edge and waves of pleasure roll through my body.

"That's it, baby," he growls at my ear, rubbing his thumb through my slick skin as it pulses against his touch. A deep moan escapes me as he forces me to take every last burst of nerves firing between my legs and deep into my body.

I'm limp in his hands and on his lap by the time my orgasm finishes, but I want more. I want all of him.

I slip my hands behind me and feel my way to the button on his jeans. I work it open and draw his zipper down, finding him bare underneath his pants.

"You're so hard and hot," I moan, lifting myself enough to allow my hand room to palm his shaft. It flexes under my touch. It makes me crave him inside of me. I squeeze him in my hand, and his hands grab my biceps and hold me still. His lips graze against my ear and his breath is hot.

"I'm going to fuck you until you beg me to stop," he says, his voice a gruff whisper.

"I don't believe in quitting," I challenge, stepping up from his hold and turning to pull my shirt and bra over my head.

His tongue peeks out and he shakes his head slowly as I strip for him. I work my jeans down my hips first, stepping free of them so I'm wearing nothing but my white lace thong. I start to pull it down my hips, too, but Cutter sits up sharply.

"No, leave it. I have plans." He stands from the chair and I take a few steps back, toward the wall of patio windows.

Cutter glances over his shoulder toward the front door and the stairs, checking our privacy, I assume.

"Do you want to take me into the bedroom?"

He shakes his head.

"No. I want you here. And if someone decides now is a good time to get a glass of water, let them get a show." He grabs his cock and strokes it a few times before reaching into his jeans and pulling out a foil packet.

"So, you were planning on fucking me tonight?" I tease.

He grumbles a needy laugh.

"Laney, I've been carrying a condom around since I came in my sweatpants and had to take a long shower." He tears the packet open with his teeth, then works the latex over his cock.

My back hits the cold glass and I let out a short cry. Cutter holds his finger to his lips as he closes the distance between us.

"*Shh*, don't be too loud or we'll have company," he says, turning me around so my tits press against the chilly window pane.

I gasp, then bring my knuckles to my mouth to mute myself. Cutter's palm centers on my spine and he paints his fingers down my body until they wrap around the thin string crossing my lower back. He gently tugs my panties toward him then coaxes my shoulders to lower with his other hand. I drop my palms to the glass and rest my head against it as I bend over and arch my back to give him access.

"Goddamn, Laney. Your ass is a work of art." He smacks it, leaving a light sting before he bends to kiss the spot he claimed, and my center swells.

"Is that okay?" he asks. I nod and pant, "Uh huh."

He steps out of his jeans but keeps his palm on my lower back. His length rubs against my ass and I shift my hips on reflex, guiding him where I need him most.

"*Shh*. Patience, baby," he mutters before jerking my thong to the side and running the tip of his cock through my wet folds. My knees weaken so I press more of my weight on the glass, my hands streaking against it. There's no way Ivy is looking at these hand prints tomorrow and not instantly knowing what happened.

"Say what you want, Laney. Tell me," he commands, slowly teasing me with his cock as he covers himself in my wetness.

"Oh, God. Fuck me, Cutter. Fuck me now," I moan, no longer able to wait.

"Okay," he says, pushing into me with a long, slow stroke. I move my hand back to my mouth and cry out against it, my body stretching to fit him while also thanking me for giving it the relief it wanted.

Cutter pulls back, leaving me completely. Without even thinking, I utter, "No."

He chuckles and bends down to put his mouth at my neck.

"Miss me already, huh?" He nips at my ear then stands and pushes back into me. He rocks his hips and his cock slides in and out slowly at first until I grow comfortable with his fit and push back with each stroke.

"Fuck, Laney. You're so wet. So tight. Fuck," he groans, his hips moving faster. His thighs slap against my ass cheeks as he pummels me from behind, gathering my hair into his fist, holding me still.

Wanting to feel him in a new way, I stand with his chest

to my back and he continues to drive into me while I reach around and loop my arms around his neck.

"Fucking neighbors are going to be sorry there's a fence." He chuckles, his hands sliding around my body to grab my tits as he continues to fuck me senseless.

My body is overwhelmed with sensations, my nerves firing from my clit to my nipples, my bottom lip growing numb from the pressure of my teeth biting down so hard. I whimper as another orgasm builds. Cutter must sense I'm close because he drops a hand to my pussy and his finger circles my wet clit, driving each wave closer and closer to the brink until I crash.

"Oh, Cutter. Yes! I'm coming!" My cries are loud, but I don't care. Cutter pumps into me from behind while he works me with his hand in the front. Clutching me against him, he rocks his hips hard and fast until his breathing halts. He flattens his palm against my center as he drives his cock into me a few more times and it swells with his orgasm. He slides against my insides while the pulsing subsides, until finally pulling out and stumbling a few steps back.

"Fuck me, Laney," he huffs.

"I believe I did," I pant, bringing a smile to his lips. He pulls the condom from his cock and ties it, then hooks a finger in the air to call me to him.

I step in close and he snakes his hand up my neck and into my incredibly messy hair. He kisses me hard and holds my bottom lip between his for several seconds before his mouth stretches into a smile that breaks our touch.

"We're going to run out of furniture to spoil in this house," he says through soft laughter.

"I'm pretty sure we need to clean the window."

"Uh uh," he contends, shaking his head. "Leave it. That's

what Matt gets for making me clean up after his fucking party."

I smile at his devious plan, though I doubt Matt will ever notice. He's clueless, and I don't want Ivy finding the evidence of tonight. But I'll let Cutter have his way until he falls asleep, then I'll sneak out here like he did and play cleaning fairy.

LANEY'S BEEN PUTTING off this call with her mom for three days, but I finally convinced her to suck it up and take the first step. It's hard for me to totally understand the strained relationship she has with her parents because it's so opposite of what I experienced growing up. Even now, when my mom is not at her strongest by far, she's the one person I know I can call and count on.

Well, maybe not the only person. I'm starting to feel more like Laney is one of those people too. My person. I need to find the right time, the right way, the right place to tell her that. Laney requires impeccable timing.

"Okay, I've done it. First stone cast," she says, walking back into the bedroom with a proud look and her phone in her palm.

"Uh, not sure casting a stone is the right reference for an apology, but I'm glad you were able to talk to your mom. Do you want to talk about it?" I've also learned that Laney does want to talk about hard things, but she likes to leak them slowly until she's ready to gush.

"I left a message. That's about it."

It's not, but the rest will come in due time.

"Okay, well, are you ready?" I ask.

Laney tugs on the hem of her warm-up jersey and shrugs.

"I mean, yeah. I'm dressed for game day and I think we're going to kick Midwestern's ass. But am I ready for everything after the game? Uh . . ." Nervous laughter spills from her lips, so I bring her into a hug.

My family decided to come up a little early, likely thanks to the twins and their big mouths. They did a little sleuthing and found out Laney has a home game the day before mine, which means they can scope out their own evidence in this whole Caney-ship thing they've become obsessed with. Maybe I'm a little obsessed with it too. Sure feels a lot easier to let my brothers make the case to Laney for me, though I'm not entirely sure they'll be the best at selling my positive attributes. They did spend most of their lives sitting on me and poking grass up my nose until I said they were the best hockey players.

I always took it back when I got away.

Laney grabs her gear and rather than letting her continue to spiral internally I decide to swoop her up over my shoulder and carry her out to the Jeep in a rush. When it evokes her perfect raspy laugh, I know it was the right move. I know she wants to get there early, but I also know that she's overthinking meeting my family after her game, and I don't want anything distracting her when she steps on the court.

Still giggling in my arms, I swing her around then back her up to the Jeep's hood. I set her on top so I can step between her knees. Her giggling subsides and her hands land on my shoulders as I snuggle in between her legs, and rest my hands on her hips.

"Listen," I say. Her eyes snap to mine and she sucks in her top lip.

I don't want you to think about anything other than putting that ball down for the next four hours. My family? We're easy. So put us off to the side for a little while and be selfish. Think about you and your goals. That's all you need to focus on.

She nods but a short laugh slips through her tight lips.

"That's easier said than done," she admits.

I nod.

"I know. But I'm serious. I can pretty much guarantee they will all be wearing matching hoodies because that's how we roll. McCrearys don't care about judgement or opinions, and they are not looking to impress anyone or be impressed. The only thing that matters to us is that people are real, and you, Laney Price, are the realest person I've ever met. There's no mincing words with you. You're direct. You know what you want. You fight for it. And today you are going to show the world what a versatile badass you are."

Her mouth ticks up on one side and she drops her hands to the strings of my hoodie, tugging me in for a kiss. Her lips land on mine with a sweet stillness until they spread into a wide smile against me. Our foreheads rest on one another as she grabs two fistfuls of my hoodie and gives the material a gentle shake.

"So, is this the sweatshirt, then?"

I lean back and quirk a brow.

"The one you all will be wearing so you look like you just rolled off *Family Feud*?"

I lean back with a belly laugh, then stand straight and drop my chin to read the blue lettering on my Tiff sweatshirt. I shake my head then help her slide off from the hood.

"No, I don't match the rest of them. One of us has to lead."

She rolls her eyes, but I know in that moment her mind is right. The edge has been taken off. And my brothers are going to be so fucking jealous.

We get to the school in half the time it usually takes, probably because most of the day classes are done and the parking lots are near empty. I feel bad for poking fun of the volleyball attendance before, but it's true that it doesn't draw nearly the crowds we do, or basketball for that matter. It's too bad because honestly, our women's volleyball is about as close to Olympic level that one can get without having to fork over a few hundred dollars to sit in the nosebleeds.

I help Laney pull her bag up on her shoulder and tuck her court shoes into the open zipper. She scans the parking lot, turning in a slow circle until her gaze reaches mine again.

"Forget something?" I ask.

"No, it's not that." She looks down at her feet and chews at the inside of her cheek before taking in a deep breath through her nose and popping her gaze back up to mine. "I asked my dad to come again. So he could actually *see* something. See me play, I mean."

My stomach tightens in sympathy and I scan the lot behind her, clueless to what I'm looking for. The other night Laney showed me a few websites about her dad, and I did my own deep dive into his company and his beach career while she was asleep. She looks a lot like him. Not just in her height, but her build and the color of her hair and eyes. I could tell she's been thinking about him a lot since he showed up. It's good she asked him to come again, but it's not great that she doesn't seem to see him here now.

"It's early yet," I offer in excuse.

She lets out a heavy breath and her shoulders drop.

"Yeah, but he probably won't come. He said today would be tough but if he doesn't make it he'll for sure come to the next home game." Her eyes dart toward a car that approaches us to the right and my body shoots up with adrenaline and hope for her. Her quick deflation lets me know that car isn't his.

"Like you said. Probably the next game, then. And you'll be even more ready to prove to him exactly how focused you are." I cup her face. I caress her cheeks with my thumbs and she leans her head into my right palm, then closes her eyes and turns enough to press a kiss to the inside of my wrist.

"Okay, I've gotta go," she says, pushing away and clapping her hands together as if she's dusting me off like chalk. "Geesh! You're bad for my punctuality."

I wait until she ducks through the gym doors before I get back into the Jeep and check the time. My family should be at Patty's in about twenty minutes, which means I have just enough time to get there first and threaten anyone I know against telling embarrassing stories about me to my very convincing brothers and even more convincing mom.

NOW I KNOW it takes approximately two and a half beers to get my brothers to shut up about me having a girlfriend. Of course, now they refer to Laney as "the girl formerly referred to as Cutter's girlfriend," which is not much better. Actually, I think that's worse.

"Is that her? Damn, bro. She's hotter in person," Flynn

says, standing at the top of the bleachers and pointing to Laney as she stretches in the center of the court.

I know my face is red. It's so red I feel it.

"Dude, try to be a little less Flynn for the next two hours! I'm begging." I gesture with my palm for him to sit down, which of course only leads to Todd joining him and standing at his side as they dance-ish to the music filling the gym.

"Cutter, when are you going to learn that your brothers cannot be tamed?" My mom pats my thigh. I put an arm around her and squeeze. She's wearing a pink knit cap to hide her thinning hair. It's the first time I've seen her wear one, and though she always told me that losing her hair wouldn't bother her, I think it's different now that she's in the middle of it.

"I can't wait to meet her in person. I've never actually seen you defend a girl to your brothers so she must be pretty special." My mom gives me one of her know-it-all looks, a puckered smile on her lips. That's all I need to take my red cheeks one shade brighter.

"She is pretty special," I admit. Saying the words out loud eases some of the tightness in my chest.

I haven't told Laney about my mom's cancer battle. It's not one of those easy things to bring up, and there have been so many other things going on with Laney and her family and her role on the team. I didn't want to bury her with my stressors. That, and I don't think of my mom as a burden. She's my privilege. Of all the boys, I'm the one who gets to be closest to her and help her through this as best I can.

Now that I see my mom's state, though, I know that her battle is likely going to be visibly obvious to Laney when she meets her. I hope she doesn't think I was hiding it from her. I just wasn't sharing, and there really is a difference.

The lights dim in the gym, so I help my mom to her feet and my brothers pack in around us. It's too bad Andrew couldn't make it. I know a brother shouldn't choose favorites, but Andrew is definitely the one I have always looked up to most. I leaned on him a lot when I was in junior high and figuring out what kind of man I wanted to grow into. Andrew always made smart choices, and he was always honest. He even gave himself up when he broke things around the house or drank the last soda in the fridge. But he never ratted us out. He'd simply give us that look, not dissimilar from our mom's, and we were usually guilted into telling on ourselves once he leveled it.

Laney would like him. And he would love Laney. Maybe . . . after I tell her how I feel . . .

"Wow, Laney's really fucking hot!" Todd shouts as Laney jogs into the spotlight during the starter announcements.

"Todd!" my mom chastises. "That's your brother's girlfriend."

"You mean the girl formerly known as Cutter's girlfriend," Patrick points out.

I flatten my palm against my oldest brother's chest and he laughs hard. Being oldest definitely doesn't make him the most mature.

For the next two hours, Laney proves to every single person watching exactly what this team has been missing in her absence. From the opening rally that ended in her stuffing a block so hard that the ball rebounded back into the attacker's face until just now when she put the final point away, nailing the ball off a slide set that sent her leaping one way and the ball another. Three straight sets in record time, and my brothers aren't referring to Laney as anything other than the greatest volleyball player in the history of all history.

Patrick rented a large SUV, so I show my family where to park next to me in the student area so we can wait on Laney. We pile into the grass just outside the gym doors, and the second Laney exits the door she stops in her tracks, blinks a few times, then bends over with hands on her knees while she laughs.

I wasn't kidding about the matching sweatshirt business. And when I mentioned something about Tiff Tuff to Patrick, he got busy putting in a special order from one of those mail-in places and had special sweatshirts made for everyone—me and Laney included.

Laney walks over to our coordinated little cluster and presses a quick kiss to my cheek as she scans the chests of every single McCreary one more time.

"Wow, you guys went all out."

"Oh, honey. If there's one thing to learn about us, it's that we don't do anything half way," my mom says, stepping across me and holding out a hand for Laney.

I hold my breath and wait for it, but Laney's good at masking the quick breath that leaves her the moment she truly looks my mom in the eyes.

"I'm Allison, Laney. Cutter has told us only what we've been able to drag out of him about you." My mom—I can always count on her to kick things off.

I chuckle as Laney shakes my mom's hand, then glances to me. I catch the quick signal in her eyes as they widen that she's put my mom's diagnosis together and is maybe a little miffed about my omission. I smile through tight lips, hoping it relays an apologetic excuse.

"Probably about as much as he's told me about you all,"

Laney responds. My chest tightens, but she's quick to shift the tone. "Though he has told me about you two." She moves to shake Todd and Flynn's hands next.

"Oh, I'm sure. Sorry you got the leftovers with that one. The gene pool ran out of good looks and charm since we came out twins," Flynn says.

"And that one is Flynn. The charmer," I say in introduction. Before Flynn can make it to Laney, Todd cuts in front of him and introduces himself, practically tripping over himself. Patrick sits back and waits while the twins act like buffoons but make Laney laugh, then he steps in to play adult.

"Patrick. Patrick McCreary," he says, tacking on a throat clear as if to be punctuation. We all grow silent and I hold in my laugh as best I can until Ma, of course, puts Patrick in his place.

"What are you, James Bond? Jesus, the girl isn't interested in any of you. And you're married. *Lordt!*" Everyone cracks into hysterics except Patrick, who immediately presses the key fob to unlock the SUV and usher us on our way.

My family piles into their vehicle while I take Laney in mine, which gives me the privacy I was hoping for to tell her how proud I am of her.

"So, where should I start? The block? The kill at the end? Seven aces? I could go on." I like gushing about her, and it's clear she likes to hear it by the way she sits up tall and fills her chest with air as she grins.

"It was a pretty great block wasn't it?" Now is not the time for Laney to be humble.

"Uh, yeah!" I pull us onto the main drag to head toward Baker Joe's, our favorite BBQ place. The twins haven't been there since graduation and begged that we head there for dinner.

Laney recants her game to me play-by-play, explaining the little details that she thinks I missed. I may have missed some, but not many. I studied her. I was locked on her. And I see how she makes this game so exciting.

"Did you know that the only reason they had to give Chelsea a shot was because her family is the one that owns Mickelson Electronics? Like, *those* Mickelsons."

I grimace and glance at her as I drive. It takes her a few seconds to pick up on the fact that I did in fact know that.

"Why didn't you say something?" she huffs.

"Uh, I could tell you it's because it slipped my mind, but honestly, I think I was afraid of what you might do if you knew." I glance at her again and her eyes have hazed but she's not totally shooting lasers at me.

"I see that's not the only thing you were afraid to tell me." Her lips purse and she blinks a few times. I turn my attention back to the road. She's talking about my mom.

I run my palm over my face, then leave it over my mouth and chin as I take a deep breath.

"There's not really a natural segue into saying, 'Oh, by the way, my mom has breast cancer.'" I glance at her with a sheepish smile and her eyes soften. She pulls her torso free of the safety belt as we approach a stoplight and when we're stopped, puts her arms around me, her head on my shoulder.

"I'm sorry."

I look down as her eyes flit up to me.

"Thank you," I say before pressing a kiss to her forehead.

"Is she . . ."

I know the start of her question comes with multiple possibilities. Is my mom all right? Is she winning? Is she going to be okay? So many more.

"She's in good hands, and they caught it early. She'll

finish chemo next month, and then some more tests to see what's next. But her prognosis is very, very good."

I think maybe saying it out loud to Laney is the first time I believe it myself. My mom has told me thousands of times, but when it's your mom—your rock—it's hard to see the good odds. You only see the fraction of a chance that life goes wrong.

Laney stays close to me, hugging my bicep and leaving her head on my arm as she runs her palm along my skin. It feels . . . nice.

"You're a good son," she says after nearly a minute of silence.

"Yeah?" I ask as she lifts her head.

She nods.

"I knew it from the first mention of your important Sunday dinner date." She smiles, and I let it soothe the old aches I've been carrying around. That Sunday dinner, the one we postponed because she was in the hospital. Laney didn't ask pointed questions that night, but she knew something was wrong. She knew, and she cared.

"Hey, when my family's gone . . . can we . . . talk?"

Laney sits up and slips her seat belt back on. Her eyes widen as she says, "Oh."

"Nothing bad. Just some stuff I've been thinking about, and you and I talk, but we don't get to *talk* talk." I lick my bottom lip, then suck it in as I give her a sideways glance.

She tucks her hands under her thighs and her knees bob for a few seconds.

"Yeah, we can talk," she finally says.

That tightness in my chest? I'm pretty sure I just gave it to her, too.

We luck into a live music night at Baker Joe's, which

eases the tension between Laney and me throughout dinner. I sit with my mom while Laney and my brothers finish a diehard battle of horseshoes, which she is winning.

"She's really something," my mom says, pulling my attention from Laney but only briefly.

"Yeah, she is," I sigh out.

"Uh oh," my mom adds.

My brow drops as I turn my gaze back to her.

"Uh oh, what?"

"I know that look. You're in love." She picks up one of her French fries and dips it into the ranch dressing she insists on eating, then pops the potato into her mouth. My mom has the ability to chew with the smuggest expression, a skill she's showing off right now.

I roll my head, then my shoulders, as I look the other way. I squint into the sunset and let those words settle deep inside. They feel right. And I know I asked Laney to talk, but also, I thought maybe I would ease into it with her.

"You should tell her, Cutter. You never know unless you throw caution to the wind and give big stuff a shot."

I laugh and my mom hugs me, turning my attention back to her side.

"She's a lot like them, you know." I gesture to my brothers, who are currently strategizing a way to get an impossible number of points at a game that basically boils down to throwing heavy metal at a large nail.

"That's why you like her so much."

I swallow at her words, then nod.

It is.

It is.

19 /
laney

WHEN MY MOM called back last night I was still at Baker Joe's and having too much fun with Cutter's family to dive into the work she and I have in front of us. But since she called back this morning, I don't feel right putting her off again, though I very much would rather head to Cutter's game early with them.

"I can stay back with you," Flynn says, but his brother Todd yanks the sleeve of his T-shirt to pull him out the door.

"He's like a pet you'll never get rid of. Make your phone call and we'll save you a seat," Todd says.

"Thanks." I hold up the shirt they made for me to wear so I could match everyone, and promise to put it on. It says Cutter's Fan Club, and as much as my feelings about him have changed—dramatically—I still don't think I can put that shirt on in public. Maybe under something.

I wait until I hear them pull from our driveway after having joined us for breakfast, then head to the beanbag that Matt usually takes while he plays video games. He's out of town again, and Ivy's working a shift. Cutter's on the ice for pre-game. I'm truly on my own. No more excuses.

I dial my mom's number and she answers instantly.

"Thank you. Oh, Laney, thank you for calling back." She sounds winded but I think it's just relief.

"Of course I would call back." I catch myself—*that's not true.* "I mean, this is important. And I should call more often."

My mom sniffles.

"That would be . . . nice."

I lay back to stare at the ceiling and we both hold on with silence for a few long seconds. Where do I start? Maybe she will.

"I'm so incredibly proud of you, Laney. I always have been, and I'm so sorry I don't say it enough."

"You don't really say it ever." I wince at my own words because they sound harsh, and that's not how I want this to go. "I mean that in an honest way, not to take a dig."

"I know," she says in a hushed tone. "And you're right. I do brag about you to anyone who will listen, but perhaps I've been saying the good stuff to the wrong people. Wrong *person.*"

More silence.

"Thanks. It's nice to hear, even now."

"I got the campus profile today."

"Oh? Did you read Dad's quote?" I figure that's where this is going.

"I did. It was pretty funny. But that's not why I mention it. I cut the first page out and framed it. You look so strong and so fierce. And the words they have next to your photo. 'All I want to do is win.'"

We both say the line together.

I breathe out a soft laugh.

"Yeah, how many years have I said that now?"

"Well, you're twenty-two, and you started talking just after your first birthday, so . . . twenty-one years."

We both laugh softly.

"Seems about right," I agree.

I swallow hard, my throat closing due to how anxious this call is making me. I don't like how things are with my mom, but breaking the pattern is hard. And saying things that hurt her has left a bigger stain on my conscience than I thought it would.

"Mom, I'm sorry I was so angry the other day," I finally let out.

"Oh, honey." Her voice cracks, and I give her a few seconds to compose herself. A tear strikes at the corner of my eye and I dash it away with my Cutter Fan Club shirt.

"I'm the one who is sorry. I've put the pain from your dad leaving on you your entire life. Not intentionally, but I think somewhere deep down it made me feel less alone to share it with you. That wasn't fair. I'm working on it. I've been talking to a therapist, and I'm learning a lot of things about myself."

"That's really good." I sit up, my chest opening a little. This conversation is hard but it's good. I feel good having it.

"It is. And I want you to know that I encourage you to make your own choices. To choose your circles, to pick who to love. And Cam was good on paper, so I forced it and I shouldn't have. To hear he made you miserable . . ."

"It wasn't all bad," I sigh. I look out the window where a bird is sitting on the thinnest branch. It somehow holds his weight, and that somehow feels like a metaphor for everything in my life. I pile things on myself, even when I can't hold it all. But Cutter forces me to share. He scares me. The way he can coax me into opening up. His patience? It's terrifying. Along with the fact that he shows up for me, forcing me to accept his help.

"You know that photo you framed?" I grin imagining it.

"Uh huh," my mom responds.

"That hockey guy you poked fun of? The one I'm living with? He took it."

I chew at the inside of my lip and blush a little when my mom says, "Oh."

I can hear the sound of something sliding against the wall and imagine her pulling the frame down for closer inspection.

"He's talented," she says.

"He is. At that, and at his sport. And he's smart, and pretty funny, and—"

"And he's quite the looker," my mom butts in.

"Ha, I mean . . . yeah, he's pretty handsome." I cover my face even though I'm all alone. I imagine Cutter's face, the sharp line of his jaw, his chest, his . . . other attributes. I bite my thumbnail.

"You really like him," she says.

I nod but eventually say it out loud.

"I do."

I've caught feelings. I've caught them hard.

I pull my phone out for a beat to check the time. I need to get moving if I want to see the start of the game.

"Hey, Mom. I have to go, but maybe we can talk more tonight. Or tomorrow. And maybe we can plan a weekend for you to fly out? See some games and maybe spoil me with dinner?"

My mom laughs, probably amused at me weaseling dinner, but she quickly agrees.

"I wish I could get you out next weekend. I did something

crazy and invited Dad. I don't really know what to say to him, and since apparently you're talking now, it might be nice to have you play moderator."

My mom puffs out a snarky laugh at my suggestion.

"I think it will take a while for us to work into a full-fledged family weekend. And since you don't plan on grad school, I'm afraid we don't have enough time for that."

I smile and nod.

"You're probably right."

"I love you, Laney. And I'm so proud of you. For everything." A new round of tears prickles my eyes, and I quickly blot them away with the shirt.

"I love you too, Mom. And thank you . . . for everything."

We both let the quiet settle in for a few seconds, maybe letting the butterflies land in our chests as we prepare to end the first totally cordial conversation we've had in years.

We say our goodbyes and I dash into the bedroom to slip on some leggings and the stupid fan club shirt. I try tucking it in at first but pull it free, realizing no matter what I do, the words are still going to be there.

"Gah!" I chuckle at myself as I stretch it out as if somehow it won't feel weird walking around in a Cutter billboard. I'm already half of Caney-ship. Do I have to eat all my words I ever said about the man?

I glance to the bed and find my favorite Tiff Hockey sweatshirt of Cutter's and decide to put that on over the shirt rather than the zipper jacket I was planning to wear. I grab my wallet and keys, then head out for the game.

I make it there just as the announcements finish, and Cutter's mom spots me as I scan the rows of seats in the family section. She waves her hands as she stands on the seat and I head up the steps toward her. Flynn jogs down to me, ignoring that I know where I'm going, and I muse internally over how spot-on Cutter was with his descriptions of his brothers. When I make it to their row, I follow Flynn and take the open seat by their mom and a man I don't think I've met yet.

"Laney, I'm Andrew. We didn't get to meet last night since I just got in." *Andrew. Cutter's favorite.*

I take his hand and hold it with both of mine as we shake. His palm is warm and he notes how cold my fingers are.

"You don't come to a lot of hockey, do you?" he asks.

I shake my head. He looks so much like Cutter it's as if I'm getting a glimpse into the future. He's more professional looking but probably only because he's close to thirty and has a perfectly trimmed mustache and beard. And a sweater with a tie underneath. That part helps too.

"Here," Andrew says, handing me a small square bean-bag made of felt. I squeeze it in my palms and it heats up.

"This is the greatest invention I've ever seen," I gloat. The McCrearys all laugh then hold up their own squares, everyone but Andrew that is, since he gave me his. I'd offer to give it back but that would just be stupid.

I settle into the seat between him and his mom, and the game gets under way. The puck is in Cutter's control within seconds and I get lost for a while watching him work. Everything has me on edge. Each trip he makes along the ice, sliding the puck through bodies and sticks all before being slammed into the glass and having it stolen. He's the embodiment of grit, the way he gets right up and storms right back. Our goalie makes a massive save to end the first period, and I feel like I've been holding my breath for twenty minutes straight.

"We picked a good one, huh?" Cutter's mom says.

I fall back into my seat and wipe my brow, which seems as though it should have sweat on it despite how cold I am. That was hard work.

"I mean, I think I prefer the blowouts, but yeah."

She pokes my arm with her elbow and silently laughs.

"Yeah, those are easier on the heart, for sure."

The boys take advantage of the time between periods and slip from our row to hit the restrooms and get second beers. I notice that Allison has half a beer in her cup holder and she must catch my gaze looking because she says, "I can have a small amount."

"Oh, I didn't mean to question you. I was curious, though."

"No, it's all right. I like talking about it, actually. My daughter-in-law is the reason I finally went and got checked. I had a suspicion I felt something but I ignored it. I guess I thought that would make it go away, but when I brought it up to her, she insisted. And she saved my life." Her eyebrows raise in emphasis.

"Was that Andrew's wife?" I vaguely remember Cutter telling me that Andrew was a teacher and his wife was a nurse.

Allison nods.

"Sure was. My boys pick smart women." Her eyes dance over me for a few seconds, and I get the insinuation. It warms my cold face, which is thankfully probably already red from the temperature.

"It must be hard having them all spread around the country."

She nods and pulls her phone out to show me pictures of her three grandchildren. I may be seeing things at this point, but I swear everyone in that family looks a little like Cutter.

It's the eyes, I think. A lot of greenish tints, and they crinkle at the edges when they smile.

"I miss them all when they're gone, but they're all happy and doing well. That's all a mom can hope for."

"It's good they get to visit sometimes."

She nods slowly then lets her eyes drift to my face.

"It is. But I always knew the ones who would fly out of the nest and not really fully come back." She shifts her gaze down the aisle where Flynn and Todd are balancing beers that are far too full for them to walk up steps. They make it up three before spilling down their pant legs.

"Those two, you mean?"

"God, yes. They were barely in the house when they were kids. It took hours of me yelling around the neighborhood to get them to come home for dinner and sleep. Patrick, too. Andrew, not as much. He's always been responsible and level-headed. He probably wouldn't have moved away if he hadn't fallen in love."

"And what about Cutter?" I hold my breath and await her answer about him. He seems so independent and free-spirited. I've never met someone so willing to go with the flow. Hell, he shacked up with me on a whim and a dare, and I don't think the adjustment has been nearly as hard for him as it has been for me.

"Cutter? Oh, he's like a magnet. That one, he will never leave."

I feel the weight of her words, and I know the corners of my mouth have drooped, so before she looks at me again, I force them back into a plastic smile.

"Homebody, huh?" I swallow the rocks in my throat.

"Not that he doesn't like to go out or that he's not an extravert because, *ooof*. He's the life of the party. But he's always been close to us. He likes his roots, and I think his hometown gives him comfort. You know, I don't know if he told you but I had to sell the second home he was living in. It was an investment property my husband and I bought knowing the boys would live there if they all went to Tiff. But it was getting to be a lot, to pay on both houses."

"He mentioned it." I remember the first night when we butted heads in the room we now share. He didn't have a place to stay, and this is why. I knew the reason but I didn't really get it until now.

"He doesn't know this, but I put some of the furniture in storage for him. The nice stuff. He's the one who cares about it. He's always been big on memories and nostalgia. One day when he gets a place, he'll be outfitted in the dining room for sure."

I picture heirlooms and well-cared-for things, and somehow that jives with the Cutter I've come to know. He has his own version of Pete's treasure room. One from his life.

"What happens if he gets drafted somewhere far away?" *What happens if I do? And we're together?*

"Oh, I mean . . . he would have to decide, and I think he should go no matter what. But I have this feeling about him. That boy? He'll always come home."

"Todd's a dumbass!" The twins pass in front of our knees and a few drops of beer splash on my leggings. I reach forward and grab spare napkins from the cup holder and blot it dry.

"You're twins, so odds are if he's a dumbass so are you," Andrew adds, pounding fists with Patrick as the oldest two brothers slide in and take their seats.

The buzzer sounds and my attention flies to the ice where

Cutter comes streaming out and glides around the Tiff side, warming his legs and leading his teammates through a few starts and stops. He's going to get drafted. And he could go to a big market. He'd be a fool to turn that down. But also, he has so much here. I could never ask him to choose me, to pick where I end up. Especially if my career means starting somewhere like Tacoma or Dover, thousands of miles from the middle of the country, where Cutter's heart clearly is.

**20 /
cutter**

I'VE BEEN DUMPED a few times in my life. Laney likes to call me Campus Hot Boy, but before I got to Tiff, I was more or less Campus *Not* Boy. There are a few tell-tale signs when someone is trying to dump you.

One, they avoid intimacy, and not just the sex stuff but the entire concept of being alone with someone in the same space. Two, they have a strange and instant personality shift. It's almost as if the person they were right before they decided to break up was eaten by someone with a super busy calendar, bad hearing, and a super short temper. And three, they are definitely looking for a fight.

Laney and I haven't been awake and alone since my family left Monday morning. That's five days ago, well four and a half, I suppose, since it's Saturday noon. Since we said goodbye to my mom and brothers after breakfast on Monday, Laney has been the busiest student on Tiff's campus. I pretty much know her schedule of classes, and I'm not buying that she has three study groups that seem to meet all of a sudden back-to-back-to-back three evenings in a row. And when I called her to compliment her on her away game that I streamed on Thursday, she said we had a bad connection and she couldn't hear me. I gave her the benefit of the doubt, but in my gut? I knew something weird was up.

Last night? Last night was the fight. And I walked right into it like an asshole.

I had no idea Laney's ex had proposed. All I cared about was that he was an ex, and that all the reasons they broke up seemed like pluses in my favor. He didn't understand the drive of athletics. But I do. He wasn't supportive of her pushing to go pro. I, however, not only support it, I expect to be the first one wearing a Laney Price fan jersey. And where he dismissed her demons, I can't wait to help her conquer them.

Check, check, check!

Winner, Cutter McCreary.

Only, I'm not the winner. I'm on the outs. Hard.

Ivy mentioned the proposal during a round of video games, and Laney and I were competing in a pretty epic battle of video table tennis. I hit pause at the news and then let the stupidest words known to man fall out of my mouth.

"Someone actually wanted to marry you?"

Even Matt gave me the open-mouthed *you're a dead man* stare.

I didn't mean it that way. I'm not sure exactly how I meant it. I know what I felt, which was pride that Laney knew herself well enough to walk away before she was in too deep. She could have said yes and dragged the engagement out, hoping she'd feel differently down the line. She could have gone through with it and kept the hope going. She could have given up on her path to take his, especially now that I know the pressure her mom put on her.

But she didn't. She said no. And broke up with the poor lad.

And I'm pretty sure she's about to break up with me. If we're even a thing that can be broken. Maybe I've been naïve in thinking this was morphing into something real. But she met my family, and she kissed me with so much heart, and she wanted me in ways that felt like she needed me to breathe. I didn't imagine that.

I was letting my frustration and fear control my reaction last night. I said that to her out of knee-jerk hostility, out of frustration for not getting the alone time I was desperate for to tell her how I felt. I lashed out, and she fought back with a vengeance.

In a matter of minutes, I went from being a nice guy to the same selfish jock who must only be out for a good time that she thought I was a month ago. She threw her game controller down when she was done, then went to bed. And I let her.

I should have begged her last night to tell me what was really going on, but I didn't. Because I was afraid of what she might say. But now that I'm sitting here in the kitchen across from her while she violently chops vegetables and slides them into a pan with an incredibly sharp knife, I'm painfully aware that I missed my moment. And now, all I'm doing is putting things off.

"Well, I guess I may as well be the first to talk. And I guess this is going down in front of you two." I push in my stool and gesture to Matt and Ivy.

Laney's making stir-fry because Ivy was craving it. She has a game in a few hours and totally doesn't have time for this, but it seems speed cooking is higher on her list than being on her own with me. She even convinced Ivy to let her borrow her truck rather than let me drive her to campus.

"What's going down?" Matt, sweet clueless Matt, sits up tall like a kid waiting to find out he's going to Disneyland. Ivy, however, seems more in tune with the vibe in the room. She sets her phone flat on the table and rests her face in one palm.

"Just Cutter apologizing for being an asshole," Laney says, her voice clipped to match the *chop-chop-chop* with her death knife.

"That's right. Again, I am apologizing for being an asshole. I misspoke. I was in a bad mood. I took it out on you and said something stupid. And I didn't mean it. Or hell, maybe I meant it. But only because I'm so confused and want to know what all of this . . ." I whirl my finger around in a circle. "Is about. Tell me, Laney. Just break it down and tell me. Why am I back in the dirt, mud on your shoes? What happened between Monday morning and the afternoon that changed the way you look at me? I don't understand."

Laney keeps chopping, and her best friend glances between the two of us. Matt reaches for his phone and I point at it and yell, "Stop!"

"Don't you dare type up some gossip post or online poll about the status of Caney-ship! Dammit, Matt, this is my life. This is Laney's business. My business. Leave the damn socials alone. Give it a rest." I'm practically panting.

"Dude, I was just going to step outside and give you two some space." Matt holds up both palms, his phone lodged in one and his app open on the screen.

I shake my head and breathe out hard through my nose as he leaves the kitchen and dashes upstairs.

"He's a liar," Ivy says. "But the one thing he got right was leaving you two alone. So I'm going to take this opportunity to maybe shower, or take a nap. I don't know, but I've gotta go."

Laney slams down the knife, flattening it against the cutting board.

"I'm making you lunch!"

Ivy shrugs.

"And I will love it. Put it in a bowl and leave it in the microwave." She moves closer to the stairs.

"It's not the same," Laney growls, turning to the trash and sliding the newly cut veggies into the bin. She snags the pan from the stove and moves it to the sink, flipping on the water and passing it under the stream with a whoosh of steam.

"Oww!" She drops it then flicks the faucet off, backing up and sucking on two of her fingertips. I rush around the counter and flip the cold water back on, then move the pan.

"You gotta run that under cold if it's a burn. Come on," I say, waving her to step close.

She glares at me but steps up and holds her hand there for a few quiet seconds.

"Lemme see," I say, taking her wrist gently and rotating her palm until I see her fingers. The pad of her right index finger is pink, but doesn't look like it's going to blister.

"I think it will be okay. But you should maybe ask the trainer what you can put on it before the game."

She jerks her hand away and puts the finger back in her mouth, muttering, "Fuck."

I flip the water off and grab the edge of the sink, staring at the still-oily pan while my heart explodes into a thousand pieces in my chest.

"Are you trying to push me away?" I keep my back to her. It's easier this way, but only mildly.

She doesn't answer so I ask the question again.

"Are you? You can be honest with me, Laney. I've been trying to have this conversation with you, and this is not how I imagined it going, but now we're in it."

I turn around and lean my lower back against the sink as I meet her eyes. Her arms are crossed over her chest, closing her off and guarding her heart.

"I care about you, Laney—"

"Don't," she breaks in, waving her hand at me, then turning to leave the small galley space. I reach for her arm and grab near her elbow. She spins around to face me and I halt to keep the foot of distance between us because I think that's what she wants.

"I can't turn that off, Laney. I care about you. I like you, a lot. No . . . you know what? I love you. I love the way you make me feel, and I love your fire. You are like nobody I have ever met, and I want to know more. I want to learn all of your secrets. I want to help you solve your problems. I want to climb mountains with you. I—"

"Stop it, Cutter. You're being—"

"I'm being what? Real? Yeah, I am. I am being real. And I really love you." I shrug, and I see the ache pooling in her eyes. There's a piece of her that wants to choose me. There's love in there. If I can just get her to admit it. She shakes her head though, and my chest caves in.

"We want different things," she says.

"So what?" I say with a quick head shake.

She laughs out a sigh and turns her back on me again, moving toward our bedroom. I trail behind her but still give her space. I don't want her to feel trapped. I've learned things about her, and sometimes Laney has to find her own way into expressing things. It takes her time. I'll give her room.

"What happens when I get drafted by the pro league?" she asks, picking up her gear bag and stuffing her warmup sweatshirt inside, then scanning the floor for her court shoes. They're by me, near the door, so I pick them up and hand them to her. I hold on tight for a beat, pulling against her as she tries to take them, and our eyes meet.

"So what?" I repeat my response from before, which earns me the famous Laney eyeroll.

"You don't get it, Cutter. I am willing to go anywhere. Boston, Miami, Newport, Chicago, Vancouver. I don't care where I get my opportunity to play professionally. If Finland wants me to pick up and move there to play, I'm going. I worked too hard. I want it too much to quit on it."

"You don't have to quit, Laney. This is absurd!"

I don't understand where this is coming from at all.

She pulls her bag up to the foot of the bed then zips it closed. She gathers the handles in her palm but pauses, staring at her grip.

"Where do you want to play, Cutter? If you go pro, which, let's be honest, you're good. *You're so good.*"

I suck my lips into a hard line because her compliment feels more like a curse the way she's saying it.

"I don't know yet. The Boilers have sent scouts, and it would be cool to play close to home, but—"

"Right there. That's it," she cuts in.

"What's it?" I shake my head and lean into the door jamb while she jerks her bag's shoulder strap up and over her head then turns to face me.

"I want to go anywhere. And you, you want to be home. Your home is here, Cutter. And there is nothing wrong with that. You have an amazing family, and your mom and your relationship . . . *gah!* I can't even describe the envy I have. I love that you love your mom so much."

I push from the wall and take a step closer to her.

"I don't have to stay close to home, Laney. But that's in the future. We aren't even there yet. We're here right now, and I love you right here. And if this blooms into ride-or-die then yeah, I'll go wherever you want. I'd do that for you."

I would, and now that I've said it, it feels so easy. The easiest thing ever. I know it in my gut.

"But I don't want to make you do anything for me, Cutter. And that's the problem. It hit me watching you with your mom. Hearing her talk about how selfless you are. I'm not like you, Cutter. I'm selfish, like my dad. I will pick me and what I want, even if that means leaving you behind."

Her eyes blink away tears and she chews at her lip. She's holding everything in. Not the negatives or her anxieties, but she's holding back the desires and the conflict. She's giving up.

"You aren't your dad, Laney."

She shakes with a quick laugh.

"I'm more like him than I care to admit, I'm afraid."

We stare at one another for what feels like a full minute, though I know only a few seconds go by. It's quiet. The house feels as if the oxygen is being sucked away.

"I guess that's a risk I'm willing to take. I'm not going to predict all the *ifs*. I want the ride and will deal with ifs whenever. We would deal with them together. Because I fell for you."

She blinks through more long silence.

"Then I guess you lose."

She shifts her weight and crosses her arms, and even though the red in her eyes betrays her, she holds firm.

"Fine," I finally say, moving past her to my side of what was our bed. I bend down and pull my empty travel bag out from under the bed. I flop it on the mattress and pull the zipper open wide before moving to the closest drawer and fishing out an armful of sweatpants and shorts. I dump them in the bag then put my hands on my hips as I stare her in the eyes. Daring.

"I'll move out, Laney. Because you're right. I lose. I lost. I fell for you. I fell fucking hard. So the room is yours. You can sleep here all alone and have all the room you want."

Her hands grab at the sides of her jersey as she hugs herself, her teeth gnawing at her bottom lip. Her gaze darts from my face to the bag as her body sways in a tiny motion. She's close. So damn close.

"Good," she finally utters, turning her back to me and marching out the door. I follow behind for a few steps, just enough to watch her basically sprint down our short hallway. The front door slams shut a few seconds later, and I'm left alone staring at my travel bag and the quiet, cozy space that was hers and mine for the best month of my life.

I fill my bag with clothes until I've cleared out most of the drawers, then zip it up and flop face first and sideways on the bed with my arms hanging off. I lay like that long enough for my hands to get tingly from blood pooling in them. When I finally roll to my back and let my head hang upside down I'm struck by Ivy staring at me from the doorway.

"It was pretty hard not to hear all of that," she says.

I run my hand over my face, then roll over one more time to sit up. My head hurts, but I think only partially from my stint upside down. I think it's taking over for my heart, which hurts like hell. It needs a break.

"Sorry," I say, flailing my hands up then letting them drop on my thighs.

"Don't be sorry. You said what you needed to and what she needed to hear. She'll get there." Ivy steps into the room and takes a seat on the bed next to me.

"I'm not sure. She was pretty adamant."

Ivy glances at her phone for a few seconds then hands it over to me. I narrow my eyes on it and she shakes it a few times.

"It's not mine. Laney left her phone on the counter. You should read it." She touches the screen with her thumb but I look away.

"I'm not going to read her private messages."

Ivy grabs my hand and slaps the phone in my palm, forcing me to take notice.

"Read. It."

I sigh but look at the screen. I'm only able to see a preview of the message that's now about an hour old.

> DAD: Sorry Lane. I'm not going to make it.
> Maybe some other time.

"Oh no."

"Yeah," Ivy concurs. "She actually thought maybe he would make it this time. And that girl hasn't had her hopes up for her father in a long time. Not since I've known her. She's going to be crushed."

I turn the phone over and press the screen to my thigh as I close my eyes and sort through what to do. As if I have a choice.

"Okay," I sigh out, opening my eyes and rolling my head

to face Ivy. "He might not be there for her, but I will. I can at least do that. Might be the last time I get to."

I grab my Tiff sweatshirt and throw a beanie on to mash down my messy hair. I shove Laney's phone in one pocket of my jeans and mine in the other.

Ivy walks me to the front door and before I step outside, she grabs my sleeve and coaxes me to turn around.

"Nobody has ever gotten that girl to dance. You're different, Cutter. For lots of reasons."

I hold her gaze for a beat and do my best to believe it. I thought I was. At the very least, I can be in Laney's corner one more time.

IT'S A BIG GAME. And my head is not in it.

"Laney, they're weak at middle block so you're going to get the majority today. That arm feeling good?" Coach asks.

I could lie. I won't. Because as messed up as I am inside right now, I still want this.

I swing my arm around and nod fervently.

"I'm good."

Sometimes the fact that *foul mood* and *game face* look nearly identical is a good thing. I'm wearing one in place of the other right now.

Coach breaks us up and we all gather by the door for our entry, the thunder already roaring in the gym. I grab one of the damp towels from the bucket and kick my feet back one at a time to wet the treads on my shoes so my grip is solid.

"You're going to kill it today." Chelsea holds a fist out to my side, and as sharp as my grudge still feels, I push past it and lay mine on top.

"You too," I say. She nods at me, her game face intact.

It's not her fault she has leverage. Still, feels weird to me not to earn something with talent. But maybe it all happened for a reason. Last week was one of my best game days ever. It was big enough to put me at the top of the national rankings. As a middle hitter who has not played middle since her kneepads were school-issued and she wrote her name on the back with a Sharpie.

I push through the doors and the team follows behind me. There's a decent crowd here today. I can't see faces yet because the lights are dimmed, but I can tell the seats are full. And I can hear them.

Maybe he came?

We pass the stands on our first lap and I focus on the family section, looking for anything familiar to stand out. His jeans, or his hair. Maybe he'll have a hat on. Any man in his early fifties who looks like me. I'm not able to spot him on the first trip, so I try again on the second. This time, the lights are on bright, and I get a better handle on the attendance. Our stands are nearly full, even the balcony. And it's when I glance up as I finish my jog that I see Cutter standing on the front bleacher upstairs with his hands cupped around his mouth as he shouts what I imagine is, "Let's go, Laney!"

I can tell that he knows I'm staring at him by the way his hands drop to his sides for a few sways side-to-side. He starts to clap, then looks to either side of him and forces students to join in. They're stomping and clapping and obnoxious the way I've only seen our student section behave for basketball. It feels incredible, and also, it's tearing me up inside.

I drop my gaze as we circle up in the middle of the court to stretch. I scan the bleachers at my level, focusing on the middle, down the net—where my dad likes to sit. Nothing.

"Hey, you ready?" Kiera brushes into me, a ball tucked under her arm.

I nod.

"Yeah, let's put on a show."

"That's what I'm talking about," she says, a hop in her step as she moves to the setter position for warmups. She tosses the ball to me and I hit it on the floor a few times with a healthy slap. I can see I'm hitting it hard yet somehow, I don't feel it. It's like my hand is foreign, not a part of me. I suddenly feel as if I'm watching from the bench, outside of myself.

I toss the ball to Kiera for a quick and somehow put the ball down hard in the far right corner. She screams, "Yeah!" It sounds as though it's piping through a tunnel.

I jog to the back line and stretch my legs more, pulling my feet up behind me as I scan the bleachers again. He isn't here. Of course he isn't here. Why would he be here?

Stupid girl.

I drop my right foot from my stretch and I can't feel it hit the ground. Bouncing a few times, I tell myself everything is fine. I shake my head and return to the court to take another swing. Another quick. This time I send it to the left corner, pounding the line.

I'm floating and everything feels slow.

Chelsea passes me a ball as I jog back to get in line for another hit and I dribble as I run. The gym feels smaller all of a sudden. And hotter. I glance to my left, scanning for familiar faces. *A* familiar face.

Breathing through my nose, I zip my focus back to Kiera. She's waving a hand at me to take another. She's yelling something. I can't hear her. I'm hot yet cold. I'm—

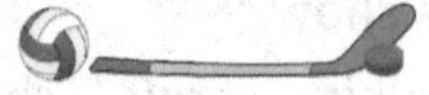

I COME TO PRETTY QUICKLY. The first sound to break through my ears is the squeaking of shoes rushing at me along the floor. Kiera's on her knees at my side, and someone else is holding my head up.

"Laney, can you hear me?" That's Coach. I recognize her.

I roll my head and squeeze my eyes shut then pop them wide to try and focus. Everything feels extremely bright, but I find her face to my other side. She has a washcloth on my head and she's pressing it to my skin, dabbing.

"You might be dehydrated. Let Tracey check you out."

Tracey's our trainer. I'm not dehydrated, but I don't know how to get those words out yet. And since I'm the one lying on the floor, I doubt my opinion holds much weight.

"Laney, Laney!" That's my mom's voice.

My mom?

Shit, I'm still knocked out and dreaming. My mom is standing by my coach and working her way down to me, dropping to her knees. Her bright pink purse slides from her arm and she tosses it to the side before moving her hand behind my head. She looks scared.

This is real.

"I'm okay," I croak, bending my knees and flattening my feet on the floor. I can't see far behind the immediate circle around me but I can tell people are kneeling. It's warmups and people are kneeling for an injury timeout. *Oh, my God, this is embarrassing!*

"I'm fine, I swear," I repeat, bullying my way through the

hands trying to keep me on my back so I can sit up. There's a water bottle squirting into my mouth the second I do. I drink, though most of it splatters around my lips and teeth. I push it away.

"Let me do it," I demand, holding out my palm. I take the bottle and drink. When I look up into concerned faces, I drink more. I'm not thirsty. I fucking panicked. Because . . . my dad isn't here. And Cutter is. And maybe I'm fucking up everything.

"Has she done this before?" Coach asks my mom.

Our eyes meet and my mom says no even though I have. Maybe twice. It's been a while, but both times were in high school and after my dad blew me off.

I try to tell her *thank you* with only my gaze. Her mouth softens from the worried frown. It's not quite a smile. I can sense her meaning, though. She gets me.

"I think I was just overhyped for this game. I set big expectations on myself." It's not totally a lie, and when my eyes meet my coach's she's on board with my excuse.

"She seems fine," Tracey says as she lets go of my arm from taking my pulse. "I want you drinking basically nonstop, though. I don't care if you piss on the court."

I blurt out a hard laugh and everyone around me joins in. Coach holds out a hand and Kiera holds out another to help me to my feet. Everyone claps when I stand, which is . . . *embarrassing*. I hold up a hand and jog back and forth a few times. I wonder what the student broadcasters are saying. Thank God Matt is out of town. The last thing I need is to become a sports meme.

My mom grabs her purse from the floor then heads back to the bleachers, stepping into the spot where I hoped my father would be. He's not here, but she came. She booked a last-minute flight and showed up. For me. Like she has my whole life.

"You sure you're good?" Kiera threads her hand with mine and shakes a little juice into my muscles. The tingling is gone.

I nod.

"I'm good. Let's get it!"

She reaches up and grabs both sides of my head and shouts, "Yeah!" I join in. Kiera and I are cut from the same cloth.

I move to the sideline and ready myself for the announcements, jogging down the line of teammates when they call my name last. I slap hands with my starting sisters, then turn to my right for the national anthem. My gaze wanders as the song plays, and I drift back to the balcony. Cutter's no longer standing front and center, and my chest starts to burn.

He left.

I'm aware of everything and I take a deep breath and return my gaze to the flag on the wall. I squeeze my hands to make sure I feel them. I wiggle my toes to check that the blood is there. I listen and hear clearly.

When the song ends, I drop my gaze to the entry to the gym and spot Cutter standing just inside. He nods at me and claps. He stayed. I want to nod back, but I don't.

Coach asks me five more times if I'm feeling good while we pre-game in the huddle. I finally flatten my palm on her clipboard on the sixth time and her glare whips at me.

"I'm fine," I insist.

She stares deep into my pupils, and there's a shift in her expression, all concern wiped away and replaced with command. She brushes my hand from her board and leans in close.

"Then let's go."

We break and I jet to the middle of the court, every muscle in my body teeming with an abundance of fuel. I feel stronger, maybe even taller. I span the net with my arms and imagine covering it all. I can feel the ball against my palm seconds before it happens. I see it all play out in my mind, and then it transfers to reality.

My first kill is dominant. Straight down. Inside the ten-foot line. The kind of kill they usually only see on the men's team. The announcer shouts, "Boom!"

Cutter rushes along the stands to my right, clapping—hyping.

"Thatta girl!"

The next set comes and this one I send through the block and into the chest of the libero with a thud.

Boom!

I glance to my right. Cutter's standing next to my mom. They're talking. *They're talking!*

"Let's run a slide," Kiera says at my ear. I nod and refocus. A play later, I put the ball away again, just inside the far corner.

Three sets. Three kills. Three points.

"MVP! MVP! MVP!" The chant starts with a handful of fans at first, but by the third set, it's grown into a howl that I bet can be heard from the parking lot. I know in my heart where it started. With Cutter. It fuels me, and it lifts me higher. And for the game, Kiera sets me one last time and I put the ball down in center court for kill number fifty-two.

My team rushes around me, and I look up at the ceiling and consider what an epic moment this is. That's the new record for Tiff. Maybe for the NCAA. My dad fucking missed it, and I don't care.

I let my smile spread while my teammates pull and tug on my jersey, hugging and slapping my back. They praise me and my cheeks warm with a blush. We shake hands with the Midwestern girls then cluster on our side of the court for more screaming. I scan the crowd behind them, looking for him. He's by the door again, his smile the embodiment of pride, and finally I let myself reciprocate and smile back. My body jostles against the others and everyone continues to celebrate. Eventually, my teammates peel away one at a time to get to the bench. Someone nudges my arm to my left and I startle as I look. It's a reporter. Someone with *The Times*.

"Laney, great game today. Mind if I get a quick word? You set a record and we'd love to get a photo for the story." Reporters always talk to the men's teams. And now, this guy is talking to me.

"I'd love to. Can I have one second?"

He nods and holds his recorder flat against his pad of paper.

I turn back to search for Cutter, but he's no longer in the doorway. I step toward the remaining fans still milling at the bottom of the bleachers and I scout for his beanie, or a glimpse of his sweatshirt. But he's not there. The balcony has emptied. The only people left are family members and regulars at our games. And my mom.

"Laney, I'm so . . ." She wipes her eyes. She gets emotional a lot more easily than I do. Though seeing the pride reflected in her glossy eyes and stretched smile does crack open my heart a smidge. I fall into her embrace and hold her tight, letting her cry into my ear.

"Thank you for coming, Mom. Thank you so, so much." I bury my face against her shoulder and breathe her in. I've missed her. I've missed this.

"I knew he wouldn't make it. I couldn't let—" She pulls back and shakes her head. I don't let her finish that thought.

"I'm glad you were here." I squeeze her shoulders and look her in the eyes and we make a silent agreement that what's been said is enough. She was here because he wasn't. Like always. And I'm finally going to stop asking.

"I have to do an interview, but can you wait here?"

She nods. "I still have to get a hotel. I've literally got nowhere to go," she laughs out.

I jog back to the reporter and fly through a few questions. He takes a photo with his phone of me leaning against the referee stand while I hold a ball against my hip. It's not going to be anything like the shot Cutter took.

I hold up a finger and urge my mom to wait for me a few more minutes while I talk with Coach and gather my things in the storage room. I don't need a locker room, but damn it, I still believe we deserve one. I glance around the space and plot my next request with our athletic director. If I leave one legacy behind at Tiff, it's going to be that.

My mom is standing by the door when I walk out, waiting in the same place Cutter was standing. She puts an arm around me and holds me to her side as we walk out to her rental car together. I dump my gear bag into the back seat and climb in the passenger side, cranking the heat on and holding my hands out to warm them. It's getting cold at night, and I didn't change from my shorts and jersey.

"Oh, here's your phone," my mom says, pulling it from her purse.

I blink at it a few times and puzzle my brow.

"That very handsome man who was here and cheering for you had it. He told me to give it to you."

My eyes dart to hers. Her head falls to the side a tick.

"Cutter, right? He seems to really believe in you. He had everyone shouting MVP by your second set." She chuckles. "I had to know his name, so I introduced myself. I see why you're so—"

"Don't you dare say smitten," I interject.

My heart flutters. Because I am.

My mom's smile perks up on one side.

"I see why you like him so much."

I blink a few times and meet her gaze.

"I kicked him out." My heart squeezes and everything I said rushes through my mind.

I hold my phone in my palm and click the screen on. My father's message lights up first. Cutter must have seen it. He knew I'd be disappointed, so he came. She showed up instead.

"Mom, I messed up." I let tears fill my eyes this time. I don't even bother to wipe them away. These tears, they deserve to drip and fall into my hands, on my lap.

"Laney, I'm sure you didn't mess up as badly as you think." She turns the car on and pulls us out of the lot. I take in a deep breath and give her a hard look. She pulls to a stop before entering the roadway and meets my gaze.

"Uh oh," she utters.

"I'm too much like him," I say.

"Like Cutter?" She lifts a brow.

I shake my head and wipe my tears away as I sniffle.

"Like Dad."

My mom's head falls more to the side as she lets out a, "Oh, Laney. No, you're not."

I nod adamantly.

"I'm selfish, Mom. And I'm going to choose the game, every time. I'm going to pick me, and damn anyone else."

She shakes her head through my guilty admission, which both soothes and infuriates me.

"No, Laney. No you're not. You are nothing like your dad. And also, it's okay to choose you. You simply need to be with someone who knows that, and who maybe chooses himself from time to time, too."

I hold her gaze and soak in her words. I don't see how that would ever work.

"But Dad chose himself, and so you chose yourself."

"No, Laney. I didn't learn how to choose myself until very recently. In fact, I'm still learning. Your dad has always been who he is, and I was blind to it. But I also didn't know it was okay to dream for myself sometimes. And maybe that's Grandma's fault, who knows." My grandmother passed away when I was five, so I take her word for it. I do know she was strict and did not like my mom marrying my dad or moving to Pittsburgh from Rhode Island.

"I don't know how . . ." I leave it there, letting my words trail off because there's so much I don't know. I don't like the unknown. The lack of a plan. The zero answers.

"You don't have to. You figure it out," she responds.

So what. That's what Cutter said.

I've just played the biggest game of my career, and instead of celebrating with friends or with a man I'm pretty sure I love, I'm crying in the car with my mom. I have nobody. I made sure of it.

"Can you drop me off at my house and maybe we can do breakfast in the morning? There's something I need to do."

My mom's lips slide into a proud smile, different from the kind she wears when I compete. This is the kind that goes with adulting, I think. This one carries more weight.

"Of course I can."

I guide my mom through the few turns it takes to get to the house. The driveway is clear, no Jeep parked by the curb. *I can't be too late.*

I get out of the car and grab my bag, then lean in through the window to take my mom's hand. She gives me a solid squeeze.

"Text me when you fix it," she says.

I nod, though I don't know if I can repair this.

I let her leave the driveway before I head inside, knowing in my gut that the fact I have to unlock the door probably means Cutter is gone. He hasn't had much time, though, so he must still have things here.

I rush to our room and flip the lights on to find our bed made up for once. My chest feels like a brick is weighing on it. I move to his side of the bed and scan the floor. His bag is gone. I tug open the drawers and his clothes have been cleared out. His phone charger is no longer on his night table. My last hope is the closet, and when I find his pants and dress shirts still hung inside, I fall into them and hug them, holding them to my face as I breathe in his musky smell. He isn't fully gone. He has to come back.

Pausing in the closet, I contemplate what else Cutter has in this house. He didn't come with as much stuff as I did, but he does have gear. I dart to the front closet and whip the doors open. It's bare except for two of Matt's jackets and a single hockey stick. It's an older stick, and at first glance, I assume it's something Matt messes around with, but then the orange grip tugs at my memory.

That's *my* stick. The one Cutter let me use.

I pull it out, holding it like he taught me, and shut my eyes. They fly open the moment it hits me.

I know exactly where he is.

cutter

"YOU KNOW I LOVE YOU, man, but I'm tired. How much longer do we have to keep this up?" Chuck's a saint. He not only answered the door when I pounded on it after Laney's game, but he came with me to the rink and suited up so I could work some shit out.

Nothing with my play, of course. Just the stuff in my head.

"Maybe a few more?" I lean my head to the side and he huffs, then slides his mask back in place. He drops down and I slap a shot that he snaps up easily. I'm getting tired, too.

He pushes the puck to the side to join the others then sets up to take another.

"Mind if I take a few?"

I smirk at the sound of Laney's voice, and Chuck pushes his mask back up again.

"Oh, thank God. He's all yours." He slides the pucks out to me, and I gather them while trying not to rush Laney as she glides into my periphery.

"Laney." Chuck gives her a nod as they pass, tipping his mask like a gentleman.

She spins around so her back is to me, and I notice that she's wearing the same sweats she borrowed from me the last time we did this, along with her stolen Tiff Tuff quilted satin volleyball jacket.

When the locker room door shuts behind Chuck, she spins to face me. Her lips part with a sudden breath and her eyes are puppy-dog-like. I'm not sure if she's scared or sad.

"New record, huh?" I break the ice, so to speak.

Her mouth snaps shut and she holds a tight-lipped smile for a deep breath through her nose. Her shoulders rise then drop on her exhale as she nods.

"New record," she echoes. "You came."

"I did."

She sucks in her bottom lip and drops her hands into the pockets of her jacket as she stares at the edge of her skates. Correction, *someone's* skates.

My brow furrows and I point at her feet.

"What are those?" They're at least four sizes too big on her.

"They're Matt's. They were in the closet." She shrugs, then slides one foot forward, nearly losing her balance. She drops the stick and I catch her at her elbows. Her hands flatten on my chest, then grab at the fabric of my sweatshirt. Her stare remains on the center of my chest as one of her hands moves to grab the string from my hoodie. She tugs on it lightly, then flits her eyes up to me. Several wordless seconds pass.

"You knew my dad wasn't going to make it, so you came to make sure I had someone there."

"I did." I can't help but let my gaze roam over the curve of her cheek. She's so fragile yet so strong. She's beautiful.

"So, how would this even work?"

My eyes snap back to hers at her question. My pulse pauses as my chest opens and hope drops inside.

"Us?" *Please be us.*

She nods slowly.

My mouth tugs up on the right and I glance beyond her shoulder at the empty arena. I breathe out a laugh, then come back to her face. All I can do is shrug.

"You say you love me, too."

She blinks once then closes the last few inches between us, pulling on my sweatshirt for balance as her lips move closer to mine. Her head tilts slightly and her top lip curves up.

"I love you, too." She's kissing me the moment her words hit the air, and everything in my body relaxes. My hands move to her hips as I lift her into my arms. Her freezing palms press against my cheeks as our breaths fog up the air around us. I taste her mouth, the orange Gatorade flavor from her game still fresh on her lips. Her body a perfect fit against mine as I leave my mess behind and skate us to the team's bench.

I spin to take a seat, setting her on my thigh so I can run my hands through her hair and hold her close.

"You have to get out of those ridiculous things," I say, glancing down at the too-big skates.

"I agree," she says, followed by a sheepish laugh.

Her smile flirts with her cheeks, pushing them higher, making them rosier. She blushes from my attention, or maybe the power of the moment. It's adorable.

She leans in for a chaste kiss and grazes the tip of her nose against mine before falling against my chest and sliding her hands to my back.

"I'm really sorry, Cutter. About everything. I'm just scared."

I slide a strand of hair out of her face and tuck it behind her ear as I cradle her head to me.

"It's okay. I'm not going to up and leave. I wasn't even really going to move out. I was going to forfeit the bet."

She snuggles in tighter.

"Bets don't really work that way. You'd still owe me."

I cough out a laugh because she's right.

"Yeah, I guess I would."

"It's not you leaving that I'm afraid of." She leans back and looks me in the eyes. "I'm afraid of letting you down. Of not showing up when you need me. Of picking me over you. Because that's what my dad does, and I know how it feels to be on the other side of it."

I hold my breath and study her face for a beat, pondering the right words.

"So, I'm the one who should technically be scared. Wouldn't that make sense?"

Her brow furrows but she says, "I guess," as she shakes her head.

"And I'm not," I say, meaning it to the roots. "I'm not afraid of being hurt by you. I'm afraid of not trying for us at all. I'm afraid of regret. Of missing out on something amazing. Of being there for you when you break more records and show thousands of little girls that growing up to play volleyball for a living is possible."

"But what if I up and run?"

She blinks then stares at me with wide, genuinely worried eyes.

All I can do is laugh, then kiss her hard enough to lean her back in my arms, her hair tickling the seat of the bench.

"I guess I'd have to chase you."

Because that is who Laney and I are. Push and pull. Run and chase. Dig in and fight.

And fall in love.

epilogue
Five Years Later

cutter

"YOU KNOW, just because our boarding group is B does not mean we somehow lost. B is not for losers." My girlfriend can turn everything into a competition, including, apparently, checking in to board a flight.

"This is why we fly separately. You don't get it." She's a little grumpy because she's afraid she won't get a window seat. I've done the math, though. We may be near the back, but she'll get a window.

"I think the guy who willingly takes a middle so his girlfriend can look down at farmland gets it," I grumble, thinking about how skinny I'm going to have to make myself in order to fit. I'm bulky on my own; sandwiched between two travelers makes me feel like a hotdog in the microwave, close to bursting open.

Laney hugs my arm then kisses my cheek.

"You're right. You do get it."

Every time she tugs on my sweatshirt I panic. The ring is nestled in the front pocket, and only because I want to be able to check on it constantly. I was too nervous to put it in a checked bag, and Laney is in and out of our carry-on too much. The damn box sticks out in my joggers, so this was the best bet. Nothing feels safe from her uncovering it, though.

"We're next. Come on, we need to get to staging." She tugs my sleeve to pull me closer to the gate and I stuff my hand into my hoodie pocket to make sure the ring is safe.

"For the record, there is no such thing as staging. There is crowding. What we are doing now is crowding," I say. Laney glances over her shoulder at me, and I know that look.

Hush it, Cutter. Just get in line and let me get my seat.

"But I'm here. I'm staging." Under my breath I cough out, "Crowding."

My palms are so sweaty. I keep wiping them on the inside of my hoodie pocket and along my thighs. Laney has to notice. I'm not afraid of flying, but I look like a nervous wreck. I know I do. Because I am.

I decided about four months ago that I was going to propose this weekend. I've been planning this moment in my head, though, for about four years. It was our first year living together in Seattle after we both got drafted. Laney was the second overall pick for the inaugural pro volleyball season. I went a little deeper, and when I knew it would come down to being in Kansas City or Seattle, I did everything I could to sway things in my favor to play for the minor league team up here.

Laney has always been afraid of me wanting to go home. She fears being the one to break us apart by choosing her career, but I know in my gut that she's really afraid that I'm going to choose not to follow. Two people can make two different choices in life, and neither is wrong. Her going wasn't much different than me staying. And it was the idea of growing together then falling apart that gave her pause.

But what she didn't get is what I knew the moment I decided I loved her. I would never choose anything but her. Even now, as we "stage" our way into nearly coming to elbow blows with an older couple trying to get into the early B group too.

"Come on," Laney says, taking over the wheeling of our carry-on.

We cut the nice couple off and I turn to apologize for being aggressive to the gentleman who's now on the boarding bridge behind me.

"Oh, don't worry. She's just as competitive," he grumbles, pointing to his wife. The woman grimaces at him, then turns to me and Laney.

"I am not competitive."

The man and I exchange a glance and smirk. Nothing more needs to be said.

We amble our way through the filled rows on the plane until things lighten up toward the back. As I figured, there are maybe a dozen of completely empty rows, so I let Laney pick her favorite and climb in for the window seat. Once she's settled, I push the handle in on our rolling bag and lift it into the storage bin, pushing it in snugly. I duck my head and climb into the seat next to Laney, then feel to my right then left for the stray buckles that are mine.

"Hey, Lane? I think you're sitting on—" I stop when I see her wide eyes staring at the velvet box in her palm. Panicked, I drop the belt in my right hand and feel in my pocket.

Empty.

"Shit," I mutter.

"Cutter?" Her gaze slides over to me.

Deep breath time.

"Well, this is not going according to plan." I chuckle, or rather, *vibrate* with nervous laughter.

"This seat taken?" a woman asks from the aisle.

Seriously?

"No, it's not," I say, then turn my attention back to Laney, who is still gawking at the box in her palm.

"I can't believe I messed this up." I run my hand through my hair a dozen times, stammering for the right words to somehow fix this and turn it into something meaningful.

"Oh! Are you proposing?" The tall blonde woman who took the aisle seat leans over my shoulder. I close my eyes and pinch the bridge of my nose.

"Yeah. I guess I am," I say, cracking only one eye open and looking to Laney for a response.

Her gaze lifts to me and a slow smile creeps into her cheeks.

"Is that a yes?" Again, not the epic words I'd planned to say, but I suppose this simply fits right in with the rest of our story.

"Yes, Cutter. It's a very enthusiastic yes." She hands me the box, so at least I get to crack it open and watch her face as she takes in the platinum ring and princess-cut diamond that my mom helped me pick out in April.

"It's beautiful," she hums as I pull it from the box and slip it on her finger. She admires it, then leans into the arm rest between us to kiss me. Our audience of one has grown to six or seven, and they all begin to clap.

"Thank you." I hold up a hand and glance around, not really taking in a single face. I can't believe I botched this so badly.

"Cutter, I can't believe you had this planned. And I had no idea."

I guess that's one thing I got right. Laney is hard to keep secrets from, and I had to live with this ring in our apartment for several weeks.

"I have a favor to ask of you." I hold her gaze and let the seemingly permanent smile on her lips soothe any lingering disappointment. This can be fixed for everyone else.

I pull my seat belt together and click it as Laney says, "Anything."

"Before we land in Iowa, I'm going to need that back. And when my entire family and your mom are there to pick us up, and I drop down on one knee to propose, you have to pretend that it's for the first time."

Laney covers her mouth and shakes with a sharp laugh.

I nod.

"Yeah, they all came for this. This trip wasn't just us going home to see my mom and be there for Tiff's homecoming. Hell, we don't even have to go to Tiff's homecoming. After we close down Patty's for the party my brothers planned, you might not be up for it."

"Your brothers planned a party?" Laney's always wanted the feel of family. I think maybe it's one of the reasons she fell in love with me, and I'm okay with the fact my family is one of my best attributes. I happen to agree.

"They did. And you know how pissed Flynn is when he doesn't get his way."

She laughs.

"And you say I'm competitive."

I lift her chin a hair and press my lips to hers, stopping to rest my head against her as well.

"I can't wait to introduce you as my competitive wife," I say.

"Me neither," she replies.

I tether our hands, then lean back in my seat and imagine every moment yet to come. When the woman next to us asks how we met, I decide to let Laney tell the story; it's fun to hear it from her side. She likes to play up the enemies-to-lovers bit, and I never correct her, even though Laney Price was never really my enemy. She was my forever home.

THE END

if you enjoyed this book, you might also like:

The Varsity Series

A New Adult Sports Romance Trilogy

Begin Your Binge with Varsity Heartbreaker

Lucas Fuller is a lot of things.

He's the boy next door.

He's the first crush I ever had.

He was my first kiss.

He's also the only person who has ever broken my heart.

For two years, I've wondered what happened to the us I used to know.

We were best friends, and then suddenly…we weren't.

I tried to run away from it. I even changed schools just to make the hurt disappear.

But no matter how hard I tried to not think about Lucas, I just couldn't stay away from the high school quarterback with perfect blue eyes and so many secrets.

I'm back. We're seniors now. We've grown—all of us. And Lucas Fuller might be different, but I'm different too.

This is my time to take risks, to experience life and to fall in love for real.

I want Lucas Fuller to be a part of my story, but I know for that to happen, I need to know the truth about our past.

acknowledgments

Boy were Cutter and Laney fun to write!

Cutter is my first actual hockey-playing hero. True, Andrew in Wicked Restless plays college hockey, but he's admittedly not great at it and he's only there to be a disrupter. Cutter McCreary, however? He's good. And sexy. And one of several brothers who love and play the game. I know my sports intimately. I've worked in sports reporting. There is not a sport I don't watch (yes, this includes those on the Ocho!) but college hockey needed a little bit of research to get some of the nuances right. Workouts, schedules and such. So special shout out to Connor Dumesnil, Bakersfield's best, for giving me some of the nitty gritty details.

So many to thank for helping me to bring this book and series to you. As always, I'm nothing without my wing woman Autumn at Wordsmith Publicity. Brenda Letendre, your editing and guidance is everything! Sprinting partners . . . there were many of you with me in the trenches this time, but Rebecca Shea and Kacey Shea (not sisters lol) you helped push me through the goal line. Enormous thanks to my mom, my boys, and my dogs, who think it's weird when I dictate and it doesn't turn into a treat as we wander around the house. And the biggest thanks of all to the incredibly talented Katy Mendoza, who drew these characters to life, all the way down to the perfect stripes on Laney's knee-highs! I love you all!

I am so honored to be able to do the job I do. It's my dream, and the only reason I'm able to keep pouring time and passion into stories is because of you—my readers. You make this possible, and I am forever grateful. If you've enjoyed this book, please consider sharing your excitement with others. Posts, reviews, comments, recommendations, videos, BookToks, inspiration images, photos—all of it! Every little thing helps an author to keep going. We're an anxious bunch, and we dwell in imposter syndrome more often than we care to admit. You are the life rafts that pull us out. At least for me you do. So thank you! And get ready for two more books in the Final Score series. I hear these next couples are just as hot!

about the author

Ginger Scott is a *USA Today, Wall Street Journal* and Amazon-bestselling author from Peoria, Arizona. She has also been nominated for the Goodreads Choice and RWA Rita Awards. She is the author of several young and new adult romances, including bestsellers Waiting on the Sidelines, The Hard Count, A Boy Like You, This Is Falling and Wild Reckless.

A sucker for a good romance, Ginger's other passion is sports, and she often blends the two in her stories. When she's not writing, the odds are high that she's somewhere near a baseball diamond, either watching her son swing for the fences or cheering on her favorite baseball team, the Arizona Diamondbacks. Ginger lives in Arizona and is married to her college sweetheart whom she met at ASU (fork 'em, Devils).

FIND GINGER ONLINE: www.littlemisswrite.com

facebook.com/GingerScottAuthor
instagram.com/authorgingerscott
tiktok.com/@authorgingerscott

also by ginger scott

Final Score Series

The Tomboy & The Captain

The Wallflower & The Running Back

The Best Friend & The Short Stop

The Boys of Welles

Loner

Rebel

Habit

The Fuel Series

Shift

Wreck

Burn

The Varsity Series

Varsity Heartbreaker

Varsity Tiebreaker

Varsity Rule breaker

Varsity Captain

The Waiting Series

Waiting on the Sidelines

Going Long

The Hail Mary

Like Us Duet

A Boy Like You

A Girl Like Me

The Falling Series

This Is Falling

You And Everything After

The Girl I Was Before

In Your Dreams

The Harper Boys

Wild Reckless

Wicked Restless

Standalone Reads

The Moon and Back

Southpaw

Candy Colored Sky

Cowboy Villain Damsel Duel

Drummer Girl

BRED

The Hard Count

Memphis

Hold My Breath

Blindness

How We Deal With Gravity